" _____ tain-
i _____ imes

"Goldberg's prose is deceptively smooth, like a vanilla milk shake spiked with grain alcohol."

—*Chicago Tribune*

"[A] creepy, strangely sardonic, definitely disturbing version of Middle America . . . and that, of course, is where the fun begins." —*LA Weekly*

"Perfect . . . with all the sleaze and glamour of the old paperbacks of fifty years ago." —*Kirkus Reviews*

"Striking and affecting. . . . Goldberg is a gifted writer, poetic and rigorous . . . a fiction tour de force . . . a haunting book." —January Magazine

"Well plotted and deftly written. . . . Goldberg serves up heaps of Miami's lush life and lowlifes while exposing its drug and arms underworld."

—The Huffington Post

continued . . .

Praise for the Series

"Likably lighthearted and cool as a smart-mouthed loner . . . cheerfully insouciant." —*The New York Times*

"Brisk and witty." —*The Christian Science Monitor*

"[A] swell new spy series . . . highly enjoyable."
—*Chicago Tribune*

"Violence, babes, and a cool-guy spy . . . slick and funny and a lotta fun." —*New York Post*

"Smart, charmingly irreverent . . . pleasantly warped."
—*Detroit Free Press*

"Snazzy." —*Entertainment Weekly*

"Terrifically entertaining . . . neat and crisp as citrus soda." —*Seattle Post-Intelligencer*

"Breezy cloak-and-dagger ingenuity. [A] nicely pitched action-comedy hero: handsome, smart, neurotic, tough, funny, sensitive . . . Michael Westen is Jim Rockford and MacGyver filtered through Carl Hiaasen. Entertaining, in other words." —*LA Weekly*

The Burn Notice Series

The Reformed
The Giveaway
The End Game
The Fix

burn notice
The Reformed

TOD GOLDBERG

Based on the USA Network Television Series
Created by Matt Nix

AN OBSIDIAN MYSTERY

OBSIDIAN
Published by New American Library, a division of
Penguin Group (USA) Inc., 375 Hudson Street,
New York, New York 10014, USA
Penguin Group (Canada), 90 Eglinton Avenue East, Suite 700, Toronto,
Ontario M4P 2Y3, Canada (a division of Pearson Penguin Canada Inc.)
Penguin Books Ltd., 80 Strand, London WC2R 0RL, England
Penguin Ireland, 25 St. Stephen's Green, Dublin 2,
Ireland (a division of Penguin Books Ltd.)
Penguin Group (Australia), 250 Camberwell Road, Camberwell, Victoria 3124,
Australia (a division of Pearson Australia Group Pty. Ltd.)
Penguin Books India Pvt. Ltd., 11 Community Centre, Panchsheel Park,
New Delhi - 110 017, India
Penguin Group (NZ), 67 Apollo Drive, Rosedale, North Shore 0632,
New Zealand (a division of Pearson New Zealand Ltd.)
Penguin Books (South Africa) (Pty.) Ltd., 24 Sturdee Avenue,
Rosebank, Johannesburg 2196, South Africa

Penguin Books Ltd., Registered Offices:
80 Strand, London WC2R 0RL, England

First published by Obsidian, an imprint of New American Library,
a division of Penguin Group (USA) Inc.

First Printing, January 2011
10 9 8 7 6 5 4 3 2 1

TM & © 2011 Twentieth Century Fox Film Corporation. All Rights Reserved.

OBSIDIAN and logo are trademarks of Penguin Group (USA) Inc.

Printed in the United States of America

For Wendy

ACKNOWLEDGMENTS

I am, as ever, eternally thankful to Matt Nix for letting me add my two cents to his wonderful creation. As no book really gets written alone, I must also thank Lee Goldberg for his continued advice; my agent, Jennie Dunham, for her diligent and ever-mindful assurances; my fine editor, Sandra Harding, and the whole team at NAL, who manage to find all of my errors just in time; Chris Alessio for his excellent insight into paintball markers (anything that is off in this book is my fault, not his); Julia Pistell for finding a title for me; and, of course, my wonderful wife, Wendy, who must tolerate my muttering "When you're a spy . . ." for months at a time.

I'd like to think no one would read this book and then attempt to do anything they've read about. But, as a realist, let me remind you: Please do not attempt to blow anything up, counterfeit money, modify weapons or, well, anything else you've read here. It won't work, and you'll probably explode. You've been warned.

1

When you're a spy, the amount of time you spend in a church, a temple or a mosque depends on simple local custom: If the people trying to kill you have a healthy fear of their god, going to a church, a temple or a mosque is a great way to avoid a bullet in the head. Even the most cold-blooded killer will think twice about spraying gunfire inside of a holy place, because though the idea of sanctuary may sound like something from a genteel, antiquated past, so it would reason that even the most nonreligious person might give even more consideration to shooting a gun in a holy place when given time to contemplate his particular god's wrath—even if he doesn't particularly believe in that god.

All of which is why I always make sure to have my gun on me whenever I'm near a church. It's just better to be the one guy who isn't thinking twice about things, which is precisely why I didn't want to stop at the Church of the Gleaming Spire's youth-group car wash, despite my mother's sudden desire to be a good citizen.

"Michael," my mother, Madeline, said, "when you were a boy, you played basketball there every day after school."

"No, I didn't," I said.

"Well, you could have," she said. "And done arts and crafts, too." We were stopped at a red light down the street from the church, and there were three teenage girls with a sign for the car wash, waving at us on the corner. I kept my eyes forward. You never want to engage the enemy if you don't have to.

"Ma," I said, "I prefer to wash my own car. It's an issue of pride."

My mother ran a finger over the Charger's dashboard, leaving a trail in the dust. "Apparently not," she said.

"I don't like people touching my stuff," I said.

"Your father kept this car so clean," she said.

"No, he didn't," I said. Of course, he also didn't use the car as the frequent base of operations for clandestine missions with his friends, so maybe I had a decent excuse for the Charger being periodically dusty. In the past few years, since I'd received my burn notice and been sent back to Miami, minus my life, Dad's Charger had been set on fire, shot at, slept in and, occasionally, crashed into stationary objects.

"I'm just saying, Michael," my mother said, "that it wouldn't kill you to help those nice kids out by giving them a few dollars of your blood money."

"Ma," I said, "I have an AK-47 in the trunk."

"So don't have them clean out your trunk," she said. "And, anyway, it's a good cause. Maybe it will keep these kids from becoming gun-toting mercenaries like you and Sam."

That my mother was not fazed by the fact that I had an assault rifle in my trunk should have been disconcerting, but since I'd been back in Miami, many of the secrets of my life had been demystified. To my mother, Sam was no longer just a friend of mine from the military with questionable taste in women; these days he was also, well, essentially, a gun-toting mercenary. And my ex-girlfriend Fiona wasn't just a nice Irish girl without a discernible job (it's hard to tell your mother that the girl you're dating robs banks for the IRA), but, well, essentially, a gun-toting mercenary these days, too. That both Sam and Fiona were really just out to protect me was clear to my mother, too, but something told me she didn't think I needed protecting most of the time.

And she's right. Most of the time.

"Fine," I said. I'd already spent the previous three hours with my mother, running a gauntlet of errands—the podiatrist, Target, the hair salon, back to Target, back again to Target—and now, finally we were heading back home, so I wasn't in a mood to argue much. Sometimes it's just easier to say "Fine" and chalk the day up as a total loss.

I reached across my mother, flipped open the glove box and pulled out the SIG SAUER I kept there and the bag of blasting caps I meant to give back to Fiona. There were also about fifteen cell phones in various stages of disrepair littered on the floor in the back, but I figured those could stay in one place since I didn't see any vacuums around, anyway. I handed the gun and the blasting caps to my mother. "Could you put all of that in your purse?"

"What are these sticks?"

"They're like fireworks," I said.

"Are they legal?"

"Just as legal as the AK-47 is," I said.

"If I wasn't here, where would you put all of this stuff?"

"If you weren't here," I said, "I wouldn't be stopping."

"Oh, fine," she said, and stuffed it all in her bag.

The light turned green, and I made my way through the intersection and then pulled into the church lot. There were about fifteen kids lingering, but only two cars getting washed. I pulled behind a yellow station wagon—the kind that was last sold in America when Carter was president—and then both my mother and I got out. My mother immediately lit up a cigarette, which clarified why she'd wanted to stop the car so desperately.

A teenage boy walked up to the car with a bucket and a towel and his hand out. "It's five dollars," he said. He had all the urgency of molasses.

"What does the money go toward?" I asked.

"We're trying to earn enough money to go to Disney World."

"Why?"

The kid shrugged. "We go every year," he said.

"Yeah," I said. "But why?"

"I dunno. It's fun."

"Is it?" I asked.

"Do you want a car wash or what?"

I reached into my wallet and pulled out a twenty. The kid reached for it and I yanked it back, ripping it in two. "Here's the deal," I said. "I'm going to be standing right here. If you go anywhere near the trunk of the car, I'm going to keep the other half of this bill. If you manage to stay away from the trunk, I'll give you the other half, plus five bucks. Deal?"

"Why don't you just wash your own car?"

"My mom won't let me," I said.

The kid seemed to understand this universal truth and started to get to work on the Charger without another word. I stood back and watched him work for a few minutes and tried to recall the last time I'd stood in this exact spot. It was only a few miles from my mother's house, but wasn't in a part of Miami I tended to visit all that often, since it also happened to be just a few streets from my old high school. It was bad enough when my mother bumped into my ex-classmates—or the families of my ex-classmates—and told them I was back in town.

She'd invariably tell them I was free to do odd jobs for them, or she'd just give them my number and encourage them to ask me for help. This sort of help typically involved me saving them from human traffickers, drug kingpins and particularly violent gangster rappers. Frankly, it was easier dealing with the various rogue governments and jilted assassins sent to kill me than it was with people who knew me when I was fifteen.

The kids working the car wash all looked liked kids

in Florida always have—which is to say that they were all wearing flip-flops, shorts and T-shirts and had a slight sunburn on their cheeks. Their hair was slightly shaggy and they had the air of nonchalance people possess before they start paying taxes or taking palpable risk.

I can't imagine I had ever looked anything like them.

"Why didn't I ever take part in any charity car washes as a kid?" I asked my mother.

"I always wanted you to," she said.

"What does that mean?"

"Well, you and your brother, Nate, were always so industrious. I just thought it would be wonderful if you were engaged in some of the philanthropic events I was interested in."

"What were you interested in?"

"Well, Michael, that doesn't matter," she said.

"No. Now I'm curious."

"Well, I always *wanted* to be involved with that thing where you went to another country and did things."

"The Peace Corps? You were interested in joining the Peace Corps?"

"Yes," she said. She exhaled a huge plume of smoke and stared at me. "Don't give me that look, Michael. I was a very active person when you were a child. You don't remember, obviously. You didn't just develop your sense of wanderlust on your own."

"I didn't have wanderlust, Ma. I had a desire to escape."

"And look where that got you," she said. "Right back where you started from."

"Ironic," I said. For a moment we both watched the kid working on the Charger. He kept trying to buff a spot out of the hood that, if memory served, was from a bullet deflection. The week previous I'd been involved in a small shooting incident involving an ex–KGB agent who'd come to town to settle a few scores, which, as it happened, had ended up involving me. "You can let that spot go," I told him.

"You sure?" he asked.

"Yeah," I said. "I'll touch that up myself."

The kid nodded and moved around to the passenger's door and stopped. "You've got a couple of similar-looking spots over here," he said.

"You can leave those, too," I said. I turned to my mother. "This was an *excellent* idea."

"It wouldn't kill you to reach out to some at-risk kids like these," she said.

"These aren't at-risk kids," I said. "They're going to Disney World."

"Michael, do you remember how nice it was when adults took a special interest in you?"

"Ma, the only adults who took a special interest in me were in the Special Forces."

The kid moved toward the rear of the Charger and then paused. The problem with telling a teenager to avoid something is that it only makes him more interested in doing precisely what you've advised him against. It probably would have been wiser of me to tell the kid that I wanted the trunk area to be pristine.

I held up my half of the twenty-dollar bill and waved it. "You remember this?"

"It's just that you've got a lot of, uh, dirt, I think, on this part of your car."

The kid pointed at the bumper and also indicated a spatter pattern on the back window. The car was indeed dirty, but it wasn't covered in *dirt*, so I thought it best not to have the kid investigate the matter any further.

"Yeah," I said and handed the kid the rest of the twenty and then handed him another twenty. "Let's just call it even, okay?"

"I haven't done the driver's side yet," he said.

"Your lucky day," I said.

I tried to remember what might have happened recently for the back of the Charger to have blood on it, and then recalled that Fiona and the ex–KGB agent had tussled a bit over the trunk. It had been that type of week. I patted the kid on the shoulder and then pushed him away from the trunk, lest he notice anything he might need therapy for later.

"Ma," I said, "let's go. This was a terrible idea."

My mother reached into her purse, managed not to fumble my SIG and the blasting caps out onto the pavement in front of the church, and came out with another five bucks, which she handed the boy. "I'm sorry," she said. "My son isn't very good with people."

The kid nodded—again, something he could readily understand. "Do you want a receipt? This is all tax deductible, I guess."

"No," I said.

"Yes," my mother said.

"Let me get the father over here, then," he said, and

off he went into the church, leaving my mother and me to stand there beside my bloodstained car.

"You're really going to take five dollars off your taxes, Ma?"

"No," she said, "I'm going to take forty-five dollars off my taxes."

I sighed. I rolled my eyes. Then I did both things again. I checked my cell phone. It wasn't ringing. For as often as Sam called to let me know he had a buddy who needed help dodging the mob's bullets, or who'd ill-advisedly entered into an agreement with Hamas, he never seemed to do so when I really needed him to. I was certain that it was only a matter of time before lightning would begin to crack down around me or perhaps a good, biblical hailstorm would start pelting me from above. A torrential flood also seemed like a possibility.

Instead, it was the past that came rushing toward me. Or, to be precise, it came lumbering out the double doors of the Church of the Gleaming Spire in the form of Eduardo Santiago. All six foot five and 320 pounds of him. The last time I had seen Eduardo had been at least fifteen years ago, when I was asked to help out with an "urban renewal" project that involved the capture and extinction of certain members of the Latin Emperors prison gang, who'd begun a robust drugs and extortion business in El Salvador. And even then, I'd only seen a photo of him since he was still locked up. From his prison cell, he had been purportedly calling shots that had bodies showing up on the streets of foreign countries. And now he was fifty yards away and gangster-limping his way across the blacktop toward me, which made me consider that, in light of the current order of things, my previous thoughts on churches were misguided. Who believed in anything anymore?

"Ma," I said, trying to stay as calm as possible, "I need you to hand me your purse, and then I need you to get into the car, lock the doors and, whatever happens, don't get out."

"I'm not giving you my purse, Michael," she said. "My cigarettes are in there."

"Ma," I said, "do you see that man walking across the parking lot toward us? The one with neck tattoos?"

"Yes."

"He's not a friendly person."

"Little Eddie Santiago? You went to school with him for ten years, Michael."

"What?" I took off my sunglasses and squinted at the mass of man. He didn't look like Little Eddie Santiago, but then I hadn't seen Little Eddie Santiago since the ninth or tenth grade.

"That's Eddie Santiago. He's a priest now. Don't you know that?"

"You're thinking of someone else. That man is a gangster," I said, but now I wasn't so sure, since it wasn't as if my mother was generally up on the business of churches and such. She was up on neighborhood gossip, however, and that sounded like something people would gossip about. Nevertheless, since my mother wouldn't hand me her purse, I positioned myself next to the trunk in case I needed to pop it open and grab the AK. Not that I wanted to unload an AK-47 in front of a church on a lovely summer day, but I also didn't think the alternative of being shot in the face by Eduardo Santiago sounded very appealing, either.

"Same person," my mother said. "He's very big in the community now, Michael. Don't you read the newspaper?"

"No."

"Do you ever watch the local news?"

"No."

"He's turned his life around, Michael. You should ask him for some pointers."

I'd get the chance, since Eduardo Santiago, or Little Eddie Santiago, or the man who'd shoot me in front of my mother, was ten feet away from us and about to pull something from his pocket.

"This is for you," he began to say, but then I reached out and grabbed his arm—the one connected to the hand that was shoved in his pocket and that was pulling out a gun, a knife or, well, a receipt—but I couldn't be too careful—and pressed into the pressure points on either side of his elbow, bringing the big man to his knees slowly.

"Whoa, easy there. It's slippery," I said, and bent down to his eye level, which wasn't difficult, since even on his knees Eduardo Santiago came to about my chest. "Do you know me?" I whispered.

Eduardo Santiago glared at me. Presuming he had a gun in his hand, the best he'd be able to accomplish from this angle would be to shoot himself in the foot and hope I was made squeamish by the sight of blood.

He wouldn't get that chance, however, because if I even felt a muscle twitch, I'd break his arm.

"Yes," he said. "You're Michael Westen. And I've been looking for you."

I tightened my grip and Eduardo winced. "Who do you work for?"

A thin smile crossed Eduardo's face. "God," he said.

2

If you find yourself in a threatening situation, it's best to take people's actions at face value. If someone pulls a gun on you, more than likely he intends to shoot you. If someone is strapped with C-4, it's probable she's about to blow herself—and you—up. So if someone is facing serious injury—like, say, Eduardo Santiago—and is asked a serious question, it's unlikely he'd tell a joke to lighten the situation. That only happens on television.

"I told him you were a priest," my mother said to Eduardo. We were sitting in a small business office just off the main chapel inside the Church of the Gleaming Spire, and Eduardo kept rubbing at his elbow absently as we spoke. "He didn't believe it."

"No one does," Eduardo said. "No one who knew me back in the day, anyway."

Back in the days I knew him, Eduardo Santiago was a junior-level hard knock: the kind of gangster who played sports, didn't commit crimes in his own neighborhood and still attended school on a somewhat regular basis. Even then, however, it was clear he was set for bigger and better things in the gang world. At sixteen, he was already well over 250 pounds and none of it was fat. He played linebacker on the high school team, and rumor had it that the University of Miami already had him penciled into their starting lineup. Rumor also had it that a few Hurricane alums had already put him on scholarship; the black Mercedes he drove to school seemed a bit outside of his credit rating.

The truth, though, was that he was on a Latin Emperors scholarship and was already working as an enforcer for the gang. It was a job he was uniquely qualified for and he rather enjoyed. He rose through the ranks until, by the age of just twenty-five, he was already a top dog, the kind of guy who both called shots and occasionally took some just for kicks, and to let the young ones know he was still in the game. Getting sent to prison only improved his stock, which was how I'd heard of him. That I hadn't connected him to the kid I grew up with shouldn't be much of a surprise—the name Eduardo Santiago is like Joe Smith in the Cuban community.

"Shouldn't you still be in prison?" I asked.

"The old me? Yeah. Yeah. And he still is in prison. Or someone like him, you know? But this person? Who I am today? No, man. You're looking at a man who changed. You don't read the newspaper?"

"No," I said. "No one does anymore. That's why they're all going out of business."

"You got the Internet? You should Google me. I'm a success story, if I do say so myself."

"Really?" I said. "Then why do you look like a guy who just got out of prison?"

Eduardo grinned big. He did everything big. He was still a pretty muscular guy, but he was also a guy who'd clearly spent some time in front of an all-you-can-eat buffet on more than one occasion. But beyond that, he didn't exactly dress like a success story. He had on a tank top that revealed his dozens of tattoos, tan shorts that looked like they'd been cut off from an old pair of Dickies and, just like the kids, a pair of flip-flops. He wore a huge cross around his neck, but it was absurdly blinged up.

"Michael," he said, "this is a car wash. You think I'm going to wear a suit to a car wash? And besides, this isn't even my church."

"Then what are you doing here?" I asked.

"Father Fremon took ill last week, and I volunteered to help out so he could get some more bed rest before the big Disney World trip. Plus, if I come out here, maybe a few more cars come rolling through because they know I'm involved."

It sounded plausible enough, probably because it was perfectly plausible. Still, sitting across from Eduardo Santiago didn't feel comfortable, especially not with my mother sitting there, too.

"Then I apologize for trying to break your arm," I said.

"When was the last time you two saw each other?" my mother asked.

Eduardo chuckled. "Man, what? Back when you were a freshman? I remember you being one of those kids who wasn't afraid to look me in the eye. You were a tough kid."

"And you were a thug," I said.

"I was a bad person," he said, "but the Lord, you know, he taught me the way. Live by the gun, die by the gun. All that. You take a look at the Bible, and it's in there, too, but that isn't about how I'm living now. You recognize that and change, man, and the world opens up for you. I got a theology degree. Went to seminary. And here I am."

"How much time did you do?"

"Fifteen," he said.

"Out of what?"

Eduardo got a bashful look on his face, as if this wasn't the kind of conversation he normally had in pleasant society. Either that or he'd figured out the subtext of my question: Who did you snitch out to do less time?

"Fifty," he said.

"Fifteen out of fifty," I said. "They don't usually chop thirty-five years off a federal sentence for finding the Lord."

"How'd you know I was doing federal time?"

"I'll answer that as soon as you tell me why you've been looking for me," I said.

Eduardo's gaze shifted from me to my mother and back to me. When I didn't say anything, he did it again. Life would be much easier if people just said what they wanted to say and didn't bother with nonverbal communication.

I stood up. "C'mon, Ma," I said. "Eduardo needs to tend to his flock."

Eduardo stood, as well, and extended his meaty paw

in my direction. He had scars on his knuckles from where he'd had old tattoos lasered off, but I could still make out the faint outline of the Roman numerals XII–V: the sign of the Latin Emperors.

"Why don't you come by my church tomorrow?" Eduardo said as we shook. He told me where it was located—about five blocks from the old Orange Bowl, and just blocks from Little Havana. A good central location to save some souls, I guess. "I'll show you around the campus," he continued. "Let you meet some of the kids. And then we can talk about what you know and what I know, and what I need help with."

"I can't wait," I said.

"Good luck with your car wash," my mother said, and gave me the same look Eduardo had given me moments before, and then continued to do so until I set another twenty bucks on the desk. Sixty dollars for half a car wash. That's inflation.

"Way I see it," Sam Axe said, "the only thing Eduardo Santiago could need from you is the name of your investment guy."

It was just after six in the evening, and Sam and I were eating dinner inside Perricone's, an Italian restaurant that was housed inside an old barn shipped in from Vermont, which essentially meant it was just like every other tourist in town. Sam said he liked the place because it was inside a barn and it made him yearn for his country childhood, a childhood that—to the best of my knowledge—was lived nowhere near a barn or the country. It was also one of the few places in Miami that served Peroni beer, which, I suspect, was the true reason he'd suggested we meet there on this particular evening. I'd called him after I met with Eduardo and asked him to see what he could find about the good Father Santiago.

"I gave everything to Madoff," I said, "so he's out of luck."

"My sources tell me your old buddy is a big player these days. Maybe he wants to pick your brain on fashionable sunglasses."

"He's not my old buddy," I said. "And who are your sources?"

"You ever hear of NBC?"

"That some CIA front?"

"No, the network. He's on one of those local chat shows about twice a week, talking about helping the poor and all that. Always wears a smart-looking suit. Good hair. He's got a smile that people trust, too."

"Really?"

"Well, you know, one of those local rags said he was the most trustworthy man in Miami. I read all about him at the dentist's office."

"He was a shot caller for the Latin Emperors," I said.

"And you were a spy," Sam said.

"I'm still a spy," I said.

"And I'm still a hundred eighty pounds. They're just buried under the other seventy-five." Sam took a sip from his Peroni. "I ever tell you about the time I dated a model from Milan?"

"No, I never heard about that."

"Her father owned a small fraction of Peroni. Whole house was like one big keg. I tell you, Mikey. I've made some mistakes in my life, but that relationship was not one of them."

"Where is she now?"

"Turns out she was KGB," Sam said. "It only lasted a weekend. One long, glorious weekend. Didn't find out she was KGB until I Googled her about a year ago. She's written a memoir and everything. I'm waiting for the English translation to see if I made it in."

"Your point?"

"People aren't always who they end up being."

That was true enough, but if Eduardo was really a different guy, why did he need my help?

"Apart from NBC," I said, "you pick anything else up?"

"I talked to a buddy of mine in the Department of Corrections, and he couldn't wait to talk about Eduardo. Says he's the reason he has faith in his job."

"No one talks like that," I said.

"I know. That's what I'm saying. He's not just clean. He's damn near an angel. His church is just one aspect of what he's doing. He's got a nonprofit called Honrado Incorporated that puts ex-gangsters to work doing everything from making T-shirts to running a bakery to learning how to invest their money, plus it sponsors a basketball league, operates its own Little League outlet, even has a huge bingo night and ladies' Bunco tournament. Honrado employs two hundred people, most of them either ex-cons or at-risk kids, and the board of directors is made up of athletes, politicians, financiers, artists—you name it. Mikey, they've even got their own newspaper that they write, print and deliver."

"This is a guy who used to shake down fifth-graders for their lunch money," I said.

"And there are photos of me where I look like Sonny Crockett," Sam said. "We all make mistakes."

"When did he go from gangster to gang star?"

Sam tapped my bottle of Peroni with his. "Nice turn of a phrase there," he said.

"I thought you'd like that."

"Anyway," Sam said, "looks like he got released from Coleman in 2000."

"That's a lot of progress in ten years," I said.

"He was already brokering peace deals between rival gangs from the joint," Sam said. "Wrote a children's book about the ills of gang life, and someone tried to get him nominated for a Nobel Prize. President Clinton mentioned him in a speech."

"While he was in prison?"

"I told you, Mikey, the guy is bulletproof now. He's made a complete change in his life. A standard-bearer for the good that prison can do for a guy."

"Just so I'm clear," I said, "they executed the guy who founded the Crips, right?"

"Eduardo wasn't up on murder charges," Sam said. "They had him on RICO charges—a lot of them—but he didn't have a single conviction on violent crimes."

"He got sentenced to fifty years for RICO?"

"Latin Emperors are a worldwide organization, Mikey," Sam said. "And he was near the top of the chain. By the time he got into prison, he was the top guy in Miami. So he might have been calling shots, but no one ever was able to trace them back to him."

I shook my head. "That can't be," I said. "Remember that thing we did in El Salvador in 1994?"

"With the tanks?"

"No," I said, "the other thing."

"Oh . . . with the Russians?"

"No," I said. "I forgot about that. No, the other thing."

"The urban renewal?"

"Yes. He was involved with that. He was the top of the pyramid. Even from prison, he was the guy making the calls."

"Mikey, that was a covert operation. Even if he was involved, what we did in El Salvador didn't actually happen."

"So your guy says he's a hundred percent legit?"

"It's not just my guy," Sam said. "Eduardo Santiago is known around the world for the work he does, Mike. This is a guy who is making a difference, which is a lot more than I can say for you and me."

It seemed hard to believe that a guy like Eduardo Santiago could be completely rehabilitated, but everything Sam said seemed to indicate it was true. Which I guess is why people go to prison.

"I'm still having a hard time with the fact that he got thirty-five years clipped off of his sentence," I said.

"He's got influential friends," Sam said. "Or he snitched out the right guy."

"Or a combination of both," I said.

"And what's so wrong with snitching?" Sam asked.

"He found the Lord and stopped covering for the cowards he ran with. That's good behavior right there."

"I guess you're right," I said. "You want to come with me tomorrow?"

"No can do, Mikey," Sam said. "I've got a big date."

"Really?"

"No," Sam said. "I just thought I'd see what you'd say when I told you I couldn't come. You want Chuck Finley for this?"

"I think Sam Axe will do just fine," I said.

Our waiter came by then and dropped off our dinners—veal Milanese for Sam, fettuccini Alfredo with the sauce on the side for me, so, essentially, just a plate of noodles—and regarded the growing scale of Sam's empty bottle collection. "Anything else to drink, sir?" the waiter asked.

"Whatever else you have," Sam said.

When building a fortress, it's important to understand the message you want to send. The White House, for instance, was built with the understanding that people visiting it for the first time would be awed by the size and scale and thus would feel awed by the size and scale of the American government. Your fortress tells unwelcome visitors who you are, what you're made of and, likely, what you're willing to risk to protect yourself.

It used to be that you could walk right up to the front door of the White House and ask to pet Calvin Coolidge's dog. Now, in many Miami neighborhoods, you're stopped at a gate by an out-of-work cop who demands a DNA sample before you're allowed inside. And yet Eduardo Santiago's fortress projected no such audacity. It looked, for all intents and purposes, like a college campus. A very small college, and one filled with tatted-up ex-gangsters sitting under trees, but a college no less.

"I didn't know they still had trees in this part of town," Sam said. We were a few blocks from the Orange Bowl, just off of Northwest Fourth Street, in an area mostly surrounded by stucco warehouses, three-story apartment complexes and small houses behind chain-link fences. In comparison, Eduardo's church and the buildings for Honrado were bunched around a bucolic expanse of green grass, towering shade trees and discreet water features. There were picnic tables and Adirondack chairs placed seemingly at random in different areas, though it had a designer's touch for what randomness should be, hallmarked by the fact that the chairs and tables were bolted onto concrete slabs. It was still Miami, after all.

There were seven buildings in all and each was a modern steel-and-glass structure, even the church. There wasn't a spot of graffiti anywhere, nor was there any visible security. The adults and kids who sat on the grass and walked between the buildings looked tough from afar, which is to say that they looked like they *thought* they looked tough, but really just looked like they'd been terribly misguided at some point. Who walks with a limp when they don't need to?

For the most part, however, everyone wore clothes that fit and most of the men, women, girls and boys wore identical gray polo shirts with the logo for Honrado Incorporated on the left breast pocket. If you want to build an army, the first thing you need to do is get them into uniform. This is true if you're in the marines or if you're in the Bloods. People like to feel like they belong to something larger than themselves, and even here, at a business run by a church, those rules still applied.

"What was this place before it was this?" I asked.

Sam looked around. "Nothing. That would be my guess."

"Five acres of nothing?"

"Sure wasn't a great, big park with Adirondack chairs."

"No," I said, "I would have remembered that."

"Seems to me I remember parking here before football games. It was one of those vacant blacktop lots that some industrious soul decided to sit in front of with a sign offering parking for five bucks less than at the stadium."

"This couldn't have been cheap to renovate," I said.

We made our way across the lawn to the church's administrative offices. Double doors opened into a rounded portico where a young woman with a headset on sat behind a small desk. Unlike the young women who had the same job at the hotels along South Beach or the busy offices in Coconut Grove, this woman had a ragged scar that stretched from the corner of her right eye, crossed over her nose and continued all the way over her left cheek and down across her jawline. It was rippled and red and maybe half an inch wide. It was unmistakable: Someone had slashed her face with a razor blade.

"Can I help you?" she asked.

"We're here to see Eduardo," I stopped myself, considered the surroundings, and then corrected, "Father Eduardo."

"Do you have an appointment?"

"No," I said, "but he's expecting me. Tell him his friend from the car wash is here."

The girl touched her ear and spoke into the headset. "Father Santiago? Your friend from the car wash is here. Would you like me to take them to the conference room? Yes, no problem, Father." The girl tapped her ear again and smiled up at us. "Father Santiago is running a few minutes behind schedule. He says he'll be right out to see you in a moment. Can I get you something to drink while you wait?"

"What do you have in a bottle?" Sam asked.

"Evian or Dasani," she said.

"He'll have Evian," I said before Sam could answer.

"No problem," she said. She slid a clipboard toward me and asked me to sign in, which I did. Except that I said my name was Napoleon Solo, because I thought it prudent not to have my name on the official visitor's list of any organization. I handed the clipboard to Sam. He signed it Illya Kuryakin and handed it back to the girl, who then proceeded to not even bother to look at it, which Sam clearly viewed as a shame. The girl then got up and walked down the narrow hall to her left, and I saw that her scar actually stretched around her neck, too.

Sam and I sat down in the lobby, and a few moments later, the girl returned with our waters.

"Can I get you anything else?" she asked.

"Can I ask you a question?" I said.

Immediately, the girl's hand flared up toward the scar on her face. "Sure," she said, though I could tell she felt uneasy. "I get asked questions all the time."

"Do you like working here?" I said.

"Pardon?"

"Do you like your job here? Has it been good for you to work here?"

"Working for Father Santiago is the best thing that has ever happened to me," she said.

I looked at Sam to see if he was gloating, but he was too busy trying to figure out the twist top of his water.

"How long have you been here?"

"A year. Maybe a little more. Soon as I got out, Father Santiago told me I could work for him."

Got out. So comfortable telling a stranger she'd done time. "Where were you?"

"Homestead," she said. "You ever been there?"

"No," I said.

"It's south of here. It wasn't so bad. You know. It was actually safer for me. Crazy, right?"

"Crazy," I said. "How old are you?"

"You don't ask a lady that," Sam said, which made the girl smile. "You ask how young they are, right?"

"Twenty-three," she said. "But I feel older."

"You look like a million bucks," Sam said.

The girl touched her scar. She was pretty, you could see that, even with the gouge across her face and neck.

"Father Santiago says that I could get plastic surgery for this. What do you think?"

"You could," I said. I pointed at the scar under my left eye. "I was going to get this fixed, but I decided it gave me character. Something to talk about on dates. Sam, you have any scars?"

"Let me tell you about scars," Sam said, and then proceeded to regale the girl with stories about the myriad holes and punctures and cuts that littered his body, each one another battlefield somewhere. I got the sense that the girl didn't believe a word he was saying—when he brought up that shrapnel wound from the Falklands, I actually heard her sigh with something near to resignation—but the sad fact is that I don't think he made anything up. "All of which is to say," Sam continued, "it's all about quality of life. If you think you'll have a better life without that scar, then I say do yourself a favor, sister, and get it taken care of."

"I will, then," she said. "Father Santiago says he's going to get a friend to help pay for it."

"He have a lot of friends?" I asked.

"Don't you read the newspaper?" she asked.

Before I could answer again, that no, I didn't read the newspaper, Eduardo Santiago emerged from a conference room with his arm over a man's shoulder. The man wore a beautifully tailored charcoal gray suit, a crisp white shirt and a silver tie. On his feet were wingtips shined to a glow, on his wrist was an understated gold watch with a black face and on his head was a perfectly combed field of salt-and-pepper hair.

He looked like somebody. He looked like a Somebody. But then so did Eduardo in his navy blue suit and tan shirt opened at the collar, enough so that you could still make out the tattoos crawling up from his chest.

"Who is that with Eduardo?" I asked Sam.

"The mayor," Sam said.

"Of where?"

"Miami," Sam said.

Eduardo and the mayor shook hands, laughed about something, shook hands again and then the mayor said, as he walked toward us, "And remember to let me know when I can get you stuck in that sand trap again, Father!"

Sam stood up when the mayor was just a few feet away. "Mr. Mayor," he said, and gave the politician a dignified nod of his head.

The mayor had a flicker of recognition when he saw Sam. And it wasn't a flicker that screamed with joy. "Mr. Axe," he said, and nodded right back at Sam, but also quickened his step out the door.

I looked at Sam. "You know the mayor of Miami?"

"I knew his wife," he said.

"A buddy of yours?"

"Of a kind, yes."

When you're a spy, there's no such thing as too much information. When you're someone's friend, the same rules do not apply.

"Gentlemen," Eduardo Santiago said, "please, come into my office. We have much to talk about."

3

There are offices—like the one I sat in with my mother and Eduardo Santiago the previous day—that serve a specific purpose, as a place where one person can sit comfortably to work on a computer. And then there are offices like the one Eduardo Santiago kept for himself at Honrado Incorporated, which was as wide as my loft, contained two leather sofas, a flat-screen television mounted to the wall, a small glass-faced refrigerator filled with bottled water, a round table covered in blueprints and an entire wall dedicated to photos. Eduardo with various celebrities, politicians, athletes and entertainers, certainly, but most of the photos were actually of Eduardo with kids and with young men and women out in the community. There were also framed news stories and features from the *Miami Herald*, *New York Times*, *Los Angeles Times* and even a snappy little color thing from *USA Today*. I stopped and read a few lines in each. Everything my mother and Sam said was parroted in the pages of the nation's most esteemed newspapers: Eduardo Santiago had done the impossible and now was using himself as a prime example for the kids coming out of Miami's battle-hardened neighborhoods.

"You'll have to pardon my ego," Eduardo said when he saw me reading his wall.

"It looks like you've done some great things," I said. "My mother didn't lie."

"Not this time," Sam said.

"I've been very blessed." Eduardo motioned to the round conference table. "Please, my friends, have a seat."

It was very strange. When I had seen Eduardo the previous day, he spoke to me in a kind of refined street patois, but here he spoke as if he'd gone to private schools his entire life. Perhaps that was the surest sign Eduardo Santiago was a different person now—he knew how to change his persona for a given situation. That was a talent I could appreciate.

We sat down at the table, but Eduardo remained standing at first, as if he wasn't sure this was, in fact, the course of action he wanted to take. How odd it must be to meet with the mayor of the city at one moment and then whatever, or whomever, Sam and I were the next.

The key to making someone comfortable, even in their own home or sanctuary, is to ask him questions about himself. People love to talk about themselves. This is why so many people admit to crimes when police interrogate them—they simply cannot help themselves from themselves.

I picked up one of the blueprints. "Are you expanding?"

"Oh, yes," Eduardo said. He stood between Sam and me and looked at the blueprint. "That will be our greenhouse. We plan on having more sustainable gardens here in the future, so we can begin providing organic vegetables. Do you know that the average apple you eat contains over fifty trace chemicals in its skin?"

"I didn't know that."

"And look at yourself. You should know. You're fit. You're smart. Now think about these kids in these neighborhoods. You think any of them have any idea about pesticides in their food?"

"I'd guess that's the least of their concerns," Sam said.

"You would guess correctly," Eduardo said. "Whoever you are."

"Mikey didn't tell you I was coming?" Sam said. He shook Eduardo's hand. "Sam Axe at your service. You've got the full faith and credit of the United States government right here in my handshake."

"That's not an entity I trust, but I assume if you are with Mr. Westen that you are trustworthy."

"That's not a good assumption," I said.

"Ah, but it is an educated guess," he said. "Educating someone is different from making them concerned about something. Same with the kids and the organic food. People today, they do not know the difference between education and fear-making." He sighed then and shook his head. He finally took a seat across from us. "This is precisely what I was talking to the mayor about. All of this money to teach children what to be afraid of, and no money to teach them music or art or, well, you know how it is. Do you know I learned how to play the violin in prison? It's true."

"Maybe more people should go to prison," I said.

"Just because it is true doesn't mean it isn't a shame, Mr. Westen."

I laughed.

"You find that funny?" he said.

"I find it funny you just called me Mr. Westen," I said. "I was trying to remember the last time I saw you before yesterday. And you know what I remembered? You actually turned my brother, Nate, upside down and shook all of the change out of his pockets."

"Mikey, that's what kids do," Sam said.

"He wasn't a kid," I said. "Do you remember this, Eduardo?"

"I'm afraid I do not. Not because it didn't happen, but because I did it to so many people. How old was I?"

"I don't know," I said, "maybe seventeen? Maybe eighteen? Old enough and rich enough not to need a kid's pocket change."

"It was never need," Eduardo said. "And where were you at this time?"

"I was coming up with a bat in my hand to crush over your head," I said. "Unfortunately, a teacher saw me coming and wouldn't let me."

"Unfortunately?" he said.

"Could have saved you and a lot of other people a lot of grief," I said.

"I get the sense you don't believe I am a changed person," Eduardo said.

"You sense correctly."

"I need your help, Michael," Eduardo said. "So I hope I can convince you that I am worthy of it."

"How did you even know I exist?"

"You helped a friend of mine," he said. "Ernie Paseo. He was having trouble with some gangsters."

Can no one keep a secret anymore? Ernie Paseo had been one of the first people I'd helped in Miami. He had also been sworn to tell no one that I'd helped him, and had subsequently referred people to me like I was a Merry Maid.

Ernie was not the kind of person to engage with crooks, and the mere fact that he'd mentioned me to Eduardo was a good sign.

"Ernie's been good for business," Sam said.

"Remind me not to give him any secret launch codes," I said.

"He told me I could trust you," Eduardo said. "He told me you were a good and honest man and that you weren't scared of anything. Your name sounded familiar, so I asked some of our old . . . associates . . . if you were the same person as I recalled from childhood."

Associates. That could mean only that Eduardo made some phone calls to a few of the less desirables we'd both gone to school with and maybe he'd rolled with. "No one you knew from school knows I'm back," I said.

"That's funny," he said. "You have a friend who sells guns?"

Fiona.

"No," I said.

"A girl, maybe? Wears short skirts and always has automatic weapons?"

Fiona, for sure.

"Nope. Sam, you know anyone like that?"

"Can't say I do, Mikey. Sounds like a very danger-ous person. If I see her, I'll call nine-one-one."

We both gave Eduardo our most professional smiles.

"I don't care, Mr. Westen, who you know. Just know people are aware of your presence in town. The right kind of people and the wrong kind of people. Just like you and me. The difference is that I have a path guided by the Lord, and that path tells me that at every turn I'll need to make right the sins of my youth. I don't think you feel the same way."

"I'm not a criminal, Eduardo. I never was."

"Maybe not in your eyes. But, Mr. Westen, you have killed, have you not?"

"I have," I said.

"That's against someone's law," he said.

He certainly had a way of evening the scales. And the truth is, I believed him. The evidence was all around, and his demeanor suggested a man who'd changed his life and was dedicated to helping others.

"You've done an excellent job letting me know that we are cut from the same cloth, that you've been saved and that the world is going to be just fine now that you're on the job. So, Eduardo, what do you need me for? You need help getting out of the sand trap the mayor left you in?"

Eduardo exhaled through his mouth and his entire body wilted a bit inside his expensive suit. He loos-ened his tie and took off his coat, and then held up another blueprint. "You see this?" he asked. "This is going to be our new library. Paid for entirely through donations. It will be state-of-the-art—computer retrieval system, digital library of every newspaper in America—everything—and we will be training librarians here. It's true. Library science classes will take place on Northwest Fourth Street. This?" He pointed at yet another blueprint. "This is going to be an auto shop. We had one before, but it wasn't here. It was out near the juvie, so I couldn't watch it, and soon it became a chop shop. You know? Kids, they will fall back into bad habits. So many plans. Next year, I'll have another hundred fifty people working, if everything goes as planned."

"Who is shaking you down?" I said.

Eduardo got up, went to his desk and came back with a thick manila envelope. "I can trust you?" he asked.

"I'm here, aren't I?"

He handed me the envelope and then sat behind us on one of the leather sofas. It was as if he didn't even want to be in proximity to the contents I was pulling out and sharing with Sam. But the thing was, there wasn't anything particularly incriminating in the envelope, just old photos of Eduardo with various other members of the Latin Emperors. There were several photos that featured pictures of Eduardo with guns and a few that showed drugs, but none of this was a mystery to anyone—it was, apparently, what had made Eduardo such a superstar.

"I don't get it," I said.

"Those men," he said, "most of them are dead."

"Did you kill them?" I said.

"No."

"Then what's the problem?"

"No one knows where their bodies are, either," he said.

I gave Sam a look. This was where things tended to get dicey. I reminded myself to give Ernie Paseo a call at some point to tell him to forget I ever existed. "Do you know where the bodies are?" I said.

"No, no, of course not," he said. "But someone does."

"Here's the deal, Eduardo," I said, "I need you to just tell me what the problem is. I'll tell you if I can solve it, and this will all be over in a matter of moments."

"I have divorced myself from this life, you understand," he said.

"I understand. Everyone does. President Clinton does. God does. Now, spill it."

Eduardo peeled himself off the sofa and came back to the table, went through the photos one time, very quickly, and then stopped when he landed on a picture of himself at maybe twenty-five, his shirtless torso thick with muscles and ink, his eyes hidden behind wraparound sunglasses, standing beside a man who could have been his twin, right down to the prison tattoos. "This is Jaime Gonzalez. People called him Junior. He's a few years older than me, but was held back two years. Played football, too."

"He ever smack around Mike's brother?" Sam asked.

"Most likely," Eduardo said.

"I don't remember him," I said.

"He recruited me into the Latin Emperors, jumped me in, helped me run the set. We both went up at the same time, ended up taking over the prison branch, diversified our interests."

"He help with El Salvador?" Sam asked.

Eduardo actually twitched backward in surprise. "How did you . . ." he began. "Never mind. Never mind. But yes. His mother is from El Salvador, so he had dual citizenship. It was his idea to start moving into the voids there."

It was actually a smart move on Gonzalez' part, even if it was an illegal one that caught the attention of the United States government and certain covert operatives. I didn't bother to tell Eduardo that, but I believed it to be true nevertheless.

"Let me guess," I said, "you snitched on Junior to get a break on your sentence."

"It wasn't snitching," Eduardo said. "It was a calling. It was the right thing. I didn't know it would reduce my sentence, and I, frankly, didn't care. It was the right thing to do."

I took a look at the photo again. Junior Gonzalez had muscles where other people had hair follicles. "Where was he when this all went down?" I asked. "Because I can't see him not putting a shank in you if he knew about it."

"I'd already been transferred to the minimum-security section," he said. "I was a priest, after all."

"What did you give up?" I asked.

Eduardo did that big exhaling thing he seemed to enjoy. A guy that big, when he exhaled through his mouth, it was like a jet engine starting. "Everything," he said. "Me, you know, I didn't get dirty. I kept up above the game, you know? Slang here and there. Set up jobs. Maybe move a little product myself. Maybe make a big deal about someone disrespecting us, but I didn't put a cap in anyone, you know?"

There was that weird language shift. It was funny. When Eduardo Santiago was in his element, talking about his mission in life now, he sounded like a CEO, but when he got involved in the old times, he started to sound like a gangster again.

"You talk like that when you speak with the kids?" I asked.

"Like what?" he said.

"You just sounded like you were still on the streets."

"Yeah," Sam said. "Five minutes ago, I thought you were running for Congress. Just now, I thought you were going to ask me to spot you in the chow line."

"I guess I don't even notice it," he said. "The devil, he's in all of us, or he tries to be. Maybe that's him trying to weed his way out into the world."

This devil-and-God talk was wearing thin—if I had a core belief, it was probably one my dad taught me: never write bad checks. He'd done it enough to know, but when applied to every aspect of your life, it was good advice.

"Anyway," Eduardo said. He cleared his throat, and I could tell he was about to try to tell his story without sounding like a thug. "I told the feds who Junior had killed, what shots he'd called, gave them information on the drug trade we had. But mostly? Mostly they wanted to get control of the prisons. At the time, Latin Emperors ran all the prisons up from Florida to New York. La Eme had the West Coast; Texas Syndicate was running Texas, Oklahoma—that cowboy shit. Black Guerilla Family and all those Blood and Crip sets run the South and places like Rikers. But we were political, too, and that made it different. We had clout."

"Funny," Sam said, "I don't see the Latin Emperors running some Attica game."

"Not from the outside, you don't," he said. "But it's a whole other culture on the inside. And we ran it. By the time I was running the show, I was like Obama. All hope and change and all that. Junior, he didn't see it like I saw it. He was down for crime, not empowerment. That's where we diverged. So I gave up what I gave up and things got easier for me, relations cooled inside, and eventually I got my release and now here I am."

"And where is Junior?" I said.

"He was released last year," he said.

"Blood in, blood out," I said. "So I take it he's looking for yours now?"

"More a pound of flesh," Eduardo said. "He wants in on this business, says because of our oath to each other, every dime that passes through Honrado, half is his. And he wants to run Latin Emperor business through here, launder their money through my organization. And he wants payback. I think that is the largest issue. He did twenty-five years."

"How'd he get out?" Sam asked.

"Overcrowding," Eduardo said. He gave a shrug. "Good behavior. Paid off the right people. These things happen. He may have been the kingpin all these years, but I suspect even he saw after a while that the path to getting out of prison was paved with nonviolence."

"So, call the cops," I said. "That's an easy extortion case."

"I can't," he said. "I got pulled over two weeks ago right here on the corner. I thought maybe I'd run through the stop sign. Instead, the officer came to my window and handed me that envelope. Didn't say a word. Just dropped it on my lap. Three days ago, there's a knock on my door, at my home, and it's another officer. He tells me he was just in the area and wanted to make sure I was still alive. That's all he says."

"You recognize this cop?" Sam asked.

"No, I'd never seen him."

"Thing is," Sam said, "anyone can get a cop uniform, and anyone with a little time and money can get a cop car. So you don't know if you're dealing with real police."

Eduardo squirmed in his seat. He was being eaten up by this, but there was something more. We just hadn't gotten to it yet. "You see, that's true. But the fact is, we've . . . they've . . . had police on the payroll for thirty years."

"You telling me the Latin Emperors employ crooked cops?" Sam said.

"Mr. Axe, please, tell me you are aware that the Miami PD has a rich history of being on the take. Since the days of Al Capone."

"Okay," I said, "so the Emperors have bad cops on their books. Fine. Why not call your friend the mayor?"

Eduardo did that squirming thing again. I was beginning to know his tells—he might be a pious man, but he was also a nervous man. "Junior called the other day. Understand, I have not spoken to this man in almost twenty years. He said to me that he was happy to see that I was prospering and that I was doing good things in the community, and that I'd helped Emperors that had been released from prison get jobs," Eduardo said. "And then he told me that if I didn't do as he asked, he'd go public with what he knows about our past, about where the bodies are buried—literally, where the bodies are buried."

"I thought you didn't kill anyone. I thought you never got arrested for violent crimes," I said.

"How do you get arrested for a crime no one knows was committed?" Eduardo said. "These men, they weren't missed by anyone. These are criminals, Michael, that maybe rolled down to Miami after getting out of prison, or they're people who never had families, or people whose families never expected to hear from them again. These were not good people. But the fact is, I did not kill them. I did not order their deaths."

"How can that be if you ran the gang?" Sam said.

"Division of labor," Eduardo said, "and plausible deniability, I suppose. In terms you can both understand, Junior ran the defense and the judicial, and I was in charge of the economy and outreach. Those were our skill sets."

"Obviously," I said.

"And if I am arrested again," Eduardo says, "I'm in prison for life. And that would be a short life. I would be dead within an hour, I assure you. Even though I am innocent, it wouldn't matter. I'm confident my involvement at all would constitute a conspiracy charge, and I am confident that the judicial system would happily use me as a public relations target. All of this, all of what you see here, would be gone. This is all because of me, Michael, because of my desire to atone and my desire to help these kids so that they don't necessarily make the mistakes I made. And here, my past can ruin it. I did my time. I admit my mistakes. I admit my crimes. I will not let all of the good I am doing fall to waste. And that—that, Mr. Westen—is why I cannot call the mayor or the president or anyone. You are my only hope."

The room fell silent. I frankly didn't know what I was going to do to help Eduardo, but I had the sense that he was right—no one else could help him, and without help, all that he'd done would crumble.

Plus, I liked being called his only hope. I felt a little like Obi-Wan Kenobi.

"Okay," I said. "I need time to think about this."

"And I can pay you whatever you require," he said.

"Well," Sam said, "there are going to be some expenses. . . ."

I put a hand up to stop Sam, which is a bit like hoping a feather could stop a freight train, but luckily it was still pretty early in the day for Sam, and he didn't quite have his normal midafternoon head of steam yet. "Don't worry about it," I said. "I need the karma. And so does Sam."

"One question," Eduardo said. "Are you actually a spy?"

"I am," I said. "Or I was. You and me, we've both been excommunicated from our organizations. You by choice, me by someone working behind me, trying to discredit the good I did, so I understand uniquely the situation you're in."

"How did you go from here to there?" Eduardo said. "And why are you back?"

"I could ask you the same question," I said. "We all make choices, Eduardo. I made the right ones. You made the wrong ones. And yet here we both are."

"A strange fact of life," he said.

I couldn't imagine a stranger one. "When are you supposed to have an answer for Junior?" I said.

"Two days," he said.

"You have a way of contacting him?"

"One of his soldiers is to come by tomorrow to confirm."

"No phone number?"

"No, no," Eduardo said. "I have no idea where he's even living. My people on the streets say he is not in the old neighborhoods."

"All right. When his guy comes, you tell him you want a face-to-face meeting here. When is this place the busiest?"

"All day," Eduardo said. "We have a shift that starts at seven, another at four, though we feed the workers at three thirty for the night shift."

"Tell him to be here at three thirty, then," I said. "Let him see the full workforce."

"What will we be telling him?"

"I don't know yet," I said. "But I have a few ideas."

Sam and I wound through the shaded lawn of Honrado Industries as we walked back to the car. There were flags in places where the new buildings were planned and signs, propped up with artist renderings of what the buildings would look like. The weird thing was that just across the street from this small bit of paradise—paradise built on the religious reformation of a gangster and put in peril by his past—was the real world: a teenage girl pushing a baby stroller, a homeless man asleep in an apartment complex carport, a stray dog nosing around for scraps.

"Here's what I don't get," Sam said. "Why come back here? If you're Father Eduardo, I mean. Why not just move to Idaho and start all over? He had to expect that he'd run into these kinds of problems eventually."

"Home is home," I said. "And besides, he's paying penance."

"I dunno, Mikey," Sam said. "I don't see myself running over to Fallujah when I retire just to pay penance. I could live my whole life without seeing the Republican Guard again and I'd be perfectly fine. Know what I mean?"

"You can't discount ego, either," I said. "Eduardo wouldn't be lunching with the mayor if he lived in Boise. He might be doing it all for the good, but there's still a little bit of the showboat gangster I remember in him."

"You gotta have that to make it in the God game," Sam said. "Look at Tammy Faye Baker. She wasn't exactly reserved and refined."

He was right. He usually is. "Listen," I said, "I want you to find out what you can on Junior Gonzalez. I need to know just what kind of guy we're up against."

"If he's got cops," Sam said, "I'm a little limited on my sources. People tend to talk when they think something of interest is happening, and you never know who knows who in law enforcement."

"I'm sure you'll find someone who can help," I said.

"I can go back to my guy in Corrections, but he'll only know so much. I've got a buddy who did some time at the same prison while Junior was there," Sam said. "That might be a place to start. And I'm pretty sure he's no friend of the local law. He runs a pretty lucrative post-lockup business these days, is my understanding. You know how Father Eduardo gets kids back on the road to good? My buddy, he paves the road with the papers they might one day need if they ever want to work a real job."

"What was your friend in for?" I asked, which is probably the wrong question to ask anyone when they say they have a friend who's done time.

"Oh, you know, fraud, some passport business, minor nonviolent acts meant to increase his personal wealth. That sort of thing. Good guy. You'd love him. I'll call him and see if we can meet up for drinks. He's the kind of guy who likes a little lubrication."

"I know the type," I said.

"Ah, Mikey, you only know the half. My guy? He still makes pruno at home. You'd love it. Puts a little spice in there that'll make you jump out of your socks. Of course, if he makes it wrong, it can also kill you. So it adds a bit of thrill to the evening."

"That's great," I said.

When we reached my Charger, there was a young

man of about twenty walking slow circles around it. He had on the same polo shirt as the rest of the kids working at the facility. "This yours?" he asked.

"Yes," I said.

"Nineteen seventy-three?" he asked.

"Nineteen seventy-four," I said.

"Original interior?"

"It's had a few accidents," I said, though I opted not to tell him the number of times I'd fixed bullet holes in the leather . . . or the scrubbing that goes into getting scorch marks out . . . or, well, the periodic exercise involved with removing blood. "But yes, the original interior."

"The body looks good. You should lower it," he said.

"Not my style," I said.

The kid considered this. "Then at least you should buff out the bullet marks on the passenger's side."

"I'm going to get on that," I said.

"You pull it to the auto shop around back. I'll do it free of charge. Good practice, homes. Know what I'm saying?"

Unfortunately, I did.

I looked at Sam. "You got twenty minutes?" I said.

4

Dealing with a source or a confidential informant is always a dicey proposition, but Sam Axe had made it into a kind of performance art. The way he figured it, people wanted to tell you their deepest and darkest secrets, because what fun is it knowing something salacious if you can't revel in the knowledge with a friend? And maybe over a couple of beers? And maybe, in some cases, earn some cash for what you know?

The issues were always the same with people in the know, however: The more you used them for important information, the more power they began to accrue, and thus the more demands they'd start to make for the privilege of giving you what you needed. So Sam tried not to use the same sources more than one or two times. And at all times, Sam tried to keep his sources feeling like what they were sharing was an act of friendship. What better way to show that you like someone than to give up information on a third party? It was a lesson the FBI would have been smart to pick up on—back when they had Sam informing on Michael's whereabouts, it was never even posed as an issue of friendship. It was always under a veil of threats: Do this or lose your retirement package, lose your health benefits, get audited for the rest of your life.

So when Sam called K-Dog Dorsey to see if he might want to meet up for drinks, he didn't bother to let him know that he intended to pump him for information. The last thing any ex-con wants is to be questioned. The best way to get information out of someone like K-Dog is to perform a subtle form of conversational manipulation that involves, well, making him talk about things that would make him sound like a tough guy.

Problem was, Sam had to drink K-Dog's pruno in the process of this conversation, which meant there was a high likelihood he'd forget salient details in the process. So he did what any good operative would do: He wired himself. He also took a cab to K-Dog's, since there was an even higher likelihood he'd be far past the legal limit to drive just by breathing the air in K-Dog's house. He was pretty sure K-Dog brewed his concoction in a more sterile environment than the prison toilet he learned his trade with, but, nevertheless, Sam also brought some antibiotics to the party, too.

Of all his preparations, the antibiotics seemed like the smartest move to Sam after only a few minutes in K-Dog's home. It was the sheer amount of animal hair in the place that got Sam spooked. It floated in the air. It was stuck to the walls. It covered the sofa Sam sat on. How could a person live with that much dog hair? At some point, wouldn't it get into the food supply? Sam didn't like to cast aspersions on how other people lived, but in this case he felt like maybe K-Dog needed an intervention from someone who really cared about him. Unfortunately, Sam didn't really care about him that deeply, so he was in something of a pickle.

K-Dog walked into the living room, holding a pitcher of pruno in one hand and two glasses in the other. At least all three of those things looked clean, though all would need proper inspection. "Now it's a party," K-Dog said. "Like old times. K-Dog and the Axe, right?"

"Sure thing," Sam said. It was true they'd had some old times, but it wasn't like they were best friends. In fact, they'd met under rather odd circumstances. K-Dog (whose real name was Kevin, but no one bothered to call him that, especially since he wore a gold chain with a dog bone around his neck and had a tattoo of a bulldog on both of his arms and the words "Dog Pound" etched across his chest) had run a nice fake-passport business back in the late eighties and early nineties, before he was pinched post-9/11. Sam had met a nice girl in Cuba on a mission and couldn't get anyone in the government to listen to him about what an important, uh, *asset* she'd be, and so he had to turn to K-Dog to try to get a decent batch of papers for her. It cost him a bit of dough, but it was worth it . . . or, well, it would have been worth it if the girl ever even bothered to give him a call once she got stateside, but Sam didn't dwell on that. You win some, you lose some, and sometimes you end up buying a fake passport for someone.

Over the years, though, they'd formed a nice friendship based on mutual respect and the fact that they both had things on the other person that could be used against the other. Sam even tried to help after he got picked up after 9/11, but K-Dog understood that old alliances didn't mean much in the scope of world calamity. So he did his time. And now here they were again . . . drinking prison wine.

K-Dog filled Sam's glass and then the two toasted, as if they were drinking some nice scotch. Sam took a sip of his pruno, swallowed, and then felt a burning sensation akin to drinking electricity. He had to try to keep his balance, even though he was sitting down.

"Good?" K-Dog asked.

"The best," Sam said.

"Added a little something new this time," K-Dog said.

"Battery acid?"

K-Dog slapped Sam's leg. "I ain't in prison, Axe Man. I put in a couple habanero chili peppers."

"A couple?"

"I wanted it to have that same bite I remembered from the joint. You can't get that usually unless you add something like engine coolant or acid. Thought the habaneros would do the trick."

That explained the thick brow of sweat that had already formed on Sam's neck. But it also proved the best opening Sam could think of to get the information he needed out of K-Dog.

"Who taught you how to make this?" Sam knew the answer to this already, since it was the first thing he'd asked him after their last evening on the pruno train, but Sam knew it would lead to where he wanted to go.

"Originally? My man Ernesto. We bunked for six

months before he caught a shank. Poor guy. He's pissing out of a tube now."

"Who cut him?" Sam liked saying things like "Who cut him?" It reminded him of being a kid and watching prison movies, which is probably why prisoners talked like that, too. Everything anyone knew anymore was learned on television. Sam took another sip of the pruno. It went down smoother this time, possibly because he no longer had feeling in his extremities.

"Mexican Mafia guy," K-Dog said. He took another drink, too, but made a face. "You think this needs more ethanol?"

"No," Sam said. "They have some beef? I mean, wasn't Ernesto in his fifties?" Oh, crap, Sam thought, he hadn't told me that again. Fortunately, K-Dog seemed to have been tasting his work all day long and didn't seem to notice Sam's fumble.

"Well, Ernesto, he was Latin Emperor from back in the day, and the Mexican Mafia was trying to make a move into Coleman back then, and for some reason they thought Ernesto was a shot caller. Man, he was just an old-ass man already. Read books most of the time. Didn't even lift anymore. He thought it was foolishness and got stuck regardless. Sam, my man, don't do time."

"I'm not planning on it," Sam said.

"Who plans on it?"

K-Dog actually had a misty look in his eyes. Man, pruno could make anyone feel sentimental. Sam picked up his glass and toasted K-Dog, let him know he felt his pain.

"You gotta be tough," Sam said.

"True," K-Dog said, his composure back where it should be.

"Who was the toughest Latin Emperor?"

K-Dog scratched his chin and really gave it some thought. "Well," he said, "I think you start with a guy like Junior Gonzalez and work your way down. You know of him?"

"Can't say I do."

"You should keep it that way," K-Dog said. "He's out now. Literally ran into him at Publix one day. You know, that's the funny thing. Standing in line, buying your shit—you know, Pop-Tarts, Fruit Roll-Ups, whatever—and you look across the aisle and there's some gangster in line buying the same shit, plus, you know, a big thing of Woolite, paper towels, whatever. Even a gangster needs to wash his shit, right?"

"You guys talk about old times in the parking lot?" Sam hoped he wasn't overplaying his hand, but, then, he couldn't really feel his hands anymore.

"We talked some shop. I told him I was keeping it on the narrow, got my own printing company now, all that. He told me he was ruling, which I took to mean he wasn't giving up the life."

Ruling. Interesting.

"Was he top dog in prison?" Sam asked.

"Oh, indeed," K-Dog said. Just then, one of K-Dog's three cocker spaniels came bounding into the room and leaped onto the couch with Sam. For a guy named K-Dog, it didn't really fit that he was housing spaniels, but even Sam had to admit they were cute. He could have lived without seeing K-Dog giving the one on the sofa a kiss on the lips, however. "Know what I missed most in prison? These little guys. All my life, I've had spaniels. They're just good, nice dogs. Now, Junior? He was bad news my first couple of years. But by the time I got out? He was working in the library, leading education groups, had the warden's ear on things. Complete turnaround. Homeboy had already done twenty-five, right? He learned to play the game like all the rest. Me? I just had five years, so I knew I could get out in three, four, if I kept my nose clean. Ernesto? He had my back until that shank, but even still, people didn't give me too much trouble, on account of what I could do with paper and ink. But Junior was LE to the fullest. Even if he was toeing the line, you knew he was running that gang, inside and out."

Sam reached over and scratched the dog behind its ear, which caused the dog to emit a low growl of pleasure. If only all things were so easy. He decided to move the conversation closer to the finer points, seeing as the dog's growl echoed in his head like he was at a Pink Floyd concert in 1974, minus the floating pig and the laser, though he had the feeling that any more pruno would bring those forth, too.

"Did you know Father Eduardo was a Latin Emperor?" Sam said. "I saw him on television the other day and then got on the Google, and there it all was. Can't see him doing that gang-life stuff."

K-Dog took a deep gulp of his concoction and then grimaced. It occurred to Sam that K-Dog might want to get his liver examined by medical experts, because there was no way he was human. "He was out of Coleman, time I got there," K-Dog said. "Man, those peppers. That's some burn."

"What was the word on him, though? He must have caused a stir getting out of prison like he did and becoming a big deal."

"Oh, you didn't say his name around the LE. You say his name around Junior and you were asking for a beat down. Know what I heard? After he found Jesus and all that? After he started writing kids' books and shit, he actually turned state's and rolled up on Junior and maybe ten or eleven soldiers."

"How do you feel about that?"

"Man found God," K-Dog said. "What can you do? You can't do anything, that's what. You can't very well go out and kill a priest, right? Because those LE boys, they might be gang affiliated, as they say, but half of them are Catholic, go to church on the regular, all that. You kill a priest. They bury you under the prison. So what can you do?"

"You can't do anything," Sam agreed. "But now that they're both out on the streets again, you think Father Eduardo has a reason to be worried? I just see him on TV all the time, and you tell me this Junior is a lunatic. Wouldn't that put him over the edge?"

K-Dog shook his head slowly. "See, that's the kind of thing that makes you forget dude is of the cloth and all that. Pride. Loyalty. All that crap? I wouldn't be surprised if Father Eduardo wakes up dead one day soon. You won't be able to put Junior on it, I'd bet, because he's smooth now. But if Father Eduardo trips and lands on an upturned blade? That shit could happen on the real."

K-Dog clicked on the flat-screen TV he had mounted above his fireplace, and for a few minutes he and Sam watched Bobby Flay challenging someone to make the best apple pie on earth. "This guy?" K-Dog said, and motioned at the television. "He's a real gangster. Shows up at someone's house and tells them he's gonna beat their ass in what they do well."

Sam watched the show in silence for a bit while K-Dog kept up a running dialogue about how Bobby Flay was going to lose the competition because he didn't understand you gotta put your heart into a good apple pie. All Sam had learned up to this point was what he sort of knew already, so he decided to make a leap.

"You end up doing any business with Junior after you saw him at the market?"

"Oh, sure, sure," he said. "You see a guy like that on the outside? You let him know it's all cool. Because two things can happen: He can think you're avoiding him because you're scared of him, or he'll think you're avoiding him because maybe you snitched on him or something. And either way, if you end up back in prison—not that I intend to ever go back to prison, you understand, Axe Man—that's a death sentence. And even on the street, I don't want the LE having me down as an enemy. I mean, I pay my taxes now and I'm running a legit business."

"Really?"

"For the most part. For the most part. You know

how it is, Sam. Nothing that'll put me away. So I gave Junior my card and told him if he needed any printing or laminating or what have you, to come see me at my shop, avoid those Kinkos assholes. Couple weeks later, he brings me photos he wants blown up. Dead homies and the like. I also did some invites for one of his girl cousin's wedding. He's actually a pretty steady client."

"He always bring the stuff?"

"Nah," K-Dog said, "he's got homies who do his running around most of the time." K-Dog refilled his glass and Sam's, too. Crap, Sam thought. How much have I drank? He looked up at the television and Bobby Flay was gone, replaced by the Starship *Enterprise*. How long had he been sitting there watching television? Or had the channel just changed? Sam looked over his shoulder and through the window and saw that it was dark out. He had no idea what time it was. That was why pruno was good in prison. It messed with your time-space orientation.

"Why you so interested in Junior Gonzalez?" K-Dog asked finally, though Sam wasn't sure how much time had passed since they'd actually spoken.

"You're the one who started talking about him," Sam said.

K-Dog whistled and then started to laugh like he'd been told something especially hilarious.

"What are you laughing at?" Sam asked.

K-Dog got up from the sofa and disappeared into his kitchen. Sam could hear him rummaging around for something. Sam hoped to God it wasn't more ethanol. K-Dog came out a few minutes later holding a piece of paper, which he handed to Sam. It had an address on it.

"What's this?" Sam asked.

"Where Junior's been kicking it," he said. "One of my delivery guys made a drop there about a week ago."

"Why would you think I'd want that?"

"You're wearing a wire," K-Dog said. He pointed at Sam's chest, and Sam realized he'd unbuttoned his shirt at some point. It was those damn peppers.

"Sorry," Sam said. "I didn't want to forget anything."

"It's all right," K-Dog said, "I'm not gonna remember that you were wired up, either. That's the joy of pruno, right?"

"Right," Sam said. He read the address aloud so that it would get on his wire, since he was pretty sure he'd lose the paper before all things were said and done with K-Dog.

5

The aim of terrorism, in all its forms, is maddeningly simple. If you blow up a plane or yourself or a car parked in front of a busy hotel, or even if you just walk up and shoot a political figure, the reasoning can usually be broken into one of three things:

A desire for revenge.
A desire for acknowledgment.
A desire for publicity.

On the occasion that terrorism is used for strictly religious purposes, it's very rarely what any god has told someone to do, but rather the skewed interpretation that a god seeks revenge for being put behind the eight ball of some other religious idol.

The difference between a terrorist organization and a prison or street gang is negligible. The Latin Emperors didn't rise in prominence because of their political bent in the late nineties; they rose because they controlled a vast network of drug dealers and gave back to their own community—which is to say, they hired people in their own neighborhoods to do menial tasks, handed out money on holidays and gave the people of the projects a sense of identity and even a little bit of hope. When you're hopeless, even a gang seems like a good idea. The difference between Hamas and the Latin Emperors isn't that large: for both, it's about defending a piece of land and defending a particular identity, and the conflicts between power and preeminence.

How you defeat terrorism is more complex. But it begins with counterinsurgency. The level of violence— or the threat of violence—determines the response. Blow up the World Trade Center, for instance, and expect to have your country, or countries, invaded. Threaten the president via e-mail, and expect to have a Secret Service agent outside your door in about five minutes, just to make sure you're not producing anthrax in your mother's basement. Begin organizing an anarchist organization that believes violence is the only way to achieve the aims of the revolution—what this revolution will entail is anyone's guess—and expect to have a new member within a few weeks who, eventually, will be writing your FBI file.

As it related to Junior Gonzalez, I suspected we'd need a little of all of the above to stop his campaign against Father Eduardo.

"Why don't we just shoot him?" Fiona asked. I was at her place fixing her sink and explaining the situation I'd decided to enter all of us into, and, as per usual, Fiona had a very simple solution. That she had it while I was under her sink wasn't my choice. I called her that night and told her we needed to talk about a new client, and she told me that she'd love to discuss our latest venture over dinner, except that she was having a household problem and only I, with my superior skills, could fix the issue.

I thought she was speaking euphemistically.

She wasn't. So with wrench in hand, I told her all we knew.

"He hasn't actually done anything yet," I said. "He plans to extort Father Eduardo. He plans to blackmail him. He's maybe planning on killing him, but there's nothing criminal in what he's done yet, apart from maybe having some cops on his payroll, and that sort of makes it difficult to kill him, too."

"But let's be honest, Michael. Eventually he will put himself in a position where it would be easier if we just shoot him or put a bomb in his house. Why not just jump ahead? Darwin would approve of this plan. And so would Sam."

Fortunately, Sam was off getting information on Junior and wasn't there to nod his head or tip his beer in assent. Unfortunately, I wasn't in a position to really start arguing with Fiona, seeing as I was on my back and attempting to unscrew the elbow joint of her sink. Since she's prone to sudden violence, I thought it would be wise to keep things, you know, calm.

"I see your point," I said. "But no." I finally popped the joint, and a slow drip of water came out. I reached into the pipe and pulled out what looked to be clogging her drain: an eight-inch knife that could gut Bigfoot. "Have you been looking for this?"

"I knew I left it somewhere," she said.

"Were you expecting ninjas to come after your stamp collection?"

"Michael, you can never have enough sharp objects in your home. You know that." She took the knife from my hand and admired it a bit. "I bought this in Switzerland. It can cut meat, vegetables or human flesh with equal acuity."

"That's wonderful." I rescrewed the joints together and then stood up.

"Anyway," she said. "My point here, Michael, is it would be nice not to play these games. You're always saying you want your job back. Yet you never exactly used due process when you were a spy."

"Which is precisely why I can't go put a bullet in Junior's head," I said.

"But it was so much sexier when you could," she said.

"I guess we all lose, then," I said. I went into Fi's fridge and pulled out two beers and a blueberry yogurt I'd left a few days previous. It's always smart to store rations in a safe place. I opened Fi's sliding door and stepped out onto her patio and sat down at her picnic table. It was just after seven in the evening, and there were a few people out on the water in small boats, oblivious to the plots and scenarios of the bad people. That wouldn't be such a horrible thing, I suppose.

A few minutes later, Fiona came out with a plate of fruit and some cheese.

"I thought you were making dinner," I said. "I thought that was why I had to fix your sink."

"No, you had to fix my sink because I asked you and you're unable to say no to me." She pushed the plate toward me. "Eat some solid food. It will be a shock to your system."

I took a piece of cheese and gnawed on one corner.

"Something the matter, Michael?"

"I'm a little concerned about the fact Junior has cops on the take. That's not good for Eduardo, but it really isn't good for us, either. Last thing we need is some crooked cop deciding to make a name for himself by arresting someone like you."

"They'd never take me alive," she said.

"Fi, that's noble, but let's not get crazy here," I said.

"I didn't mean that I'd die," she said. "I meant that they'd never be able to take me and live."

"Great."

"Does Sam know anyone on the police force?"

"Not really," I said. "At least not since that trouble we ran into." A rather adept Miami officer, Detective Paxon, thought she might find something of interest in my life a few months earlier—turns out that if you blow up half the city and leave a few bodies on the streets of Miami, eventually people tend to notice—and since then, Sam was a bit worried about his contacts there. But it's not as if a bad cop sits around the locker room, telling everyone about the great gig he has working for a prison gang. "If Junior has cops working for him," I continued, "I'm going to guess that it's not as easy as paying someone off to deliver messages or look the other way when crimes are being committed."

"You think the Latin Emperors have a mole in the police?"

"Moles. That's what I'd do. Hell, that's *what I do*. It would make sense for the long-term survival of the gang—get some boys loyal to the gang to go in to the police."

Fiona took an orange from the plate and sucked the juice out of it. It had been a while since we'd been intimate with each other—we go through cycles where we want to love each other and where we want to kill each other, and where we just want to be near one another but not put that huge emotional investment at risk by actually having any real emotion—but that doesn't mean I didn't think about the possibility on a fairly regular basis.

"What would be the benefit for the bad cop?" Fi asked.

"Same as for anyone. Money. Power. Influence. A little street fame, maybe. And if they're loyal to the gang, it's either do what's asked of them or take a permanent vacation from this life. At least this way they get health benefits and get to carry a gun legally."

"That's a long distance to go just for something childish like a gang."

"You robbed banks for the IRA," I said.

"That's been slightly misrepresented. I just helped some fellow countrymen who needed money for a charity event."

"Fiona, I know your file," I said.

"And I know your file," she said. "And as I recall that's what cost you your job. A few discreet lies."

"It might be what costs Father Eduardo," I said.

"Do you believe he's a hundred percent clean?"

"I do," I said. "He reformed, and he's doing good things, Fi. Better things than we are. That's for sure. But I also know that there are probably a lot of people who look at him and can't separate who he is now from who he was then. My mother, she took him at face value, but I had to get a full tour of his facility, sit down and talk with him and pull out a dreadful secret in order to believe that he's not doing it all for some lower purpose. What's wrong with me?"

"You've seen a few things that might cause you to question other people's motives," she said. "And you have inherent father issues." That was the great thing about Fiona: She always knew the right thing to say. "And," Fiona continued, "your mother sees very deeply into people."

"No, she doesn't," I said.

"You don't give her enough credit. Maybe she's a psychic."

"If she were psychic, she'd know when her car was going to run out of oil, and I wouldn't need to pick her up from the Lube and Tune tomorrow morning." Sometimes my mother can be a little frustrating. But, then, whose parents aren't frustrating? "The mayor certainly didn't have a problem with him. He's doing all the right things, and then something like this shows up. I just can't let him fail now."

"So what's the plan?" Fi asked.

Sun-tzu may have said, "Keep your friends close, and your enemies closer" more than fifteen hundred years ago, but that notion still applies when forming a strong counterinsurgency plan. If you really want to defeat a terrorist organization, which a gang certainly is, you need to understand their methodology, their aims and just how far they are willing to go to get what they want.

The best way to deal with a terrorist is to dictate the terms of the fight. If there are rules of engagement, it's not all that terrifying to face an adversary. You know what kind of guns they have, you know what parcel of land they are after and you know just how much they are willing to lose. So to fight someone who leans on your fear, you need to bring him to a place where you have no fear at all.

"We give Junior what he wants," I said. "We give him every single thing he demands. And then we make him wish he'd never stepped foot back in Miami again."

"Oh, Michael," Fiona said, her glee barely contained. "That sounds like a potentially violent and dangerous thing to do. Would you like me to get some armor-piercing rounds out of storage?"

Before I could answer, my cell rang. It was Sam.

"What do you have?" I asked.

"A hangover," Sam said. "Or what do you call that feeling before a hangover when you're not happy anymore?"

I put my hand over the mouthpiece and said to Fiona, "Brew some coffee. And do you have any bread?"

"I think I have some English muffins," she said.

"Maybe run over to the store and get a loaf of something. Oh, and some Mylanta. Get some Mylanta for sure."

"Will we be entertaining later, darling?"

"Sam's been drinking pruno," I said. "He sounds . . . off."

That's all Fiona needed to hear. "Say no more," she said, and disappeared back into her house.

"Where are you?" I asked Sam.

There was a pause on the other end of the line. "Oh, hell, Mike, I think the cab left me at the wrong place. I told him to take me to your mom's place, thinking maybe I'd get a bowl of oatmeal inside me, maybe some soup, maybe something made of lard, and then I sort of thought about that sofa in the living room, which always is very soft in the small of my back, and . . ."

"Sam," I said. "Focus. Where are you?"

"In front of that strip club Mom's Place. Over by the airport. Some very nice ladies seem to work here. Have you ever noticed how loud airplanes are, Mikey? It's like they are filled with jet fuel or something. Just one big roaring noise." Sam stopped speaking for a moment, which concerned me, until I heard him say, "Hello to you, sweetheart. What's that say on your back? Oh? Oh, I'm a bad boy? You're a bad girl. . . ."

"Sam!" I shouted.

"Oh, sorry, Mike. You know what I like? Those tattoos women get on the small of their back. Never stops being sexy."

"Sam," I said, "I want you to step away from the strip club. Is there a gas station nearby? Something with a mini-mart?"

"Let me tell you something, Mikey. Those mini-marts are ruining the mom-and-pop stores. I won't go into them anymore."

"Sam," I said, "you go into them every single day."

"I'm having epiphanies tonight, Mikey. Things are changing, for sure."

"How much did you drink, Sam?"

"It's not about how much. It's about how long. And I don't know that answer, either."

The reason people in prison drink pruno is so they can forget—for just a little while—why they are in prison. The downside, however, is that alcohol in pruno is so abusive, it can make you forget the day after you drank it, too, and maybe the next week or two if you're not careful. And, of course, if it's made incorrectly, it can just shut down your kidneys and then forever isn't a very long time. Fortunately, K-Dog sounded like the kind of guy who had good recipes, and Sam didn't sound like he was in renal failure, just regular failure.

"I want you to stand at least ten feet from the road," I said. "I'll be there in fifteen minutes. While you're waiting for me, don't go inside the strip club and don't give anyone any money. And, Sam, please don't drink any more."

"Nothing to worry about, Mikey, because I'm never drinking again," Sam said, which made me think this was much more serious than I ever could have imagined.

6

A properly trained operative understands that immediate tactical questioning of a detainee is the best way to get desired information. Wait until a person has been imprisoned for a few days, and you're more than likely going to get useless patter. The reason is simple: If you've been taken into custody by U.S. officials, there's good reason to believe that they aren't going to kill you. It's all about having the moral high ground, and enemy combatants have a pretty good idea what Americans will and will not do. However, if you detain someone on a roadside, put a gun to their head and demand information, fear tends to override rationality.

Unless, of course, the person you're questioning is drunk on pruno. After I picked up Sam from the strip club, I brought him back to Fiona's, stood him up in her front yard and hosed him down. This wasn't in order to sober him up. Rather, Sam demanded he be hosed down because he was covered in dog hair and smelled of ethanol and peppers. Sam just wanted the hair off of him, but once Fi caught a whiff of him, she thought it best to give him a thorough cleaning out-doors versus inside her home.

Wash-down complete, I tossed Sam a towel, and Fi came out with a cup of coffee and an entire baguette.

"You have a nice evening?" I asked him once he was sufficiently dried and was happily chomping on the bread.

"Let me tell you something, Mikey: There's nothing right about a drink you can make in your toilet, even if you're not making it in a toilet anymore."

"Good to know," I said.

Sam riffled through his pockets and came out with his recorder. "I wired myself," he said, and handed me the device. It was a digital device, which meant it could hold up to twelve hours of conversation. I checked the remaining time—there were only a few hours left.

"I thought you said K-Dog was your friend?"

"Mikey, I don't remember my own name right now. I taped the conversation as a precaution. It was a good thing, wouldn't you say?"

I hit PLAY on the recorder and spent about three minutes listening to Sam and K-Dog talking about how great it would be if they were a team on *The Amazing Race*. "You remember that?" I said.

"Mikey, you ever seen that show? We could win a million dollars."

"Looks like you already have a partner," I said. "You have an idea at what point you and K-Dog talked about Junior?"

"It was early," Sam said. "And then it was late. I'm

sorry, Mikey. I just didn't want him to be offended, so I kept drinking with him."

"When in Attica," I said.

We went inside, and while Fiona tended to Sam—which is to say, while Fiona made Sam eat Tums and bread and forced him to drink a gallon of Gatorade—I tried making my way through Sam's tape of himself. It turns out there's nothing less entertaining than listening to drunks, particularly drunks who think they are being insightful. Eventually, I caught the thread of the conversation about Junior and even managed to make out the address Sam slurred into the recorder.

"How's he doing?" I asked Fiona.

"I'd say he's about fifty-fifty," she said.

"Of what?"

"Alcohol and animal fats. There's nothing human about him yet. Might not be for another ten hours or so."

"Is he safe to leave?"

"Only if you don't mind him choking to death on his own vomit."

"There's a field trip I'd like to take tonight," I said. I handed her the address I scrawled down from Sam's slurred words. "This is where Junior Gonzalez has paperwork dropped off. I'd like to take a look at what he's planning."

"Shall we just drop Sam off back at that strip club? Pay a nice girl named Star twenty dollars to babysit him?"

"A good idea. But, no." I picked up my cell phone

and made a call. "Ma," I said when my mother answered (on the first half ring), "I need a favor."

The address K-Dog gave Sam wasn't in the projects where the Latin Emperors have operated for years with impunity, or even in Miami proper, but in a new development of family-style houses in Homestead, about forty minutes south of downtown Miami and only a few miles north of the southern Everglades, and a few miles west of the air force base. And only a few miles away from the women's prison my new friend the scarred receptionist spent her idle time in before getting a job with Eduardo.

"Are you sure we're in the right place?" I asked Fiona. We were parked on the side of a road that headed into a planned community called Cheyenne Lakes. The blacktop we'd been driving on previously had turned into cobblestone pavers, and there was a not-very-discreet up-lit sign that proclaimed THE KIND OF LIFE YOU DESERVE IS RIGHT AROUND THE CORNER perched on a low berm of green grass that rolled . . . right around the corner.

"These are the directions you printed out," Fi said. "It would help if you had GPS in this car instead of an eight-track deck."

"GPS didn't come standard in Chargers until 1975," I said. "Let me see the directions." Fiona handed me the paper. Everything was correct. This didn't smell right. "What is a Latin Emperor doing living out here?"

"Golfing?" Fiona said.

I checked my watch. It was near 10:00 P.M. I rolled down my window and listened for a moment. You could almost hear people snoring already. A golf cart came from around the corner, where my better life presumably lived, and I could make out the form of a security guard, even in the dark, behind the wheel. Security guards tend to sit with a supererect posture, as if they've been taught at rent-a-cop school that good posture equals authority.

"Company," I said.

"Do you want me to shoot him?"

"Let's talk to him first," I said.

The cart pulled up next to my driver's-side window so the guard would be face-to-face with me. This is something they probably also teach at rent-a-cop school: Park your golf cart like cops park their cars when they're talking in the Denny's parking lot. "Lost?" the guard said. He didn't even bother to say hello, which I found rude.

"Sure am," I said. "I was stationed at the base out here, oh, gosh, ten years ago? Eighty-second Airborne. And I wanted to show my girlfriend the old lover's lane. We're down from Atlanta for the week. Guess it's been paved over?"

The guard nodded gravely. He had a short haircut and the square jaw of a military man, but also possessed the unmistakable body of a civilian: a perfectly round gut, arms that showed the care and confidence of a man who spent his time at the gym doing only curls and a watch too gaudy to be real. He also had a name tag that said his name was Lieutenant Frank, which I took to mean his first name was Frank, because he certainly wasn't an actual lieutenant in any real service. Being a lieutenant for a rent-a-cop firm is like being a chef at McDonald's.

"Yeah, yeah," Frank said. "Been a couple years now." He didn't betray any emotion, which either meant he thought I was suspicious or he didn't have any actual emotion. Or maybe he just hated his job, which was a distinct possibility, too. He did have a police scanner on the dash of his golf cart, which seemed odd, too.

"You get much action out here?" I asked.

"That's a bit personal," Frank said.

"No," I said. "I mean criminal action." I pointed to the scanner. "Seems like an expensive accessory on your cart."

"It's important to our residents that we be able to let them know if there's any activity outside the development that might require their attention, in terms of police actions or military activity."

Fiona leaned across me and smiled at Frank. She'd been sitting quietly up until that point, but I knew as soon as Frank concluded his speech that she'd have something to say. She can only go so long.

"Pardon me," she said, a bit of Southern twang to her voice, playing the part, grasping her inner Southern belle . . . provided Southern belles these days packed nines. "But what you just said positively gave me the chills. Is there a chance of a terrorist attack nearby?"

"Oh, no, ma'am," he said. "Men like your boyfriend keep us very safe from that sort of thing."

I gave Frank a firm nod of my head. It's the kind of

thing men like to think they can get away with in lieu of speaking, but it really only works on people who aren't terribly adept at conversation as it is.

"Oh, well, thank God," she said, and leaned back in her seat and fanned herself with her hands. "I think I almost caught the vapors for a moment."

"I do have to tell you, Lieutenant, that a few buddies of mine still in the area have said that there is a criminal element in these parts now," I said. "Damn shame, if you ask me."

Frank took an exaggerated look over both of his shoulders, which I found particularly odd, as not a single car had even passed by since we parked. And if I couldn't see them from where I sat, I would have assumed that they actually rolled up and stored the sidewalks at dusk. "I only say this because I respect your service to this country," Frank said, his voice low, "but I believe immigration is one of the biggest blights on this nation. That I have to now protect people who aren't even Americans is the reason why I no longer believe in the two-party system."

"Couldn't agree more," I said. "This is a nation that should preserve its identity and not let in people who weren't from here originally. If you can't trace your roots back to before 1492, then you don't belong. I mean, what is America if it's filled with people who are from other countries?"

"The idea of a melting pot makes me positively sick," Fiona said. "I particularly find the Irish repulsive. Don't you know? It's so bracing to be around people who share our values."

"I may wear this on my chest," Frank tapped at the rent-a-cop badge on his chest, "but if it were up to me, I'd have the flag right here. Not everyone in this development would agree with me. There are subjects here who, if I understand, have spent time in prison and who are possibly illegal in their entire nature. But, apparently, just about anyone can move in where they like these days."

Frank was the strangest combination of conservative talk radio, conspiracy theories, faux law enforcement and outright racism I'd encountered in some time. If I gave him an opening, I'm sure he would have been happy to discuss the finer points of the Illuminati with me. He also, apparently, didn't have a clear sense of American history or the basic laws of the land. That he was providing security for anything was frightening, but at least he was an easy and able cipher of the information I needed. Somewhere in the development, the Latin Emperors had taken hold. Or at least Junior Gonzalez had.

"Well, I could sit here all evening and trade war stories with you, Lieutenant," I said, "but if you don't mind, me and the little lady are going to take a drive around my old memories for a bit. Is that okay with you?"

"Of course," Frank said. "There's a very nice gazebo on the west side of the lake that you might enjoy sitting in for a bit. It's where I write my blog when I get off."

I gave Frank the nod again, and he actually saluted me. I rolled up the window and tried not to peel away from the curb.

"You should have let me shoot him," Fiona said.

"Guys like him," I said, "shoot themselves every time they open their mouths."

We wound through the development as we headed toward Junior's house, and every few seconds Fiona would gasp or moan about something. It wasn't as exciting as it sounds, since her noises had mostly to do with terrible choices in lawn decoration, though her loudest protest was about the fake city square that dominated the center of the development, replete with a clock tower, a sunken lawn amphitheater and diagonal parking spaces for the shops and businesses that had yet to move into the empty buildings. A sign declared: CHEYENNE LAKES IS THE PERFECT PLACE TO DO BUSINESS . . . AND LIVE.

"What is this?" she said.

"The future," I said.

"That looks like the past?"

"I think that's the idea. Or it was in 2006."

"I suspect your friend Lieutenant Frank would blame this on the immigrants?"

"Surely," I said. "But particularly those swarthy Irish people."

"Did you like that?"

"It was a nice touch."

We continued on, traveling deeper and deeper into the development. Cheyenne Lakes might have been designed as a mixed-use, master-planned community, but the more I drove through its labyrinthine streets, the more I recognized why Junior had made it his base of operations: It would be possible to have lookouts at all the possible angles without drawing any interest from the average citizen. For the cost of rent, Junior had a ready-made fortress. It would be disturbingly easy to run a very safe and secure base of operations for the entire Latin Emperors nation of prison and street gangs.

Once I finally found Junior's street, I turned the car around and headed back to the fake city center, which was a good half mile away.

"What are you doing?" Fi asked.

"I have a theory I want to test," I said, and explained to Fiona my thoughts, and told her I thought it might be best to approach Junior's home on foot so as not to raise any flags of suspicion. I grabbed several of the cell phones and their assorted parts, too. If my assumptions were correct, we'd need them.

"If I'd known we were going for a midnight stroll I would have worn different shoes," Fiona said.

"It's not midnight," I said. "And I've seen you fight a Chechen terrorist in higher heels."

"It's this place!" Fi let out an exasperated sigh. "It ages you by osmosis." She slipped out of her shoes and then removed her top, too, revealing a plain white tank top underneath. "What?" she said. Apparently, the look on my face had a question attached to it.

"I was just wondering if you were going to take off your jeans, too."

"Not tonight," she said. "Besides, I'd better look the part, right? And what says 'casual walk in the neighborhood' more than no shoes and no bra?"

"I couldn't agree more," I said, so I took off my

shoes, too. I'd have taken off my shirt, but then the butt of my gun might have been a bit too clear an indicator that I wasn't just out to enjoy the lovely night air . . . which, that evening, carried the strong scent of the Everglades blowing up from the south.

We got out of the car and walked, hand in hand, back toward Junior's house. Had I known the plan for the evening, I would have found a dog to fill out the portrait of domestic bliss.

It wasn't until we started walking that I realized every street, avenue, road, court and cul-de-sac was named for some aspect of Native American culture, another element that must have escaped Lieutenant Frank's keen eye. We passed Natchez Court, Cochise Lane, Anasazi Road, even the requisite Seminole Street crossed Pueblo Way. But what Fiona and I were really looking for were things Lieutenant Frank probably wouldn't take note of.

"That house up on the corner of Seminole there has a lovely window dressing," Fiona said. "And some very nice rocks, too."

It sure did. The house in question was fully illuminated, which made it odd, as the other houses on the block were completely dark. I guess people in Cheyenne Lakes didn't bother to watch the late-night news, either. The house was pointed at a diagonal from the entrance to Acuera Street, which was where Junior's house was located. We were coming up from the right side of the lit house, and I could see through the cheap blinds that there wasn't any furniture in the room, which could mean nothing. Plenty of banks keep the lights on inside foreclosed homes to discourage squatters and the like. But this house didn't look like it was foreclosed upon, especially not with the two Honda Accords parked in the driveway.

The rocks, however, were the giveaway: They were fake rocks with security cameras installed inside them . . . and not very well. They were the kind of fake-rocks-with-a-security-camera-in-them that anyone can buy at Target, and so the neighbors probably paid no mind to them, not even when the cameras pointed away from the house. I looked up toward the roof and noticed a satellite dish, which was probably just the wireless receiver for the cameras. Junior was beaming security footage from down the block directly to his house. Smart.

But not smart enough. Fi and I stepped back around the corner and found a park bench beneath an old-style lamp. It sure was a charming place for a gang leader to live.

I handed Fiona two cell phones. "Take these apart," I said.

"How romantic," she said. "What are we building?"

"Jamming device," I said.

"Michael, you know I love the dirty talk," she said.

Blocking a standard, unencrypted, wireless video signal requires only two things: another video signal and enough battery power to cause an alteration to the electromagnetic waves. Three cell phones with video capability can achieve this without much problem. If you have an old cell phone, it's much more difficult than if you have the new 4G phones, which generate more power than was originally used to run NORAD. If you have three 4G phones, all you need to do is wire the batteries together so that they feed into a single phone and then begin shooting video. Place the phones next to the video source, and all that will be transmitted is blackness.

If you have the proper tools—in this case, Fiona's earring studs, a paper clip from my pocket and a credit card—you can build this device in about five minutes. It won't last very long, since the batteries will cook the master phone in about thirty minutes, but if you need to jam a signal longer than thirty minutes, you'd have better tools and material from the get-go.

When we finished up, we walked back toward the house with the cameras, this time from the opposite side of the street. From this vantage point, I was able to get a better view of the rock camera. It was fixed in position and wasn't motion activated, which told me there were probably another three or four cameras catching other angles from the illuminated windows.

I circled back on the street and came up along the side of the house again, so that I was diagonal to the first rock. It wouldn't be able to catch me because it was fixed, so I simply removed the back of the rock—they come with a handsome tab latch and several arrows to indicate just how to disable the device, which is nice—and placed the wired phones directly atop the electrical pack. I would have just unplugged the entire device, which would have been simple enough, but I saw that there were cables running the length of the house and up into the roof, which meant that it was all circuited together. This would jam the entire transmission, not just one camera.

I walked back around and met Fiona on the sidewalk.

"Sophisticated?" she said.

"No," I said. "A good idea. Bad execution. Someone has given him good advice, but there's a serious lack of skill involved here."

As we passed the driveway, I knelt down to scratch my foot, but also to get a look at the space beneath the Hondas I'd noticed earlier. There wasn't a single spot of oil I could see, and the tires on both cars were only slightly worn. The cars also had dealer plates, which I suspected meant that they'd been stolen.

If you're going to steal a car, steal a car with dealer plates. Dealers move their plates from automobile to automobile, so it's impossible to track them down to a specific car. Police also don't care about a car with dealer plates—it's a car that no one owns yet, so there's nothing of criminal note for them to pay attention to.

In this case, the cars were probably stolen and the plates were probably stolen, but not stolen together. It was a perfect (and easy) crime to pull off in a community like this, where you could set off a nuclear bomb at 11:00 P.M. and no one would realize there was a problem until the next morning, when they stepped outside to fetch the newspaper. It was unlikely that anyone paid any attention to anything unless it directly violated the HOA's codes.

I stood up awkwardly, just in case anyone was watching, which I doubted. It was so quiet you could hear time.

"Is it your Achilles, darling?" Fiona asked.

"No," I said, "just a slight irritation, my sweet."

I didn't think our voices were being recorded, but as we walked we kept up a running dialogue about the weather, the Johnsons' new pool, Mr. Jones' new goiter and our collective desire to spend the next Christmas in Spain. It was the kind of domestic conversation I imagined real people had all the time, but that was about as foreign to my domestic experience as I could possibly get. I tried to remember what my parents used to talk about when they were together, and then I remembered that they didn't *talk* about anything. They *screamed* a lot, but there wasn't much in the way of meaningless conversations about the life they were living. Not a great way to prepare young men to grow up into chatty adults, which neither I nor my brother, Nate, really were. Oh, we could talk . . . we just didn't chat very well.

As we got closer to Junior's house, I noticed yet another empty home, this one directly across the street from Junior's. This one wasn't lit up like it was on fire, as the house down the block was, but I could see a dipole sound antenna mounted above the storm drain. It wasn't a complex system Junior had working—in fact, it was about as rudimentary as they come, and could be so easily hacked into that I could see the wheels in Fiona's mind already turning—but if you're in a safe area, surrounded by people who mean you no harm, you don't exactly need satellites sending you the positions of Russian subs every morning.

"Follow my lead," I said to Fiona, and then turned up Junior Gonzalez' front walk. His house was modest— a one-story ranch style with a neatly trimmed lawn. A bed of roses was beneath the two picture windows that likely looked into the living room, though the drapes were closed, and there was a wicker basket with fake flowers sitting atop a distressed wood bench in the portico, just adjacent to the ten-foot-high front door.

When we reached the door, I attempted to open it. I could tell immediately from the complete lack of movement that it was secured by more than just a mere dead bolt. That the front door was actually metal overlaid with wood was also a pretty good clue.

If you have a metal front door, it's because you expect that one day someone is going to try to break it down. If you're smart enough to build a metal door into your house, you're probably smart enough to have a camera on the door, too—Junior's was buried in the fake flowers, another Target special—and maybe you're even smart enough to not answer the door when a stranger starts kicking it and making a bunch of noise.

"Jeff? Jeff? It's Marvin! You locked the door! Jeff!" I pounded on the door a few times, which didn't make much noise on account of the dulling nature of the metal, so I started slapping at the wall. And then Fiona started shouting, too.

"Mary? Mary? I'm freezing out here! It must be seventy degrees out here!"

I stepped back from the portico and slapped at the living room windows. Double paned. Nice. I slapped them again and shouted for Jeff. Fiona stepped out onto the lawn, fished around for a rock and then threw it at the garage door, and screamed some more for Mary.

"More?" she mouthed.

I shrugged. Why the hell not? Fiona picked up another rock, but before she could throw it, the front door opened and an exceptionally large Latino man stepped out. He wore only a robe and shower shoes and a confused look on his face. "Why are you screaming and throwing things at my home?" he asked. It was a rather pleasant entreaty from a man who'd spent twenty-five years in prison and had either killed or ordered the deaths of probably dozens of men.

"Oh, crap," I said. "All these houses look alike. I thought this was Jeff's house. We're visiting him, took a walk down to the gazebo and I guess we got lost. I'm really sorry. I thought this was Jeff and Mary's place. Honey, do you know what street they live on? This isn't the right house."

Fiona, still with a rock clutched in her hand, sat down on Junior's lawn. "How can you be so stupid?" she said.

"Honey," I said, "this is not a big deal. We'll find the house." I turned to Junior, gave him one in my new series of looks meant to convey instant brotherhood—this one was my "Women, what can you do with them?" smile—and then took a step toward him so that I could give him a loud stage whisper. "There can't be that many houses in the development, right? I think it was on one of those Indian streets. Apache, maybe?"

"Please, get off my lawn," Junior said. "I just had it reseeded."

"No problem," I said, and then Fiona began to cry.

"Why is she crying?" Junior asked.

"We both had a little to drink tonight," I said, and then I gave him the "We're both in this together look" men often share in situations that involve crying females. "I hate to ask this, but would it be possible to come inside and use your phone? It's awfully dark out, and I don't feel like there's a great chance my lady friend and I will ever find Jeff and Mary's house."

"No," he said.

"What?" Fiona said. She was up now and storming toward Junior. "No? What? What kind of person are you? What kind of values do you have? We aren't going to come inside and steal your plates, you asshole. We just want to use the telephone. And if I don't get to a restroom in the next five minutes, I'll be back on your lawn! And then what will you do?"

I caught Fiona in my arms before she could begin doing whatever crazy, drunk, Southern women are prone to do to hulking ex-convicts, which is probably whatever they damn well please. "Easy, honey," I said. "He doesn't want us in his home. That's fine. It's his right."

Fiona crumpled down on Junior's feet and began to sob even more. That probably would have been fine, really, but when she began to wail and lights started turning on down the street—or, well, more lights than our screaming and hurling of rocks had caused to turn on—Junior said, "Fine, fine. Come in."

The inside of Junior's house looked like a model home. The front door opened into a wide entry hall that fed directly into a great room combination of kitchen and living room. There was a beige sofa covered in multicolored throw pillows, a chocolate brown coffee table that was scattered with magazines and news-papers, and a leather occasional chair with a chenille blanket slung over one arm.

"Your wife has a beautiful eye for detail," Fiona said. She wandered about the living room, touching things and, I assumed, pocketing whatever she could. That was her skill set. Unfortunately, her jeans weren't ex-actly baggy. She'd find a way to make do, I was sure.

"I don't have a wife," Junior said. He walked into the kitchen and picked up a cordless phone and handed it to me. "Make your call."

I dialed Sam's cell phone.

"If this is Yvonne," Sam said, "I'm not in a position to take your call."

"It's us," I said. "We're lost. But a very nice man let us into his home to use the phone."

"Mikey," Sam said. "How did I get to your house? And why is your mother with me?"

"I'll have to explain that later," I said. "In the mean-time, if you can just give me your address, we'll get right back over there."

"Did you go to Junior's place without me?"

"I did," I said.

"And this is his phone?"

"It is," I said.

"Came up blocked on my cell," Sam said. "Only person who calls me from a blocked number is Yvonne, usually. I don't think you've met her. Great lady. Phone is her thing, if you know what I mean."

"Great, great," I said. "Well, let me get this nice gentleman's phone number in case we get lost again, maybe you can call him and retrace our steps." I pulled the phone from my ear. "Excuse me, sir, can I get your phone number to give to my friend? He's worried we're never going to get back to his place. Apparently, not too long ago there was a gator attack in these parts, so you can imagine his fear."

Junior stood in the middle of his living room, watching Fiona weave drunkenly about his house. He wasn't paying the least bit of attention to me, and I couldn't tell if he thought Fiona was suspicious or if he was worried she'd break something. I also couldn't believe that the man I'd seen in the photos Father Eduardo showed us was living in this house and that he seemed, oddly, just as professional and put together in only a robe as Father Eduardo had been in his office. Either they'd learned quite a bit from each other, or Junior had realized that in order to make it big, he'd need to clean up. I could still see that he had tattoos on his hands, and though his hair was thick and wavy, every time he ran his hand over his scalp in exasperation as Fi came close to toppling one thing or another, a flash of ink showed on his head. You can only cover so much of your past.

"Excuse me," I said again, this time a bit louder, and

Junior turned around. "Can I get your phone number? My friends are worried we might get lost again and they'll never be able to find us." Just then, Fiona did a nice pirouette into the leather chair and tumbled into it, her legs kicking up into the air and then wrapping around the long, flowing white drapes that hung across the living room windows. She tugged with her feet and down they came.

Fiona has very strong feet.

"555-9819," he said.

I gave the number to Sam.

"You want me to run incoming and outgoing?" he asked.

"That would be good, if you could," I said, "and hopefully we'll find our way back to you in a moment."

I clicked off the phone at the same time Junior walked over to Fiona, picked her up with one arm and dragged her out of the chair. "Your girlfriend pulled down my drapes," he said.

"Let me pay for that," I said. "As soon as I get back to Atlanta, I'll send you a check. You just let me know the cost."

"Price is irrelevant," he said. "I just want you out of my home before she breaks anything else."

Junior shoved Fiona in my direction—his first action that actually betrayed his true personality—and when I caught her, I had to hold her back from, well, doing what Fiona does.

"Thank you for your hospitality," I said, but he

didn't respond. He just walked back to his front door, opened it wide and waited for us to walk through.

It wasn't until we were sitting inside the Charger again that Fiona felt it prudent to speak. "If he ever touches me again," she said, "I'm going to break all of his fingers. And then—then I'm going to really hurt him."

"No problem," I said, since it's usually better just to agree with Fiona in these situations.

She reached into her pocket and pulled out a silver BlackBerry. "Plus, he won't be so upset about missing this when he doesn't have workable digits. I understand it's hard to text with your toes."

"I knew I could count on you," I said.

She reached into her other pocket and came out with an envelope with a bank logo on the return address. "I thought this might be helpful, too," she said.

"That's my bank robber," I said.

And from the small of her back she pulled out a set of car keys. "This I just did to be mean."

7

When dealing with an adaptive enemy, making contingency plans can be a fruitless endeavor. An adaptive enemy is one who can morph his defenses on the fly, can change his goals to meet the situation and is willing, above all else, to make extreme sacrifices in pursuit of victory. In order to have a Plan B against this kind of enemy, you'd need to imagine every possible scenario while also acknowledging none of the things you've imagined might actually be the right answer.

In the case of Junior Gonzalez, everything I'd expected to learn about him was wrong. That he was living well in a planned community, that his home looked to have been decorated out of Pottery Barn (albeit a Pottery Barn that offered handsome metal doors covered in a wood veneer) and that he was initially polite (until he wasn't polite) and uniformly well-spoken . . . All of it ran counter to my expectations. I shouldn't have been surprised in light of who (and what) Eddie Santiago had become, and yet it all had come as a surprise to me that a career criminal could change his outward persona.

Spend enough time locked away in prison, and it's only natural that you'll begin fantasizing about the life you'll lead once you're free and the lengths needed to fulfill that fantasy. Maybe it will be a life of revenge. Maybe it will be a life of peace. Maybe it will be a life lived out of a catalog. Or, just maybe, it will be a life lived out of a catalog and that is filled with a desire for revenge.

Pottery Barn and revenge seemed like strange bedfellows, even to Fiona. It was the next day, and we were sitting poolside at the Ace Hotel, waiting for Sam. He'd asked us to meet him at the hotel, which was odd, but he said it would all make sense once he arrived. I had a suspicion that it would only make sense to Sam, but there we sat, Fiona in a bikini that contained roughly the same amount of fabric that goes into a cotton ball, and me wearing an Armani suit, because I assumed we'd be sitting inside. And because I look good in it.

"For a brute," Fiona said, "he did have a lovely set of chenille throw pillows. How can you want to hurt people when you can put your head down on chenille throw pillows?"

"It's a great mystery," I said. I had Junior's Black-Berry in my hand and was busy going through all of his e-mail and phone contacts. Fiona was busy absorbing UV rays.

"Would you mind getting my back?" Fiona asked. She flipped over and undid her bikini top.

I'd spent the better part of the last hour putting suntan lotion on different parts of Fiona's body, enough so that I was pretty sure she could walk on the sun without getting a burn, but then Fiona was always partial to putting on a show for the tourists, and there was a new batch of young men sitting across the pool, ogling her. The Ace was one of those hotels designed to look like it had been built in the 1970s, except that all of the things that were deemed dreadful in the seventies were now covered in glitter and made to look exceptional. Even the drinks had names from the seventies, like the DY-NO-MITE! Mudslide and the Jim Jones, which was basically a Long Island Iced Tea. Most of the pool denizens were born in the 1980s, so the significance (or insignificance) of it all was likely lost on them. But Fiona's near-naked form certainly wasn't.

I squeezed out a dollop of coconut-scented tanning oil into one hand and rubbed it into Fi's back while still perusing the BlackBerry with my free hand. It's not the kind of multitasking they teach at spy school, but I was able to make do.

"Here's something interesting," I said. "Last night, Junior received an e-mail from someone with an Honrado Incorporated e-mail address."

"Aren't all of the people working there ex- or current criminals?" She reached around to the small of her back. "Did you get this spot, Michael? I don't want an uneven tan."

"You're all covered." I opened up the e-mail. It was blank but contained an attachment, which I opened. It was the visitor sign-in sheet that Sam and I had signed as Napoleon Solo and Illya Kuryakin. "This isn't good,"

I said, and handed the BlackBerry to Fiona. "It's the daily sign-in of people coming to see Father Eduardo."

"It seems that the Man from U.N.C.L.E has been compromised," she said.

"And the mayor," I said.

"The problem with employing criminals," Fiona said, handing the BlackBerry back to me, "is that they tend not to be very trustworthy."

The e-mail was from the blanket info@honradoinc .com, which was probably accessed by several people, but it was unlikely that more than one person had immediate access to the sign-in sheet. The receptionist was the only one. I'd have to check with Eduardo on that, but even the process of snooping for that info might tip off the wrong people. Better to take care of that on the down-low.

I scrolled through the rest of the e-mails, but they went back only two days and didn't provide much in the way of apparent action items. But if you really want to know about a person, read his nonpersonal e-mails, like the e-mails from Amazon.com noting the upcoming delivery of items, which, in Junior's case, provided even more insight than I could have imagined.

"Would you like to guess what books Junior has headed his way?" I asked.

"I'd like to think he's got some of those Chicken Soup books. Did they make a *Chicken Soup for the Violent Criminal's Soul* yet?"

"Not yet," I said. "But he does have *The Art of War*

and *The Revolutionary's Cookbook* on a three-day delivery."

"What is it with men and *The Art of War*?"

"Have you ever read it?"

"No," she said. "I don't need to. Do you want to know what the art of war is, Michael? *Kill the other person*. It's really very simple. No reading or extra training required."

It wasn't really *The Art of War* that concerned me. *The Revolutionary's Cookbook* wasn't dangerous as a book, but it was a favorite of garage-based terrorists for years. Most of them didn't know what to do with it, really, but someone like Junior, who was brighter than I'd given him credit for, just may. At the very least, he had the muscle and the means to acquire the goods required for large-scale explosions that didn't require weapons-grade explosives. Worse, though, was that if he didn't know precisely what he was doing, there was a good chance he'd blow up his own neighborhood by accident.

"How did you learn to blow things up, Fi?"

Fi started to turn over—well, she actually gave a half turn, to the delight of the tourists, which I suspect was her plan all along—and then remembered her undone top, which she retied before sitting up so she could see me. "I love it when you ask me personal questions," she said. "I think my brother taught me. Or maybe some kids down the way, but probably my brother. It was so much fun growing up back then. You could play outside all day and no one complained if you accidentally incinerated an empty shack or three."

"What did you use?"

"Whatever we could find. Bleach seemed to work well when mixed with other things. Pools of hairspray proved quite flammable, too."

"What could you have done with a book like *The Revolutionary's Cookbook*?"

Fiona thought for a moment. "Personally? I think I could have brought England to its knees, but then I was always a very active child."

Anyone with an Internet connection can figure out how to build an atomic bomb, or at least procure the steps needed to put it all together, but not everybody has access to enriched plutonium. And anyone with an Internet connection can order *The Revolutionary's Cookbook*, but that doesn't make him capable of actually creating a device that can do anything more than maim himself, but the mere idea that Junior was pondering this was cause for some concern, particularly since he was apparently receiving the list of visitors Father Eduardo was seeing each day.

I couldn't imagine a reason why he'd want those names unless he planned to shake them down, send them materials related to his blackmail scheme or to stick a pipe bomb in their mailboxes. None of the options were particularly appealing.

"You know what I wonder?" I said. "Just how much Junior really wants to run through Honrado, and how much he might just want to be respected like Father Eduardo. If he really wanted to bring him down, why not just kill him already? There must be easier businesses to run his money through."

"You said he hasn't read *The Art of War* yet," Fiona said.

She had a point, but it still didn't quite make sense to me. But, then, revenge isn't always about the quick fix. Sometimes it's about torture. Junior had spent twenty-five years in prison. That's a long time to spend pondering someone else's suffering.

And if anyone knew about suffering, it was Sam . . . or at least that's what his general countenance suggested when he walked up to where we were sitting, tore off his shirt and essentially beached himself facedown on the chaise longue we'd held for him. He had a manila envelope stuffed into his back pocket, which made him look like a delivery man who'd been murdered.

"Always so graceful," Fiona said.

"Sweetheart," Sam said, not bothering to turn over, "I'm doing battle with some demons today. Unless you have a pocket exorcism kit with you, I'd appreciate a bit more tenderness from you."

"Can I get you a drink?" Fiona said.

Sam lifted his head and turned it to face Fiona. "Now, that's my girl," he said. "How about a Jim Jones?"

Fiona slapped Sam's flank. It sounded wet. "You're fine," she said.

"I could do without the kidney slaps," he said.

"This is a great hotel," I said.

"Isn't it?" Sam said.

"There a reason we're here?"

"Blue skies and pretty girls aren't enough for you, Mikey?"

"No," I said, though it wasn't a bad place to scroll

through someone else's BlackBerry. I told Sam what we'd learned.

"You think Junior is working with THRUSH on this to finally get Solo and Kuryakin in their crosshairs?"

"I don't think so," I said.

"You think it was the girl with the handsome scar who sent in the list?"

"It could be anyone," I said, because the truth was that I didn't want it to be her. "Can you turn over? I feel weird speaking to the hair on your back."

"Your true colors always shine through, Mikey," Sam said. "Here's what I learned while you two were out here enjoying the free vitamin D from the sun, the reason for which shall be made clear as soon as I can move my torso." He rolled himself—which took some effort—until he was mostly flat on his back, and then pulled the envelope out of his back pocket and handed it to me.

"Are you having some kind of problem?" Fiona asked.

"I think I injured myself last night," Sam said.

I opened up the envelope and pulled out several pages of telephone records. "Quick turnaround," I said.

"Have I ever mentioned my friend Yvonne before?"

"Last night, actually," I said. "And in more detail than I was comfortable with."

"I did?"

"You did."

Sam shook his head like he was trying to dislodge his brain from a fork. "Well, anyway, she works for the phone company. She's a good source in times of trouble, and a good friend in times when you just want to be alone, but don't really want to be alone."

"More information than I'm comfortable with, too," Fiona said.

"No one wearing that much oil and that little clothing can have an opinion on what constitutes too much information," Sam said.

Junior's phone was registered to someone named Julia Pistell. "Any idea who this Pistell woman is?" I asked.

"According to Yvonne, there's exactly one person in the United States named Julia Pistell with another phone record," Sam said. "And she's a college student in Vermont."

"So she's not a Cuban gangster?"

"Doesn't appear so," Sam said. "I'm going to guess she's been the victim of identity theft, particularly since I ran her credit and she's now the proud owner of ten credit cards, all in good standing, mind you, so that's good for her."

There was one number that appeared at least twice a day for a week; some days, it appeared close to a dozen times. There was another number that appeared five times in one day and then not once after that. Sam had circled the most frequent number in red pen, the other number in blue. It was far more organization on Sam's part than I was used to. "Who's this in red?" I asked.

"You're looking at him."

"He called you?" Fiona said.

"No," Sam said. He waved his arms about. "This him. The Ace Hotel."

"This isn't a him. It's an it," Fiona said.

"Sister, I'm not real strong on the pronouns right now," Sam said. "You're lucky I'm not speaking in tongues anymore."

"Why is he calling this hotel?" I said.

"He's got a villa here, or his friend Julia does," Sam said. "It's been rented for a month."

"I want to say, Michael, that I am liking this man more now than I did yesterday," Fiona said. "He does have good taste in kitsch resorts."

Renting a villa at the Ace Hotel for a month would cost upwards of ten thousand dollars, but that's not what had me wondering what his motive was.

"Who is in it?" I said.

"No one answered when I called," Sam said.

"You get a room number?" I asked.

"I managed to make sweet eyes at the girl behind the counter," Sam said, "and when that didn't work, I gave a bartender a hundred bucks and told him to meet us out here when he had the information, and that you'd compensate him then, as well."

Sam was always happy to spend someone else's money. "What about this other number?" I said.

"Ah, yes," Sam said, "the plot thickens. Seems your friend Barry took a few calls from Junior, as well."

Barry is a friend to a lot of people in Miami, particularly people with money to launder. If you want the best man in the business, he's the man to go to. But I had a hard time believing Barry was working directly with an organization like the Latin Emperors. He tended to prefer to work with sole proprietors. Less chance of getting snitched out by someone . . . or getting shot. Barry could get you what you needed, but he wasn't the kind of guy to consort too much with the more violent members of his profession, mainly because he wasn't exactly handy around a gun, or a fist, for that matter.

"How do you know this is Barry's number?" I said.

"Hours of intensive sleuthing," Sam said, "and then I called it and he answered."

"What did he say?" I said.

"First, that he was happy to hear my voice. Second, that he was curious regarding Fiona's current romantic status. And third, that he was scared to death of Junior Gonzalez," Sam said.

"That's wonderful," I said.

"I told him you'd call him, see if you could ease his beating heart a little bit."

A common misconception about people on society's fringe is that they have some indelible sum of street smarts that Joe Public does not. The truth is that you usually end up on society's fringe because you lack a certain facility with the idea of cause and effect. Having street smarts really just means you don't know how to exist in the real world where people are ruled by the idea that what they do will engender consequences.

That was Barry, in a nutshell.

"I'll add that to my to-do list, right after saving Father Eduardo's life," I said. "What was he doing for Junior?"

"That's what he wants to talk to you about," Sam said. "He said it was just a consulting gig."

"A consulting gig?"

"Ecomony's tight, Mikey. Everyone's taking on new job duties these days."

"It's true," Fiona said. "I'm pondering a move into corporate sales and service. Like Blackwater, but with better outfits."

Luckily, a hotel employee approached us before the conversation could continue between Sam and Fiona. He wasn't young or hip enough to be one of the bartenders (all of whom wore tight black T-shirts and black pants trimmed in white, which made them look like lost, if fashionable, mimes), especially not with his gray hair, salt-and-pepper mustache and rather nervous demeanor. As he walked, he kept looking over his shoulder, as if he thought a tsunami was approaching, and even when he faced forward, his eyes continued to dart. His name tag said PABLO.

"Are you the people with the money?" Pablo asked.

"This your guy?" I asked Sam.

"No," Sam said. "Where's Louie?"

"On break," Pablo said. "He sent me."

"Why are you so nervous?" I asked.

"I need the money first," Pablo said.

I pulled out my wallet and examined the contents. I only had about sixty dollars. That wasn't much of a payoff, but I hadn't hit the cash stash prior to our visit to the hotel. I handed Pablo the money, anyway, and waited while he counted the ones, fives and the lone twenty.

"This is only fifty-seven dollars," he said. "My life is not worth only fifty-seven bucks."

"That's all I have," I said.

"I'll take your watch," Pablo said.

"No, you won't," I said.

Pablo looked from me to Sam to Fiona. He lingered on Fiona for a moment too long.

"The leering you are doing would cost you fifty dollars at any reputable peep show," Fiona said. "And if you stare a moment longer, it's going to cost you your kneecaps."

Pablo whipped his head back in my direction, which caused beads of sweat to fly from his scalp. It was nice outside, but not nice enough to make this man a sweaty mess.

"Your sunglasses," he said to me. "Your sunglasses, and we're even."

When you're a spy, you sometimes make sacrifices for the greater good. I could buy another pair of sunglasses, so I handed Pablo mine. He put them on immediately. They weren't quite his look, but he seemed content. "Follow me," he said. That he didn't also say "if you want to live" was a great relief.

8

Work for the government long enough and what you realize is that there's no such thing as absolute privacy. Every moment you spend holding your cell phone is a moment that can be tracked. Every Web site you visit on the Internet can be tracked. Every search you enter into Google can be tracked, so if you spend a lot of free time searching for ways to blow up airplanes, be aware that there's someone who is now looking for reasons why you might want to blow up an airplane. Everything you do behind the privacy of your front door is really just a sham: If the government wants to know what you're doing, they might need a warrant to kick down the door, but they rarely need anything more than a couple of keystrokes to get a great idea of what you're plotting.

If you want even a modicum of privacy, stay in a hotel. The government can't as easily bug a business as they can a person. And when you're in a hotel, there are plenty of people willing to do your bidding, so that you may feel even more secure. Plus, the sheer amount of people who might stay in a room, in addition to the number of people who have access to a room, and the amount of government-mandated cleaning that goes on, makes a hotel a forensics nightmare for investigators. Too much opportunity for pollution equals reasonable doubt.

At a place like the Ace Hotel, where looking the other way is a selling point, you could probably do a whole lot of illegal things, provided you kept the right people paid and didn't make too much noise. And even then, well, you'd probably be just fine.

The Ace Hotel was located just off Collins Avenue in South Beach, and the local lore was that it was once President Kennedy's Miami getaway, a place he'd go to meet with Marilyn Monroe and the Mafia and probably Castro, too. It was a small hotel—only four stories—but it made up for its lack of size by offering fifteen two-bedroom villas that faced the Miami Beach canal. It was one of those great mysteries of tourism: Why spend thousands of dollars to sleep in a villa that was likely not as nice as your own home?

"It is that one," Pablo said. We'd followed him out of the pool area and around the back of the hotel and through the (intentionally) overgrown botanical gardens, which subtly hid the villas from sight. Nothing says "privacy" quite like plants grown to twice their normal size. That and water features burbling away in some hidden crevice—boutique hotels are always big on hidden crevices that contain very small fountains— make celebrities and the very rich feel like they are one with nature.

"Which one?" Sam said.

·

Pablo pointed in the vague direction of a twelve-foot thrust of fountain grass. "There," he said. He was still sweating profusely and my glasses kept sliding down his nose, so that he had to continually push them up. He turned to me and handed me a room key card. "Take this," he said.

"One minute," I said. He hadn't said a word since we left the pool and had grown consistently more nervous as we walked, which made me think we were walking into an ambush. "What's in the villa?"

"Bad men," he said.

Fiona groaned in exasperation. She reached over and snatched my glasses off Pablo's face and handed them back to me. They were a bit too damp for my taste. "Pablo," she said, "I'm not as patient nor as willing to spend money on frivolous information as my two simian friends. So I'm going to need you to speak only in complete sentences now. I know you're scared of something, but if you aren't more forthcoming with information, you will actually have a reason to be scared, versus the normal, unfounded fears of your sex."

"Uh, Fi," I said, but she waved me off.

Pablo's sweaty fear was now wide-eyed anguish, so that was a nice change. "The man who rents this room? He tells me not to come and clean. But you understand, if I do not clean the rooms, I can lose my job. They track our security cards, so they always know if we've gone in the rooms and villas, you see. So they know. And I cannot lose my job. Do you understand?"

"I understand," Fiona said. She put her hand on Pablo's wrist. Very gentle. Very caring. She had that ability for kindness, too, but she could also snap his wrist if she decided she didn't trust him. "Please, continue."

"So I wait until I see the man leave and I go and just slide my card in, so it registers. You see? But then the door is open and curiosity, you see, it gets the better of me."

"Killed the cat," Sam said, which was entirely the wrong thing to say at that moment.

"I know. I know. I know," Pablo said. "I find guns. Many, many guns. And much money. Much money. But it isn't real. The money, that is. I find this out the wrong way."

"Please, tell me you did not steal counterfeit money and then use it to pay your water bill or something," I said. Pablo's eyes got wider, if that was possible. He wiped his face with his sleeve, but he didn't say anything. Whatever he did with the money, it was the wrong thing to do. "How much did you take?" I asked.

"One thousand," he said. "I bought a round of drinks at the bar here and paid with a fifty that was apparently not such a good copy. So, so, I try to take the money back, but by that time, I'd already spent maybe five hundred, so I cannot afford to pay back another real five hundred."

"When was the last time you went into the room?" I asked.

"Three days. I slide my card, but I do not go in. But the men who come and go, they do not look like the kind of people I'd like to anger."

"And what do we look like?" Sam said.

Pablo stammered for a moment, but then Fiona applied a slight bit of pressure to his wrist, which seemed to focus his attention. "I figure you are good guys, or else why would you want to know what's happening?"

I handed Pablo back my sunglasses. He needed them more than I did. "Fiona," I said, "give him your earrings."

"What?"

"Your earrings," I said.

"They're diamond," she said.

"Did you buy them?"

"They were a gift," she said.

"From who?"

"From a gentleman who didn't have quite enough money for a fair-priced assault rifle."

"Consider it karmic reparations," I said.

Fiona took off her two rather large diamond studs and handed them to Pablo, who didn't quite know what to do with them, mostly because Fiona was making noises in her throat like a cornered tiger. It can be slightly disconcerting to those who don't know Fiona's noises.

"What am I to do?" Pablo said.

"Go home sick," I said.

"For how long?" he asked.

"Forever," I said.

Pablo looked down at the diamond earrings in his hand and then back at Fiona. He plucked up one of the earrings and tried to hand it back to Fiona. "Maybe one is enough?"

"They're a matched set," Fiona said.

"Go," I said to Pablo, "before I change my mind."

Pablo deposited the earrings in his pocket and then scurried out of sight in what must have been record time.

"Guess it's true," Sam said once Pablo was gone, "that you can't trust the help at hotels not to go through your shit."

I handed the key card to Fiona. "Why don't you see if you can accidentally open the door to the wrong villa," I said.

"And get shot?" she said.

"No one shoots a pretty girl in a bikini," Sam said. "And besides, with all that oil on you, a bullet would slide right off you."

"Or I'll instantly ignite," she said.

I had a better idea. I called the front desk and asked to be connected to the villa. I hung up after five rings. "There's no one there," I said.

"Would you feel better if Uncle Sam was standing next to you with his big, mean gun, Fiona?" Sam said.

Fiona gave both of us one of her patented "I could live a better life without both of you" glares and stomped off toward the villa. Sam and I followed behind her at a slight distance, and then lingered out of sight in the nuclear-treated fountain grass as she approached the door. Though Fiona didn't have a gun on her—hard to hide a gun in a bikini—I was certain she could handle herself in the face of danger. Plus, Sam was right: No one shoots a pretty girl in a bikini. It just goes against nature.

Fiona slipped the key card in just as anyone might when they're returning to their villa—which is to say, she portrayed no nerves in the least—and opened the door. I listened for screams or gunshots or even a muffled yelp, but heard nothing. The door closed behind her with an audible click.

A few seconds later, my cell phone rang.

"Darling," Fiona said when I answered, "why don't you come back to the room? I'm lonely."

"I'll even bring a friend," I said.

Sam and I checked for unwelcome visitors and then headed to the villa. Fiona stood in the doorway, sipping a bottle of water.

"Where'd you get the water?" I asked.

"The mini bar," she said. "Just four dollars."

We stepped inside, and Fi closed the door and bolted it behind us. The villa was decorated just like the rest of the hotel, which is to say, at some point the designers began thinking of the 1970s as a period worth revisiting. For added kitsch factor, the walls inside the villa were covered with framed, blown-up photos of B-list celebrities—Zsa Zsa Gabor, Barbie Benton, Ricardo Montalbán, the guy who played Potsie on *Happy Days*—partying in Miami during the period.

"Who would pay to stay here?" Sam said. "I had to *live* in the 1970s. And let me tell you, it was no vacation."

"Hipsters," Fiona said, "love to revisit the time period their parents suffered through."

The living room and small galley kitchen looked lived-in, but not messy. There were cups in the sink, the garbage had take-out containers and coffee grounds in it and the sofa in the living room was dented from people sitting on it. There were no guns and no stacks of money, at least not in the open. The room was well lit by the sun coming in through a sliding glass door, which opened out to a small patio overlooking the canal. I opened the door and stepped outside. On the patio table was an ashtray overflowing with cigarette butts. Two chairs were pulled slightly away from the table, as well, which told me more than one person had been here.

I came back inside in time to see Sam open up the fridge. "Uh, Mikey," he said.

"You can have a beer when we're done," I said.

"I know," Sam said, "but you'll want to take a look at this."

"Please, tell me it's a human head," Fiona said.

"No," Sam said, "just a lot of dead presidents."

Stacked inside the fridge and the freezer were bundles of bills: twenties, tens, fives and ones and nothing larger.

I pulled out a stack of twenties and examined it. They were pre-1996 bills, which meant they didn't have the plastic security strip embedded into the fabric of the bill, nor the extra details such as Andrew Jackson's hidden watermark photo or the shifting color palettes.

I licked my thumb and ran it across the face of the bill. Surprisingly, no color came up. Surprising since these were clearly counterfeit bills, but ones that would easily pass in the circles where they were likely to be passed—in bars and clubs, the streets, maybe even foreign countries—though certainly not in banks. It was doubtful they'd even be accepted in a soda machine.

If you're going to make your own American currency, the first thing you need to know is that in all likelihood, you'll get caught. After you get caught, you'll go to federal prison, and after you're released from federal prison, you'll be audited for the rest of your life by the IRS. If you're still going to make your own American currency, you need to have access to a high-density printer, rag paper and the ability to compress your paper with tons of pressure in order to make it as thin as the common dollar. An automobile wrecker would do the trick.

And then? Then you'll probably still get caught, because if you're dumb enough to try counterfeiting currency, you're probably not smart enough not to spread the money around to people or businesses who might take notice of your fake bills, because even the best fake bill just doesn't feel like a real bill. Nor does it smell the same. There's no way to replicate the process an actual bill goes through from the mint to your wallet, nor is there a way to re-create the wear and tear of the bill's life span—the average fifty dollar bill lives for a decade, a twenty for half that time.

Junior—or his people—had been smart enough to use rag paper, and it looked like they'd had some success pressing the paper, too, as it had almost the right consistency. And by putting the money in the refrigerator and freezer, they'd even managed to add moisture to the bills, which helped seal in the aging chemical

they'd apparently used, too. It wasn't terribly sophisticated, but it was decent enough to fool someone who
didn't know any better or, more than likely, someone
who just didn't care.

"Not bad," I said. I tossed the bundle to Fiona. "Go
get yourself something nice."

"Like twenty years in prison?" she said.

"In your hands, as a foreign national," I said, "I'd
say you'd be looking at closer to thirty."

"How much would you say is in here?" Sam said.

I counted thirty stacks in the fridge—there was also
a half gallon of milk, the remnants of a Caesar salad, a
six-pack of Coke and five Stellas—and at least twice
that many stacks in the freezer. "A couple hundred thousand," I said.

It was enough to pay some bills, but it wasn't a real
operating budget. No reputable dealer of anything the
Latin Emperors would want—like drugs or guns or
antiaircraft missiles, if they really wanted to diversify
their business interests—would be fooled by the fake
stuff. This was money to be spread around the bottom
rungs of the ladder.

"You two might want to look at this," Fiona said.
She'd walked down the short hallway that led from
the living room and now stood in the entryway to the
first of the two bedrooms. "And maybe don't touch
anything else."

Sam and I walked down the hall and peered over Fiona's shoulder into the room. There was a stripped bed
in the center of the room, surrounded by two night-
stands, both of which had been knocked over. At the

foot of the bed were the sheets and linens. They were stained with blood.

"I don't suppose that's just the latest spring style," Sam said.

I nudged the ball of sheets with my foot, looked to see if there was something other than blood—like a head or an arm—but there was nothing solid.

"Anyone who bled that much," Sam said, "probably isn't bleeding anymore."

"Hard to say," I said. "It could be from more than one person."

"That's a pleasant thought," Fiona said.

"Wait here," I said, and stepped into the room so that I could examine the bed. If someone had been murdered on it, the mattress would be soaked, too, but that didn't appear to be the case. The room also didn't smell like death, which was a good sign. It doesn't matter if you die pleasantly or die violently; if you die in a room, you're going to leave a lasting olfactory sensation.

I opened a door to what I assumed to be the en suite bathroom, and instead discovered the Latin Emperors' money factory. There were several printers, laptops and reams and reams of paper scattered on the floor and into the exceptionally large walk-in closet, which housed an automated paper cutter.

I looked inside the machine and found the reason why there wasn't anyone about today and why there were a bunch of bloodstained sheets: Two fingers, cut off at the middle knuckle, sat among a stack of freshly cut five-dollar bills.

"Sam," I said, "did you say that Father Eduardo has Honrado creating its own newspaper?"

"They hand it out to all the community centers," Sam said. He and Fi were still in the hallway. "And I think once a month it comes stuffed inside the *Herald*. Why?"

"I've got a feeling the Latin Emperors might have some printing needs."

I made sure the paper cutter was unplugged and then called in Sam and Fi for a look. Fi took a quick glance but didn't seem overly interested. Sam, however, spent a good, long time staring at the mess.

"You have a theory, Sam?"

"I'm just curious why they didn't have K-Dog do some of this stuff," Sam said. "Seems like he'd at least know how to do it without losing important body parts."

"Maybe he actually is trying to stay straight?" I said.

"Maybe." It didn't sound like Sam believed himself. "Poor guy," Sam said eventually. "I'm gonna guess the Latin Emperors don't offer workmen's comp."

"Unlikely," I said.

"So I guess we're looking for a three-fingered man now?" Fiona said.

"No," I said, "I think the man I need to talk to is Barry." Things were starting to make a lot of sense. Father Eduardo wasn't just getting blackmailed; he was also about to be the victim of a hostile corporate takeover. And I had a feeling that this wasn't a plan originally hatched by Junior Gonzalez, since the scope of it had suddenly begun to take on a grander scale. Something maybe a "consultant" might have had some input on.

"Will you be torturing him for information?" Fi said.

"No," I said. "Knowing Barry, I think he's probably torturing himself as it is."

"Too bad," she said. "It's been so long since I've been given the opportunity to interrogate anyone. One of my rarely utilized skill sets."

That gave me an idea. "Sam," I said, "I want you to take Fiona down to Honrado, point out where our scarred friend works and then let Fiona interrogate her."

"Abduct and interrogate?" Fi said, ever hopeful.

"Use your best judgment," I said, which was probably a mistake.

9

Not much really annoyed Fiona. Oh, there were the little things—men who didn't open doors anymore, bullets jamming in expensive automatic weapons, undercooked fish—but by and large she thought that the best way to live was to be mildly cynical, but not actually to the point that every small injustice became an issue. Dealing with Michael had made her aware that even the stupid things men did—and they did plenty— could be mitigated by occasional acts of nobility.

Chivalry didn't excuse stupidity, of course, but it went a long way toward reminding Fiona that at base, men were just slightly above chimps in terms of their emotional development, and thus needed to be rewarded when they did something vaguely human.

Even Sam needed positive reinforcement periodically, which is why she told him, as they sat parked next to each other across from the Honrado campus, waiting for the woman with scars on her neck and face to depart for lunch, that though she was unsure of what she was about to do, she was certain she didn't need him wasting any more of his precious time on her. She'd be fine. He should go off and do whatever it was he did when he wasn't tracking down leads or shooting guns or drinking beer poolside or, well, whatever.

"Fiona," Sam said, "Michael told me to make sure that if anything went down, you had backup."

"What could possibly happen between me and some girl?" Fi said. "You think some girl is going to cause me a problem, Sam?"

"Well, no, no, clearly," Sam said, "but, uh, I guess what I'm saying is that maybe I should stick around in case, uh . . ." Sam didn't finish. He didn't need to. The problem with Sam and Michael was that they believed her when she said she wanted to shoot *everyone* and blow up *everything*. Six or seven percent of the time, she didn't mean it literally. But she'd been placed in so many situations recently that could have been solved with a well-placed explosive charge that it just seemed so silly that now everyone was so into *diplomacy*.

"I promise not to hurt her," Fiona said.

"I didn't say you would," Sam said.

"And I promise not to put her into any kind of cage or underground fortress."

Sam hemmed and hawed for a bit and then finally started his engine. "You remember who the target is?"

"The woman is cut like a spiral ham, as I recall," Fiona said. "I can't imagine there will be another one quite like her."

Sam eventually drove off, and Fiona was finally able to relax. If it was up to her, she'd be sitting poolside and negotiating a gun deal for some Peruvian revolutionaries—something she'd had to cancel from her itinerary for the week when this new job came up, and which, upon reflection, seemed like a fairly good idea. She'd never liked doing business with Peruvians. They always had such inferiority complexes. Now, *that* was annoying. Besides, what could be more exciting than viewing the world through a pair of high-powered binoculars while waiting for some girl to come walking out of a building?

It took another twenty minutes, but eventually Fiona spotted her mark. She focused the binoculars on her to make sure, but Fiona could tell just by how the girl carried herself that she was the one. If you live inside a pressure cooker, you're bound to have some outward signs. In the girl's case, it was the way she immediately exhaled when she walked out of the building. Not just a release of breath, because that would be impossible to see, but one of those full-body experiences favored by sixteen-year-old girls in front of their parents. She then looked both ways, like she was crossing the street, though she was just standing in the middle of a grassy expanse, and then trudged with her head down toward Fourteenth Street.

Fiona wondered what Junior had on the girl, because she didn't seem like the perfect corporate spy. Too much angst, for one thing, though Fiona supposed that angst was most likely the default emotion for many of the tough kids who end up in Father Eduardo's care—you can only pretend to be bad for so long.

It didn't matter to Fiona what the girl had done in the past, only what she was doing now. That was another way to keep from getting annoyed: focus on the present. Fi got out of her car and walked a safe distance away from the girl. Fi was maybe fifty yards behind her, which was fine, since both were walking at a normal pace down a straight road. The girl had reason to believe she was being followed—clearly, her nerves told her this much—but didn't have any reason to believe she was being followed by an Irish woman wearing a Betsey Johnson dress and still smelling of suntan lotion.

At the corner, the girl ducked into a beauty shop. Perfect. Fiona liked beauty shops for all of the promises they offered—blemishes hidden, sexier lips, new hair colors—none of which seemed to materialize in quite the manner you'd expect once you got the products home.

Fi lingered in front of the store for a moment and pretended to talk on her cell phone. Inside, she could see that the girl was regarding a long wall of lotions and creams. She'd set her purse down at her feet, a sure sign that she was in for a long haul and, more importantly, comfortable in her surroundings.

The store wasn't one of those well-lit chains staffed by matching women in matching black outfits and matching attitudes. Fiona hated those places. The women who worked in those places truly were annoying. You can't have airs and work retail. It simply wasn't allowed. No, Fiona could tell even from the street that this was a small business, the kind built out of someone's savings, low rents in a neighborhood that wasn't exactly considered prime property and stock aimed at the very people who lived and worked in walking distance. There were also two hair stations in the back that, Fiona assumed, were staffed by women who regularly dyed people's hair a color they'd regret sometime later in life.

She pushed open the doors and was immediately overwhelmed by the smell of hairspray, enough that she began to cough almost immediately, which made the girl look up with a frown.

A good opening. Fiona continued to cough until the girl had to say something.

"Are you okay?"

"Fine," Fiona said. "Just swallowed wrong."

"Oh, I hate that. Makes me feel stupid."

"Me, too," Fiona said. "Like, what, I can't even swallow right?" The girl laughed. Pleasant. Just two girls talking about saliva.

Fiona realized she had an avenue and had to keep it up. It was so silly sometimes, the lengths we have to go to get information from people, Fiona thought. Bugs, breaking and entering, torture . . . sometimes just talking to a person can yield so much more than any covert operation. Now, granted, it wasn't as if Fiona intended to portray herself as precisely who she was, but it was her intention on this day to be as normal as possible, because Fiona believed most people responded to normal.

"What are you looking for?" Fiona asked.

"I don't really know," the girl said. "My skin, you know, it gets so scaly sometimes. Around these scars on my neck especially."

Fiona pulled a bottle of Neutrogena off the shelf. "I use this," she said, and handed it to her. "It keeps me feeling silky smooth."

"Oh, that's too expensive for me," the girl said. "And I can't have anything with too much scent in it. I'm allergic."

It was odd how much the girl was willing to divulge of herself to a complete stranger in a beauty supply store, but, invariably, that was what people holding on to other big secrets ended up being like. Every alcoholic or drug addict Fiona had known was, during the course of his life, always quick to admit some other damning piece of information at a moment's notice. And then the ones who were clean always wanted to tell you about how they got clean, or how much they'd used, or how many people they'd slept with to get to this new enlightened version of themselves. It wore Fiona out most of the time, but in this case, with this poor girl, Fiona couldn't help but feel a pang of sympathy for her. She'd clearly been through a lot, and now she was going through something else, too. She was probably lit to pop with guilt.

"Have you ever just put vitamin E oil on your scars?" Fiona asked.

"That doesn't really work," the girl said. "I've tried everything. But I'm going to get surgery one day. So, yeah, it's all good."

It's all good. If there was ever a sentence young women uttered that meant the direct opposite, it was that one. No one said it when things actually were all good, only to deflect what was clearly a bad situation.

Fiona thought that if she abducted this girl, tied her up and began questioning her, within minutes she'd get every secret she'd ever been told or ever uttered.

"Are you saving up for it?" Fiona said.

"No. I work at Honrado. Down the street. And they've got doctors who volunteer to remove tattoos and fix things. So I'm just waiting on that to come through. It's a good job, right?"

"Right," Fiona said. She kept trying to get a feel for the girl, get some insight into why she'd be in business with Junior when she had such a good deal with a person like Father Eduardo. Fi decided the best way to bridge that gap would be to set that bridge on fire. "How'd you get a job there? When I got out, I would have killed to get to work with someone like Father Eduardo."

The girl looked shocked. "You did time?"

"Five years," she said.

"For what?"

Fiona decided to keep it as real as possible. "I robbed a bank," she said.

"And you only did five?"

Fi leaned in to the girl, close enough that she could smell the girl's cheap perfume and an underpinning of sweat. The girl leaned, too, sensing that they were about to tell some secrets. "I gave up my ex. He was the one who got me into it. No sense letting him off easy if I was doing real years."

"You didn't feel any guilt about that?"

"No," Fiona said.

The girl bit down on her bottom lip and seemed to

be thinking about something. "You wanna get some coffee or something?"

The honest truth was that Fiona really did not like hanging out with other women. They were usually so . . . girlish. Always concerned about who was talking about them, what they were wearing, who had the bigger whatever. Now, certainly, Fi liked wearing nice things, and she didn't like people talking about her and could appreciate big things; she just didn't require the requisite estrogen-fueled drama that went along with those desires when women got together to discuss them.

But sitting with this girl—whose name was Leticia, she'd learned—wasn't so bad. Leticia was twenty-three and had a seven-year-old boy that she still called a baby. And, unfortunately, the father of the baby was a Latin Emperor whose nickname was Killa.

"Killa?" Fiona said.

"He got it on the street," Leticia said, "and it just stuck. Now whenever someone gets killed anywhere near him, they bring his ass in. It's stupid."

"You call yourself Killa," Fiona said, "it's bound to cause suspicion."

Leticia took a sip of coffee. They were sitting outside at Café Flordita, a Cuban coffee shop just a few blocks from the Orange Bowl. They'd been there twenty minutes, and in that time Fiona had learned everything she really needed to know to understand why Leticia was snooping for the LE: Either she did their bidding, or Killa told her he'd take their son and she'd never see him again. This wasn't a custody battle, just the basics of street life, which Leticia understood even if Fiona couldn't wrap her mind around it entirely. Different rules for different streets, she supposed.

"I wanna get away from him, from this whole life, you know? I did time. I got this shit all over my face and you know, for what? It's stupid. I just want to take my baby and get out of Miami."

"Then you should do that," Fiona said.

"Father Eduardo? He's got me training to be a dental assistant starting in the fall. Paying for it and everything. So I need to be here for that. I couldn't pay for that out of my own pocket." Leticia sighed, and Fiona saw that her eyes had welled up. "I just, you know, I got this thing to deal with first, and then I can do whatever I want. It's not even illegal, and, you know, Father Eduardo is LE from back in the day, so I think that, you know, it's all good."

If anything was patently not *all good*, it was certainly this situation. Fiona wanted to tell Leticia that she was going to help her out of this situation, that there was a way out of it all that wouldn't involve her working with the Latin Emperors. But Fiona also knew that the poor girl was unsteady on her feet right now, giving up all of this information to a perfect stranger, which meant she'd give up even more to people who really had hooks into her.

Women. Fiona just didn't get most of them. She was, she had to admit, *annoyed* by many women. Leticia wasn't weak—she had those scars, after all, and was out in public doing her thing, even if her thing was filled with regret, and that took a spine and a will and Fi respected that, God knows—but she compromised emotionally. She probably loved Killa, too, even if she said she didn't. Or loved him enough not to run to the police and tell them she was being blackmailed by him. Though for a girl who'd done time, just being around . . . Killa . . . probably constituted a violation of some kind. The poor girl had made a series of bad choices in her life, or made a series of no choices whatsoever, and now here she was, about to be in the thick of a criminal conspiracy, too.

"If I were you, you know what I'd do?" Fiona said.

"Rob a bank?" Leticia actually smiled when she said that, which made Fiona happy. Somewhere was a person inside there.

"No, I'm not doing that anymore," Fiona said. "I'd pick up your son from school tomorrow and I'd just keep driving. Don't stop until you get to Atlanta or Charlotte or New York or Canada. And then when you get to wherever you are, you call Father Eduardo and tell him that Killa was making you do things you didn't want to do and that he threatened to take your son and that you're not coming back until he's gone."

Leticia nodded and then welled up again. "That's my dream. But that takes money, and I don't have enough to even get gas in my car to make it to Sarasota."

"If I could get you money," Fiona said, "would you go?"

"Why would you do that? You don't even know me."

"I was you," Fiona said. That wasn't strictly true,

but it was for the role she was playing, and it was also what life could have been like if she'd been the type of woman who let other people rule her.

"Anyway, I got a parole officer," she said. "I can't just relocate like that. It would take a lot of paperwork. And you know Killa? He's got visitation rights. It would be kidnapping, wouldn't it?"

That someone named Killa had any rights made Fiona sick. But the reality of the situation made Fiona sicker. She needed to do something for the girl. She'd just have to tell Michael that she'd picked up another client for him.

"Let me talk to some friends I have," Fiona told the girl.

"Why are you being so nice to me?"

"Someone has to be." Fi reached into her purse and pulled out a pen and a scrap of paper and scrawled out one of her safe numbers. "This is my cell," she said. "You find yourself in a bad position, you feel like you need help before I can get you the help you need, I want you to call me."

"This is crazy," Leticia said. "You don't even know me."

"We tough girls have to stick together," Fiona said.

Leticia smiled faintly, and for the first time she looked to Fiona like the young girl she absolutely was. She took the piece of paper with Fiona's number on it and slipped it into her own purse. "I better go or I'll be late to get back to the phones," Leticia said. "I don't like to disappoint Father Eduardo if I can avoid it."

10

When plotting a counterinsurgency, it's important to recognize that not all of your decisions can be based on what would be considered, in everyday life, acceptable ethics. Breaking the law for the good of the country is practically a right of passage for American presidents, so imagine how often it happens with spies.

But if you're leading a counterinsurgency operation, you must gauge the moral well-being of your subordinates after these activities and be prepared to act as a sounding board for them or, if needed, remove them from duty. What this means is that in a war zone, you may need to order a Black Hawk in to medevac a soldier to an appropriate mental facility. But if you're fighting in close quarters, with a small fighting unit, a good leader may have to serve as the mental health provider.

Which is why when I called Barry—a man with exceptionally questionable ethics and usually very little guilt about it—I could tell that he needed the equivalent of two Xanax and a good nap, but that he was pondering something more along the lines of a guy with two guns showing up at his door and offering him a dirt nap. So I did the one thing I could think of: I invited him to my mother's house for lunch. Sometimes a guy just needs a sandwich with crusts cut off to feel better about himself.

Plus, my mother's house was a safe place. If anyone from the Latin Emperors happened down the street, the neighborhood watch commander would scuttle an F-16.

I'd been at my mother's for only a few minutes when Barry knocked on the door. My mother opened it, saw him looking pitiful there on the front porch and did the one motherly thing she could do in this instance: She gave him hell.

"Did someone kill your dog?" she asked by way of greeting.

"No, Mrs. Westen," Barry said. "I've just had a hard week. Busy time in my line of work."

"You think you have it any harder than anyone else?"

Barry looked over my mother's shoulder at me—she hadn't let him in yet—and I gave him the universal sign of surrender. "No, Mrs. Westen," Barry said. "I guess I don't."

"Well, then wipe off your feet, take off those ludicrous sunglasses and come inside. Michael's been waiting for you for hours."

It's not that my mother had no concept of time—since I'd been there only fifteen minutes on the outside—it's that she'd been saying the same thing to me and my brother, Nate, for so long that it was just second nature. Someone was always waiting for hours to give us hell.

Barry did as he was told and then sat down across from me at the kitchen table. He had bags under his eyes, and his normally sculpted facial hair had a bit more scruff than usual to it. "You look good," I said.

"I haven't been sleeping too well."

"Conscience bothering you, Barry?"

"Before I make my confession, would it be possible to get something to eat?"

"Ma," I said, "can you make Barry a sandwich?"

My mother came into the kitchen and gave Barry another once-over, as if she hadn't seen him just a few seconds earlier. "You look like hell," she said. "When was your last proper shower?"

"Two days," Barry said. "I've been staying on a boat."

"The Atlantic Ocean out of water now?" she said.

Barry looked at me for help, but I'd been on the blunt end of this weapon before and knew to stick out. "Could I get a grilled cheese?" he said.

"Could you?" she said.

"May I?"

"That's better," my mother said. "I've got two types of cheese: American and Velveeta. Which would you like?"

"Velveeta isn't a kind of cheese," Barry said. "It's a brand. Right, Michael?"

"Popular misconception," I said.

"Then I guess I'll have both?" Barry said, more than a hint of hesitation in his voice. He'd finally caught the drift of my mother's tough-love approach ... which usually contained a lot more tough than love. "And could I get a glass of milk? You don't happen to have any strawberry Quik, do you?"

"I think there's some in the pantry," she said. I was going to tell her that that strawberry Quik had been in the pantry since 1983, but opted not to. If a dying man wanted strawberry Quik, who was I to withhold his wish? It was just a good thing he didn't ask for a San-ka, because she had a vacuum-sealed can of that, too, that hadn't seen the light of day since Carter was in office.

While my mom prepared Barry his schoolboy lunch, I thought it might be prudent to figure out just what the hell he'd done.

"I haven't seen you in a while," I said.

"That's a good thing, right? Means both of us have been able to live our lives without need for too much trouble."

"Sam tells me you're in the consulting business now."

"I thought I'd try to diversify my interests. Make sure I've always got a good revenue stream. It's just smart business. Like how sometimes for you, you're helping little old ladies or sick kids, or other times it's someone who's got pimp problems or just escaped a Russian prison. Same kind of thing."

"Right," I said. "I see that. Exactly the same thing." I got distracted for a moment by the smell of burning paper. I turned and looked, and my mother had started a small fire on the counter where she was making Barry's grilled cheese. She'd gone for the old-fashioned touch and was cooking the sandwich using a clothes iron. The problem was that she had the sandwich on top of a stack of newspapers. And now there were flames.

"Uh, Ma," I said. "You maybe want to shove that in the sink."

"You think I don't know how to put out a kitchen fire, Michael? You're not the only one with some training around here." My mom slid the sandwich and the newspapers and was just about to drop the iron into the sink, but fortunately, the power cord wasn't long enough and so she opted to leave it on the counter so she could electrocute herself at a later date. Barry and I both stared in stunned silence until she finally realized the near-fatal error of her ways. "What?" she said. "I didn't do it."

"Do you have peanut butter?" Barry asked.

"I have a jar of Peter Pan in the pantry," she said.

"Crunchy or creamy?"

"Barry," my mother said, "you'll eat it either way. What does it matter? And once it's in your mouth, it's all creamy." A few moments later, my mother set down a sandwich—minus the crusts—and a glass of strawberry Quik in front of Barry. "Eat," she said, and Barry did.

When he finished, he leaned back in his chair and closed his eyes. Now, this really did feel like therapy. "You ever ask yourself, Mike, what is simpler than just being at home?"

"No," I said. "Street fighting in Tikrit was simpler than being at home."

"Simple pleasures," Barry said, ignoring me. "Peanut butter and jelly. Strawberry-flavored milk. Why'd I ever leave home in the first place?"

"I'm going to guess it was to go into juvenile hall," I said.

"It even smells like home here, Mike," Barry said.

I reached across the table and grabbed Barry by his shirt collar and yanked him back to real life. "Welcome home," I said. "Time to start talking, or my mother will give you a spanking."

Barry straightened himself out, emptied the remnants of the strawberry Quik and then leaned forward on his elbows. "Truth? I wasn't made for the consulting business. I'm a hands-on, do-it-yourself kind of guy. Independent contractor."

"What did you tell Junior Gonzalez?"

"Look, he came to me, said he had some questions, could I give him some advice. And I said, 'Sure,' named a price; he came back and offered double, and we were in business."

"And let me guess—he paid you double by giving you a bag of skank bills up front."

Barry raised his eyebrows, but he wasn't really shocked. He couldn't be. If he was sitting here with me, he knew I probably had a fair idea of what had already happened. I was looking for the more salient details.

"Not just skank bills," Barry said. "'Skank' implies some basic ability. No, this was like Monopoly money."

"How long ago did he first contact you?"

"Six weeks, maybe."

"And he just came to ask you about making money?"

"Not exactly," Barry said. "You know, I've diversified my portfolio since you got back into town and began using my services. So I've been letting people know that if they have needs regarding certain government rules and regulations, well, I now have a bit more expertise and can negotiate sensitive areas."

"Barry," I said.

"So I might have told Junior about how best to avoid wiretaps, a couple of things I've picked up regarding the Patriot Act from that credit card thing we did with that terrorist bank in Myanmar, and may have navigated him toward ways he might avoid using his identity. The guy had been in prison practically since disco, so he wasn't exactly up on a lot of the new technology. And his guys—well, more like henchmen, really—weren't exactly top of their class at MIT, so, well, I might have intimated to him that I could provide additional services outside the consulting I was providing."

"Barry," I said, "there's no 'might have' involved here, is there?"

My mother came by and picked up Barry's plate, then surveyed the damage and went back into the kitchen to make him another one. That she'd managed not to sit down with us and pound questions into Barry was a sign of major growth on her part. That she was clearly listening to every word, however, and showed herself in time for Barry to come up with a suitable answer was a kind of charity I frankly wasn't familiar with.

"It's like this, Mike," Barry began, but I reached over and grabbed his collar again, which stopped him.

"Barry," I said, "we're friends. I like you. I'm happy to help you. I'm happy to get your help. But if you dance around the truth any longer, I might hurt you. So just tell me something definitive."

"Okay," he said. "Okay. Yes. There is no 'might' here."

I let go of him and said, "Barry," again, because sometimes just hearing your name reminds you that you're a real person and that you've disappointed someone. Your name is the one word in the history of language that has the power to mean about five hundred different things depending on inflection and the person speaking. In this case, I wanted "Barry" to mean "you idiot."

"I know, I know, I'm stupid," Barry said, getting it. "But, Mike, it's not like I'm flush with business right now. I've grown accustomed to a certain level of comfort and, as such, my station in life requires that I continue to grow my brand."

"Your brand," I said, "has worsened a substantial problem." I told him about Father Eduardo and Junior, about the Latin Emperor compound out in Homestead, what we'd discovered at the Ace Hotel, what Sam had uncovered and about Fiona's fact-finding mission at Honrado, which I'd learned just prior to Barry's arrival had yielded us plenty of information and, apparently, another damsel in distress . . . in addition to Barry, of course.

Barry took in all of this information without saying

much. At first he just calmly ate the second sandwich my mother dropped off; then he attempted to drink a second glass of strawberry Quik, wisely gave that up midway through and asked for a beer and, finally, began to knead his hands together.

"Just to clarify," Barry said when I'd finished, "I didn't know that Pistell girl was some college kid. I had good intel that she was a very wealthy Connecticut business woman."

"She's not," I said. That Barry was using the word "intel" was not a good sign. Apparently he'd decided his consulting business should include military words.

"Well, I can fix that one. Now that she's got such good credit, it won't be a problem."

"Is that a joke, Barry?"

"Yes. Just attempting to find some levity here."

"Tell me what Junior wanted to know," I said.

"First, just to be clear, I told him that I couldn't get involved with a criminal organization," Barry said. "I didn't come right out and say it, but I intimated to him that the snitch factor was too high for my liking, and he seemed agreeable to that. Some kid off the street gets pinched, and all of sudden I'm doing fifty years."

"Probably only ten," I said.

"I couldn't do ten minutes," Barry said. "You know you're not allowed any kind of skin lotions in some prisons? I've got an eczema thing on my knees that, untreated, could be a real problem."

"Barry," I said.

"Right. So he asked me about the best way to launder his money so that he could still invest it, so that he could make his money work for him. He actually said that. I told him the only positive illegal marketplace right now was in religious groups and faith-based non-profits. The FBI and IRS are so busy chasing all the shady mortgage lenders and refinancers and sham banks that they just don't care about the little guys when there are billions of bad dollars floating around in the banks and the automakers and the insurance companies. You don't see any churches asking for bailouts. So I told him, kind of joking—you know, levity, like I said before—that he should start a church. How much could it cost to start a church?"

"It could cost eternity," I said.

"Hey, I don't play the morality card with these people. They want to defraud God, have at it," Barry said. "I'm just offering opinions. Good, solid, fact-based opinions."

The sad truth was that Barry was correct. Running an illegal operation through a church is one of the safest routes an enterprising businessperson can take. Cash donations are difficult to track, but they are the stock and trade of many small churches and one of the easiest ways to clean dirty money. It's also one of the easiest ways to defraud people. If you want to get someone's personal information, tell them you're working for God and that you need their help. Offer to pay someone a small amount of money for a task, and they'll give you the keys to their entire life in return, all in the form of the W-2 and I-9 forms they'll need to fill out to get paid. It's a small investment for the possibility of a wide return.

It also made his shakedown of Father Eduardo all the more clear-cut: He didn't just have a church; he had an entire faith-based organization of small businesses and had the ear of important people . . . which meant the mere idea that the FBI, IRS or any other organization might decide to investigate it without probable cause seemed remote.

Of course, working the money through a church had a side benefit: It's nearly impossible to get a warrant to bug a church. It's not that the idea of sanctuary still exists from medieval times, but what someone says to his clergy is privileged, just as if he were speaking to his lawyer. Even the nice relic from the Bush administration—the warrantless wiretap—would be pretty far out-of-bounds inside a church, but particularly since this was a church that was actively helping people with the aid, probably, of government subsidy.

Junior was smart, but he wasn't smart enough to know all of this from his perch inside a prison. But Barry, well . . . Barry knew his industry better than anyone in Miami, so everything I knew, Barry had imparted to Junior, too. Junior was wise enough to go to him; Barry wasn't wise enough to run the other direction, which I told him, with more than just a little regret.

"Mike," Barry said, "it's not like the Girl Scouts show up at my house with questions about how to move their cookie money around. Good people don't need me, present company excluded."

"Did you tell Junior all of this before or after he paid you?" I asked.

"He'd already made a down payment," Barry said, though he seemed a bit unsure about that answer. "I let him put the rest on a layaway plan."

"You've become the Kmart of money launderers."

"We actually had a trade agreement at first," Barry said. "He had some credit cards he needed to get rid of; I had a guy who would buy them. I don't like to work in trade usually, because it's a dirty business. People always end up thinking that they can get more out of you than if you pay cash, which is sort of what happened with Junior. He came back with more questions, and I told him I needed to be paid this time, which is when things got dicey."

"So you received stolen property from the Latin Emperors and then sold it?"

"If you want to look at it that way," Barry said.

"Is there another way of looking at it?"

"I guess not," Barry said. "I guess it's pretty much 3-D as it is."

"4-D," I said.

"I'm not familiar with that," Barry said.

"It's called reality," I said.

"I'm just trying to find some middle ground with you, Michael. I came hear willingly to talk to you, Mike. You don't have to interrogate me."

"No, you didn't," I said. "If Sam hadn't found your number on Junior's phone records, you'd still be in the same place you were: hiding."

"What would I need to hide from?"

"I don't know, Barry. Why don't you tell me?"

"You went to his place, right?"

"Right."

"Pretty sweet setup, wasn't it? That was my consulting work right there. Pretty proud of that."

"You told him to buy that house?"

"No," Barry said. "But I told him to quit-claim it to Julia Pistell. And I told him about, you know, a lot of secret criminals-only stuff."

"You mean the rental houses, the security cameras someone stole from RadioShack and the cars with the dealer plates?"

Barry looked fairly astounded. "How'd you know?"

"I'm a spy," I said. "And the work is shoddy."

"I just told him what to do," Barry said. "I didn't go in there with a hammer and chisel."

"It's good enough to fool a fool," I said, "which means he's probably very safe there from the local police and anyone not trained at Quantico."

"Well, anyway, he was happy with that work, and that's when he gave me the money, and that's when I called him on it being crap. He didn't like that."

"So you told him how to make good money?"

"I might have given him some hints, yes."

"And what did you get for that?"

"He said he'd give me a hundred K from the fine cut," Barry said, "plus ten grand of real money if I served as, you know, a quality-control expert. So I went down to the hotel—and yes, before you ask, I told him to do this at the hotel, okay?—and saw what they were making and it was surprisingly good for a bunch of amateurs. But I told him that I wasn't going to take any of that pre-'96 money. That's like waving a huge red flag. Who has that much money all from one year, you know? You gotta get a mix from the last ten years to make it look right, but they didn't have that technology, which I told them. So I said I wanted my money all in cash, that I wasn't taking their rags."

"Did you add 'or else' when you made this demand?" I said.

"Well, I implied it."

That's what I was afraid of.

"How did you do that?"

"I said I had guys who, uh, worked for me who, uh, were, uh, ex-, uh, military and CIA and uh, other, uh, agencies of the, uh, spy variety and who, uh, might have been involved with some large-scale terrorist actions in, uh, the greater, uh, Ireland area. And, uh, that, uh, if I didn't get my money, well, he'd be hearing from him."

"Him?"

"Him. Them. You know."

"And that's when he threatened to kill you?"

"No, worse," Barry said. "The cops showed up at my mother's house. Guess that's my last known."

"That's worse?"

"I told you," Barry said, "I've got eczema on my knees. My mom was out of town, so the cops put a pretty big scare into my aunt Lois, who's down from Ocala to watch the cats, water the plants and such, so she called me and I figured it was time to lie low for a piece. So I've been sort of waiting it all out at sea. Hopped on a friend's houseboat and have been just sort of chilling in international waters for a couple days. Until Sam called. If I'd known the Latin Emperors had cops on the payroll, I'd have just kept sailing until I hit Australia. But it makes a lot of sense now, since they told my aunt that they were just coming by to see if I was still alive, which, at the time, didn't sound like what cops normally go around saying."

"Why didn't you call me?" I said.

"I didn't know what to do, Michael, on account of—well, the, uh, fact that I may have misrepresented our working relationship to Junior."

It was then that my mother finally broke and stopped eavesdropping from the sink area—where she'd been washing the same dish for the previous ten minutes—and sat down at the table next to me. She lit up a cigarette and exhaled the smoke directly into Barry's face.

"Ma," I said.

"Shut up, Michael," she said.

Barry smiled. "Wow, that was pretty cool. That's your *mom*. I guess I never really understood that she's your *mom*, so she can tell you to shut up. Wow."

"Shut up, Barry," my mother said, and he did. "Do you mind, Michael?"

"Have at it, Ma," I said.

"You know what your problem is, Barry?"

"Uh, no, Mrs. Westen," he said.

"You consort with assholes. I'm sorry for my language, Barry, but that's the truth. Did I hear you say the police came to your mother's house?"

"Yes, ma'am," Barry said.

"Do you know what that would have been like if she'd been home? You would have ruined her whole week. Maybe her whole year. Do you have any skills, Barry, other than whatever criminal things you do with Michael?"

"No," Barry said, "that's all I've got."

"Well, then, you'd better be a bit more selective with the people you work with so that Michael doesn't need to come in and save your ass like he does with everyone else. Do you understand?"

"Uh, yes, Mrs. Westen."

That made my mother happy. She stubbed out her cigarette. "Now, can I get you some pot roast, Barry?"

"Sure, that would be great, Mrs. Westen," Barry said.

She stood up, reached across the table and mussed up Barry's hair. "That was a good chat. We should do that again." She turned to me. "Michael, help this idiot out before he gets his mother killed."

And suddenly I had another unpaid client. That made three.

||

You can do all the planning you want, but when it comes to fighting a battle, eventually you're going to need guns.

Unless, it turns out, you're defending Father Eduardo Santiago.

"That's the first thing," Father Eduardo said. "And I am firm on this." He'd come to my loft that same evening so I could explain to him all that we'd learned and all that was at risk, including what Fi had learned about Leticia, which seemed to break Father Eduardo's spirit more than any other single detail. But before I could even tell him my plan, he made the proclamation about the guns, which was no insignificant thing, since I generally keep two pieces on me at all times, as does Sam. I suspect Fiona tries to form a more rounded-looking number, like six, but all of that is really predicated on her outfit.

Sam and Fiona, who were both standing in my galley kitchen, sighed audibly and in perfect synchronicity. Barry was also in my loft, because he was too scared to go anywhere else. I'd instructed Barry that under no circumstances was he to let his fear manifest into a situation where he thought he should hit on Fiona—something he does on a fairly regular basis—because I was pretty sure Fiona would react with malice. And to keep that from happening, I'd instructed Sam to fix Barry a drink containing as many varieties of rum as he could find, which in short order had knocked Barry out.

"Do you understand what you're saying?" I asked.

"Do you?" Father Eduardo said. "Seventy-five percent of the people who work for me—nearly everyone!—are convicted felons, parolees, ex-gang members. If someone under my guise comes onto my property with a gun and is anywhere near them, they could all go back to prison. I will not put them in that position."

"What about knives?" Fiona asked. "Or swords. Swords would be fun, Michael."

"No concealed weapons," Father Eduardo said.

"Grenades?" Sam said.

"I still have some C-4," Fiona said. "We could blow up Junior's car in the parking lot. That would solve this all very quickly. Make it look like an accident."

"How are you going to make a C-4 explosion look like an accident?" Sam said.

"I have my ways," Fiona said.

"No," Father Eduardo said. "No. No. No. I cannot have any of this. Do you understand? I am a man of faith. I will not let you blow up his car. I cannot have my campus turned into something on CNN. Don't you understand?"

I did. Really. It's just difficult to imagine fighting a gang without ammo.

"So, when I inform Junior what the score is going to be," I said, "and he pulls a gun, what am I supposed to do? Talk to him sweetly until he puts it away?"

"He won't pull a gun," Father Eduardo said. "He has too much to gain from this shakedown to kill anyone. And he's a coward now, from what you tell me. Hiring a person like your sleeping friend? Thirty years ago, your friend would have been like a chew toy for Junior. No, he'd have someone else kill you. Or have you picked up by the police. At no time do I want you to bring any guns onto my campus. I would rather go down myself than put these kids in jeopardy of losing everything because of my own foolish past."

Father Eduardo was probably correct on all points. Convincing Sam and Fiona of this would be more difficult.

"That's noble," Sam said. "When they make the movie of your life, this will be a very moving scene. We'll be dead then, but I'm sure audiences will love it."

"Not helping," I said to Sam. I rubbed my palms into my eyes. I'd have to figure this one out. "Okay. Okay. We'll do it your way, Father Eduardo."

"Thank you," he said. "And what is your plan?"

Just as I'd told Fiona earlier, I told Father Eduardo. "I'm going to give him exactly what he wants. I'm going to let him in."

"What?"

"Don't worry," I said. "If you want to bring him down without violence, which I promise we will not have on your property, we need to allow him to build a criminal conspiracy of his own that would so far outweigh whatever he might think he has on you that it would be fruitless for him to even try."

"But there are so many others than him," Father Eduardo said. "And there are the dead to consider. That has begun to weigh on me."

Sam and Fiona both rolled their eyes. And suddenly I had another set of nonpaying clients. This was beginning to become very complex.

"We'll deal with the living first," I said.

I explained to Father Eduardo that when Junior arrived tomorrow and saw Fiona and me—two people he would clearly remember, and two people he was probably already suspecting in light of all of his missing property—I'd explain to him that he was already entering a criminal enterprise, one run by me, and that if he wanted in, there would be a price to pay.

"And just so we're clear," I told Father Eduardo, "whatever I say, you agree with. And if I hit you, or if Fiona hits you, or breaks a chair over your head, it's not personal."

Father Eduardo had about a hundred pounds on me, maybe two hundred on Fiona, and was made mostly of muscle and menace, even at this point in his life. I had a pretty good sense that he could take a punch.

"I understand," he said.

"Okay," I said. "Is there anything you haven't told me? Anything I should know before tomorrow happens?"

This was just a routine question. The sort of question I occasionally forget to ask clients because I figure that they've told me all they possibly could, that all the avenues of intersection had been covered—and we had so many avenues already, I practically needed MapQuest just to navigate it all in my mind—and all that was left was for me to perform, which I was confident I could do . . . until I saw that Father Eduardo had broken into a sweat.

"You're sweating," I said.

"There's something I haven't told you."

This got Sam and Fiona interested again.

"Don't tell me you actually did kill these people Junior has on you," I said.

"No, no," Father Eduardo said. "It is not that."

"You're not already running an illegal business with the mayor, are you?"

"No. It's my brother, Adrian," Father Eduardo said.

Oh, no.

Brothers are difficult. My own brother, Nate, was, fortunately, in Las Vegas, which meant that in about eight days I'd get a call from him letting me know he had a problem only I could solve for him.

This, as usual, was not good. "Tell me," I said.

"He's still in the Latin Emperors," Father Eduardo said. "He's just coming up. I couldn't save him from it. Our whole family, we've been LE to the fullest forever. I am the one who got out, but only after doing my time. Now he's in and in deep. I don't want him to get hurt. I can save him."

I knew where this was headed.

"Let me guess," I said. "He's Leticia's boyfriend."

Father Eduardo nodded.

"Tell me something," Fiona said, now fully invested.

"Why would you let your brother have a street name as obvious as Killa? Couldn't you have advised him that Powder Puff or Nice Boy could have saved him a significant amount of trouble?"

"We don't talk," Father Eduardo said. "I gave Leticia her job to help her son. My nephew. I thought she'd get out of the life. I suppose I didn't account for the level my brother would go to."

"It's probably not him," I said, though I had no idea. I had hope, and that's a good thing to have if you can spare it. "Assume it's Junior's pull."

"He has to have a chance to get out of this with a chance," Father Eduardo said.

"He's not a good person," Fiona said.

"Neither was I," Father Eduardo said. "And I hope you don't mind me saying this, but I have a suspicion that you weren't exactly the best version of yourself at twenty-three, either. I know Leticia better than you do. I have known her since she was sixteen. I knew her before she was cut."

"What happened?" Sam asked.

"She sold crack for a living," Father Eduardo said matter-of-factly. "And one day, someone tried to rob her and she fought back. They left her for dead. My brother, Adrian, he took care of that . . . situation for her. So they have that bond, and she has the knowledge of what he's capable of, too. It's a different world from what you three know."

"I wouldn't say that," I said. "You don't know the things I've done."

"You're a good man, Michael," Father Eduardo said.

"Not according to the United States government," I said.

"It sounds like we've had some of the same enemies." Father Eduardo wiped at his forehead and his eyes, and I realized he wasn't just sweating now; he was also on the verge of tears. "I have worked so hard," he said, "to do the right thing. I must have this turn out, Michael."

"It will," I said. "You've told no one we are coming?"

"No one," he said.

"Good," I said. "Keep it that way. If my plan is to work, we need every move to be a surprise, even to you."

"I trust you," he said.

"You have to," I said. "No matter what happens tomorrow, understand that you should react in the only way you can, which is to say, don't fight me, and don't fight Junior. Let me do the work."

"Have you ever read *The Art of War*?"

Fiona let out a little snort. "Boys," she said, but Father Eduardo ignored her.

"Yes," I said.

"'He who knows when he can fight and when he cannot will be victorious,'" Father Eduardo said. "I have lived by that for a long time now. I have won all my battles, including my freedom, with that in mind."

"Good," I said.

Father Eduardo thanked us and said he'd see us in the morning, and began to make his way out of the loft. He paused after he opened the front door and then stepped back inside. "Your father," he said to me, and then pointed, but concentrated on some point in his mind and didn't finish his sentence.

"What about him?" I said.

"That car you drive. It was his?"

"Yeah, for a while," I said.

"Junior and I tried to steal it once from in front of the high school."

"What stopped you?"

"Your father was sitting in the front seat," Father Eduardo said, "and when we told him to get out, he just laughed at us and told us to keep on moving down the road. Those were his exact words. 'Keep on moving down the road,' just as cool as can be. It . . . unnerved me. That's the word. He wasn't afraid."

"He was probably drunk," I said.

"No," Father Eduardo said, "no, I don't think that's true. And neither do you."

"No," I said, "I guess I don't."

Eduardo Santiago, who used to rob little kids, who ran the Latin Emperors, who did federal time, snitched out his gang, found God and came out a changed man, came out a priest, smiled at me in a way I found unnerving, too. "Maybe he was a spy, too?"

"Not a chance," I said. "Get some rest. Tomorrow we go to war."

Eduardo still had that unnerving smile going. "I didn't think this was going to happen to me again. I thought this period of my life was done."

"It will be," I said. One way or the other, that was true.

Father Eduardo left for good then, so I opened up

the fridge and pulled out three beers and one blueberry yogurt.

"You gonna get a beer for yourself?" Sam said.

"I thought you weren't drinking anymore," I said.

"That was this morning," he said, and cracked open one of the bottles. "It's a new day in Australia, mate."

I slid one of the bottles to Fiona, but she pushed it away. "What?" I said.

"This Leticia business," she said. "I'm all wrapped up in it."

"We're all wrapped up in it," I said. "Even your boyfriend, Barry."

"No," she said. "That Killa is Father Eduardo's brother makes this all the more complicated for her. How does she know who to trust? I mean, really, Michael—how will she ever know who to trust?"

"She won't," I said, "just like the rest of us."

"And that poor child has a great genetic makeup. Both of his parents are criminals, for God's sake."

I couldn't remember a time when I'd seen Fiona this worked up over one of our clients. "We'll get her out of this," I said.

"Sam, can you get her into Witness Protection or something?"

Sam took a sip of his beer and then made a smacking sound with his lips. "Ah, to be in love . . . No luck, sister," Sam said, "not when Father Eduardo won't even admit there's something criminal going on. I could talk to my guys in the FBI, but Father Eduardo would have to cop to this blackmail, and he won't do that. Hell, he won't even let us have squirt guns."

Barry made a snorting noise in his sleep that echoed down from upstairs, which got Fiona's attention. She raised her eyebrows in a silent question to me.

"Maybe," I said. "Let's see if Barry makes it out of this alive before we have him getting your best girlfriend Leticia smuggled out of the country."

"Okay," she said.

"In the meantime," I said, "we need to get some guns that aren't guns. I don't suppose you know anyone, Fi, with a gross of paintball guns for sale?"

"I could get us 50 Vektor CR-21 assault rifles, if you'd like," she said, and suddenly was full of perk again. Nothing like a little gun talk to get Fiona out of a funk. "But no, nothing with paint. My clients rarely want to make an Impressionist work of art. A body is far more preferable."

"Sam?"

"I got a guy I went to basic with about a million years ago who now runs one of those paramilitary camps where accountants spend an entire weekend shooting each other for kicks. I could ask him."

"He know how to keep a secret?"

"He's ex-military," Sam said.

"Right," I said.

"Right," Sam said. "Well, I'll tell him I'm helping a bunch of at-risk kids. Which wouldn't be a lie, right?"

"If he's running a camp for rich people," I said, "he's probably been tinkering with the guns already. Tell him you want the ones he keeps for the whales in the group."

Paintball guns aren't really guns. They're markers. Get hit with a paintball and really what you're getting hit with is a paint-filled gelatin capsule traveling at three hundred feet per second, which is fast enough to bruise you or put out your eye or break your nose, all of which are good reasons to wear a helmet and goggles when people are shooting at you. If you really want to hurt someone with a paintball gun, you need to amp up the velocity to six hundred feet per second, which will generate enough force to break a bone. But breaking bones isn't usually enough if you're fighting people with guns. People with guns can still shoot you with a broken foot or clavicle. So instead of a gelatin cap filled with paint, you want to get a gelatin cap filled with pepper spray. Get hit at six hundred feet per second by a paintball filled with pepper spray and you'll have a broken bone and you'll think you're about to die. And if pepper spray isn't available, mix together bleach and ammonia and you'll find that they make a rather debilitating and disabling combination, too.

Sam drained the rest of his beer and then stepped outside to call his guy, which left Fiona and me alone with Barry's snoring. She was still upset but had on her bravest face, which only meant she was thinking of ways to do this all her way.

"Fi," I said, "tomorrow, when we face Junior again, I need you to follow my lead."

"Don't I always, Michael?"

"No," I said.

"Don't I usually?"

"It's about seventy-thirty," I said. "My plan is to attack all the angles, but systematically. I'm going to start with Leticia. I want you to know that. She's going to be at the door, and I'm going to put her into enough fear that she might run out right then."

"I don't know why this is getting to me so much," she said. "Maybe because Leticia is so young. Maybe because she has a child. I don't know, Michael."

I took her into my arms for a moment and she held on. It wasn't one of those desperate moments we've had before, where it feels like the world is about to explode. Instead, it just felt like a time when Fiona might need to be treated like someone who needed a hug.

A sound from upstairs halted the moment. Or, really, the end of a sound, as Barry's snoring came to an abrupt halt. I heard him rummaging around for a moment, and then he appeared on top of the stairs, shirtless, pantless (except for his boxer shorts) and disheveled. I could see he was trying to focus his eyes, but wasn't having much luck.

"Where am I?" he said.

"You're asleep," I said.

Barry tried to consider that for a moment, but it didn't compute. "Did you drug me?" he asked.

"No," I said. "Sam did."

"He put something in my drink?"

"Yes," I said. "Alcohol."

Barry scratched at a place on his stomach and then sniffed at the air. "Do I smell fried chicken?"

"No," I said.

"Could we work on that?"

My default answer wouldn't work here, particularly since I needed to explain to Barry that tomorrow he'd have to face his fears. That tomorrow, I had a plan for him that might involve a fantasy or two—I had a vision of Fiona smacking him, which I'm sure was a vision Barry had on occasion, too—and that if he wanted my help getting out from under the problems he encountered with the Latin Emperors, he'd need to do exactly as I told him. And I needed to tell him that tomorrow, if things went poorly, this could be his last substantial meal.

I decided to leave that last part out. Why scare the guy?

"Fiona," I said, "why don't we take our friend Barry out for a delicious dinner?"

"Why don't you take your friend Barry out for a delicious dinner, and I'll stay here and read fashion magazines and memorize your yogurt selection."

"I could stay here with Fiona while you run out and get food," Barry said. Fiona shot him a look that was equal parts warning and promise. "Easy there," Barry said. "I was just saying. I'm happy to go with Michael. If you want to make yourself comfortable, I left a warm space up there on the nice throw rug you let me sleep on."

"I'll pass," Fiona said. "And please, put on some pants, Barry. The neighborhood dogs have begun to howl."

Barry disappeared back into the darkness, which was good, since Sam walked back in from the patio then, looking far too happy. "Just talked to my guy," he said. "I'm going to his place right now. He says he's got some guns he doctored up for some boys who were doing prison control in Kabul a few months back."

"Sounds perfect," I said. "How much does he want?"

"Nothing yet," Sam said. "I'm sure there's a contingency. I'll work it out."

"Sam," I said, "no more clients."

"It's not like that with this guy, don't worry. He's an ex-SEAL. Pride of country and all that."

"Like Virgil?"

"Well, like Virgil, but with more bloodlust. Good guy. Lots of kills under his belt. This one time, in Latvia? I swear to God, he took out an entire city just by flossing his teeth and grunting. Anyway. I'll meet you here in the morning. Nine?"

"Let's do eight."

"Eight thirty?"

"Why don't you just show up whenever you want, Sam?"

"Perfect, Mikey. I'll see you then."

A few moments later, Barry came back down the stairs, looking essentially like Barry, though his hair still looked like a nest of vipers. I put my arm over his shoulder. "Barry, my friend," I said, "I have a few things to clear with you tonight that you should be made aware of before tomorrow begins."

"Oh, Mike, I don't like how that sounds," he said.

"You shouldn't," I said.

12

What Sam could remember about serving with Chris Alessio back in the day—they'd both been SEALS—was that he was never quite sure if the guy was a true-blooded American hero or just batshit crazy. He was the sort of guy who would rush a hill with nothing but a buck knife in his teeth, which is sort of neat in movies, but in real life is just a great way to get your tongue cut off. Never mind that if all you have is a knife, you're literally taking a knife into a gunfight, and they don't make up clichés like that without a basis in truth.

Crazy thing was, the guy never got shot. One time in Panama, Sam saw him rush into a Túpac Amaru hideout with just a knife and flashlight, and five minutes later there were three dead rebels and ten rebel prisoners tied up in a corner, and all Chris had to show for his troubles were a torn shirt, a knife with a broken tip and, oddly, one missing shoe. They eventually found the shoe under one of the dead bodies, which is why, for a little while, other SEALS called him Kick-Ass Alessio, until it became clear Chris really just preferred to be called Chris. And when a guy that batshit crazy tells you what he'd like to be called, well, Sam figured you heeded that warning. Why piss the guy off, you know?

Now, though, Chris Alessio operated a sprawling paintball complex called Battle: World out past Tamiami, where the city began to give way to the Everglades. A few years back, this area was just farmland and marsh, but Alessio had turned it into a theme park of sorts. For the price of admission, you and your buddies could have paintball wars in Vietnam, Tikrit, Kabul, Germany, Normandy and even the Philippines. All the major wars, except for the Civil War, were represented, probably on account of Alessio's deep well of patriotism. Or maybe because no one really wanted to kill other Americans anymore. It was too much fun killing some foreign entity . . . or at least your buddy as some foreign entity, anyway.

When Sam finally found the business office—the park had been closed for a few hours by the time he'd arrived—Alessio was sitting behind a desk of dark maple, but instead of being covered with papers, it was covered with paintball guns. It was a bit like walking into some militia headquarters. In fact, the last time they'd done any kind of mission together, Sam remembered Chris rather marveling at the nice office setup a Somali warlord had. It was that moment when Sam knew Chris wasn't going to reenlist like the rest of the team. Once you start noticing furniture, it's game over.

"That's quite an array you have there," Sam said.

"I'm just doing some cleanup," he said. "I had a group of HP printer techs out here today. Talk about guys with anger-management issues. It was like watching us take on those Russian commandos in Belarus."

"I'm not sure I remember that," Sam said.

"You might have sat that one out," he said. "That might have been a freelance job, actually, now that I think about it. It was after Yeltsin made nice, so I'm thinking it might not have been sanctioned."

"The good old days," Sam said.

"Anyway, these guys? They went after each other for hours on end today. Had to finally kick them out when they started dropping their goggles and helmets and really fucking each other up. Can't have people's eyes and teeth rolling around my grounds. That's just not good for business."

"Too much reality is a bad thing?" Sam said.

"People, it turns out, really like to shoot each other. They just don't like to bleed or see blood."

That made sense to Sam. All things being equal, not seeing blood for a few years would suit him just fine. Chris stood up then and came around the desk, and Sam marveled at how fit he still was. Where Sam had added a few pounds over the years—mostly water weight, he reasoned, mixed with hops—Chris looked like he could still be on active duty in the SEALS. Sure, Chris had a bit of salt and pepper in his hair these days, but who didn't? But his waist and belly were on the same plain. Genetics. That was it. Chris Alessio must have been one of those guys who just woke up on his first day as a human physically fit and ready to fight.

"Let's go take a look at what I got for you," Chris said. He led Sam back out of the office and then they walked out into the park. There were still a few people milling about, cleaning up the place, raking out the paint, watering down the building facades, which made it all the more eerie, since the first portion of the paintball park was designed to look like your basic Downtown USA.

"You get a lot of guys wanna shoot up their own hometowns?" Sam asked.

"We had a team of postal workers last week who went completely agro out here."

At the end of the block and just off the playing area was a building marked ARMORY, though unlike the other buildings on the block, it was an actual, fully enclosed building. Once Chris unlocked the door and they walked inside, Sam could see that his old friend had fully invested himself in branding. In addition to guns and helmets and gloves and other normal paintball accessories for sale, there were also ladies' style T-shirts, coffee cups, license-plate frames, mousepads and anything else that might be enhanced by the Battle: World logo. Hell, Sam thought, Chris had spent half of his life fighting for the freedom of capitalism; he might as well get some for himself.

"Don't bother looking at that stuff," Chris said. Sam was admiring a rack of guns that were painted pink in honor of breast cancer. They even had one of those ribbons painted on the barrel, which was a nice touch. "I keep the test guns in the back."

Sam tried to envision Fiona carrying a pink gun of

any caliber or style and decided that part of her charm was that she could probably pull it off, at least once. Sam followed Chris past racks of shirts and hoodies, past a rack of commemorative postcards and through a set of double doors, into what ended up being the meat of the building—a large warehouse stacked high with merchandise on one side, and a test firing range on the other. Sam thought it was weird to have an indoor range, particularly when the entire park was made to shoot in. Or at least he thought it was weird until Chris unlocked an upright chest and began unloading paintball guns that looked heavier and more complex than one you might buy at Sportsmart.

Chris handed one to Sam. "That's the Titan Legion Z-200 you've got there," he said. "Stainless steel. Expanded barrel. Enlarged chamber. Officially, it doesn't exist. Or not yet, anyway. They've had me testing it out here for a few weeks, and I've been adding my two cents to the designers. We've got it torqued up to go six-hundred-fifty feet per second without any problem, but I've been working to get it closer to eight hundred."

"Wouldn't that be lethal?"

"You'd have to be a sniper and you'd have to hit a defenseless person for it to have that effect," Chris said. "And even then you'd have to be pretty close."

"Wouldn't that be the point?"

"And you'd have to want to kill him," Chris said. He shrugged, and Sam remembered that this was a guy who used to really like killing people, until he started to notice the wider world outside his kill zone.

"You're not gonna kill someone shooting them in the foot. You aim at someone's head, yeah, you could kill them. Most likely, you'd just put them down for a bit. Bruise their brain a bit. But if you're coming at me to the point that I need to unload, then I'm happy to bruise your brain."

Sam wasn't really sure a person could bruise his brain, but he was certain that if he got hit in the head with just about anything traveling eight hundred feet per second, there was a good chance it would serve as a pretty good deterrent to whatever abhorrent behavior he was engaged in.

Chris loaded the gun and handed it back to Sam. "Shoot it," Chris said.

There was a full human target made of ballistics gel about thirty yards away. Chris wasn't screwing around out here. Sam took the gun and aimed it, thinking, Well, if it even breaks the skin, I'll be surprised, and fired away. It didn't have that same satisfying sound that a Glock might make, or an AK, but it did make a nice pop, and when the ball hit the target, there was a loud slapping sound. Sam had aimed for the midsection, hoping to hit the pubis bone, a spot that when punched tends to crumple an assailant.

Sam and Chris walked out to the target and examined the damage. There was a spatter of red paint where Sam had hit the body, and the flesh was torn open. Sam shoved his index finger inside the gap—it was about a third of an inch.

"Not a great place to get stitches," Sam said.

Chris waved him off. "Cuts are nothing. Who cares

about a flesh wound?" He went behind the dummy, and that's when Sam saw that it was hooked up to a laptop. Chris tapped the keys a few times and up came a series of three-dimensional re-creations of the shot. "That poor bastard you just shot? You separated his pelvis."

"Really?" Sam said.

"According to the computer model," Chris said. "He'll be in the hospital for a week. Probably will have a problem sitting for a long period of time for a while after that. No career in the truck-driving arts. I'll tell you that."

"And these are nonlethal weapons?"

"You didn't kill the guy, did you?"

"No."

"You put anything illegal into the gun?"

"No."

"Then it's nonlethal."

Sam turned the gun over in his hand. "I conceal this," Sam said. "Any problem with that?"

"If you conceal a water pistol, is there a problem with that?" Chris said.

Sam pondered this. "I need a dozen of these," he said.

"I've got three," Chris said.

"How much time would it take me to modify a regular marker to do this?"

"You got access to a torch?"

"Sure," Sam said.

"About five minutes," he said.

This was getting better and better. "Let's say I needed some CS gas balls."

"Let's say."

"You could get a person those?"

"Where's the fight?" Chris seemed genuinely intrigued by all of this, which wasn't a great thing. Sure, the guy could keep a secret, but the less anyone knew, the better, as ever.

"It's a top-secret thing, Kick-Ass," Sam said. He tossed in Chris' old nickname just to let him know they were back on military ground. You know—Band of Brothers. All that.

"Bullshit," Chris said. "If it was top-secret, you wouldn't be out here buying paintball guns."

"You remember my buddy Michael Westen?"

"Spy?"

"That's the one."

Chris put up a hand. "Say no more. Whatever you're doing with him, I want no part of that. You know how many different agencies, foreign and domestic, have come to me, seeing if I'd be interested in relieving that asset?"

Sam wasn't surprised, really. A guy like Chris Alessio would be who he'd call if he needed someone to kill a person and do it right.

"I appreciate your not taking any of those jobs," Sam said.

"Well, I value my life," Chris said, which was a surprise. Anytime an ex-SEAL can admit to being overmatched on anything was cause for a national holiday. "Whatever you guys are into, I'd just as soon put you in touch with someone who can get you some real guns."

"Real guns I've got," Sam said.

"Ah," Chris said. "I see what you've got going on. Like Latvia? Break no laws while breaking someone's back?"

"Right," Sam said. He'd told Michael about the teeth flossing, but really couldn't remember the meat of that story, though apparently it was a good one.

"Hold on," Chris said, "I've got something for you." Chris went into a storeroom and came out with a long, cylindrical box. "I got these when I was thinking about taking the park in more of a historical direction, but, you know, people just want to shoot each other. Nothing wrong with that, right?"

"Right," Sam said.

Chris opened the box, and Sam saw what looked like, well, whips. "Whips?" Sam said.

"Florida stockwhips. Cowboys used them on cows back in the day. They're considered farm implements. I got three boxes of them."

Oh, Sam thought. Oh. He took one in his hand and walked over to the ballistics dummy and snapped the whip on its knee, opening up a gash at least five inches long. Oh.

"I'll take them all," Sam said. "What can I do in return?"

"Nothing," Chris said, and gave Sam a wink. "Besides, I heard from our old friend Virgil that you do people some favors on occasion?"

"On occasion," Sam said.

Chris looked around his warehouse. "Just to say, not all of this stuff was procured by means I like to talk about. Could be I might need some people I can trust one day."

"I'm people you can trust," Sam said.

"I've got five hundred paintballs filled with pepper spray," Chris said. "Will that suit your needs?"

13

When you're combating an insurgent force on foreign soil, like in Iraq or Afghanistan, it's imperative that you work hand in hand with the nation that's hosting you. In a perfect situation, you'd have trained that nation's military force on your standard operating procedures, and there would be a great amount of mutual trust among the leaders, and the soldiers would consider each other valued assets in the fight for freedom, liberty and the greater good of whatever far-flung nation you happened to be dwelling and/or killing in. The truth, however, is that fighting on foreign land invariably means you can't trust anyone.

"You know what I don't understand, Mikey?" Sam said. It was just before ten thirty, and we were walking across the Honrado campus—Fiona had been instructed to arrive after Junior and his men, so she and Barry were watching us from her car across the street—en route to Father Eduardo's office. "Why did it take so long for the bad guys to stop wearing matching uniforms? Life was a lot easier when the people who wanted to kill you all coordinated their dress."

"All evolution is slow," I said.

"You'd think George Washington would have looked across the river and realized it would be a lot easier to beat the British if they just changed their clothes into something less identifiably American. Like, you know, a red coat or something."

"There were rules for war back then, Sam," I said. "It was much more pleasant."

"You know the only time the Americans really got their asses handed to them on American soil? Right where we're standing. The Seminoles opened up a can on the Americans right here in Florida. And you know how they did it? They came at them from all angles, and they weren't wearing stupid uniforms. You'd think we would have learned something from that."

"You might have noticed during training that we weren't given a lot of information on key losses in American history," I said.

"Which is why we've spent the last several years getting our asses handed back to us in Iraq," Sam said. "All this time, and no one gets that you don't have to have a uniform to kill someone."

Sam was particularly agitated this morning. It might have been a direct result of it being morning, or it might have been related to the fact that he set fire to his favorite Tommy Bahama shirt while we were welding the paintball guns—of which we both had two pistols each at present, while Fiona was planning on making a grand entrance with her whip—or maybe he just didn't like the idea of going into battle with a faceless opponent.

"Sam," I said, "Father Eduardo knows who in his employ works for the Latin Emperors, or at least did. We're not stepping into this blind."

"I dunno, Mikey," Sam said. "I feel like this is a situation outside our comfort zone. Who knows how many moles are in that place? We could be walking into a slaughterhouse with paintball guns and Fiona's buggy whip."

It was true. I had to trust that what Father Eduardo had was more valuable to the Latin Emperors with him alive—and with us alive—than dead.

"A bunch of dead bodies is not good for anyone's business," I said. "We're not disposable people. Junior's going to realize that as soon as he sees my face. I have a feeling that will change the way he does business."

Gangsters and terrorists are used to dealing with people who are scared of them. When you traffic in fear, you expect people will bend to your threats, and thus you're able to get things done by reputation alone. The difference today would be that Sam, Fiona and I wouldn't exactly be shaking in our shoes. Barry might have some problems, but we'd already made a plan for that.

When we reached the office building, I placed a small bug on the stucco wall adjacent to the door and then leaned down to tie my shoe. I didn't bother trying to make the bug look any more indistinct than it was already—it was the size of a flattened marble, but flat like a magnet—since it had only one purpose: to record Junior's conversation coming in and out of the building. "If you can hear me, Fiona," I said, "honk twice."

From across the street, two quick beeps rang out.

"Let's go to work," I said to Sam.

I pushed the double doors in and walked up to the reception desk while Sam stood still by the door. Leticia was on the phone, but when she saw me she hung up abruptly. "Hello," she said, just another day of her life. "It's nice to see you again, Mr. . . ." she looked at her appointments, but my name wasn't on there.

"Solo," I said. "Father Eduardo is expecting me."

"You're not on the calendar," she said.

I looked down at her calendar and saw that Junior Gonzalez had actually been penciled in. I had to hand it to Leticia. She was good at her job.

"He won't mind," I said.

She swallowed hard. "He's got an appointment at eleven," she said. "You should come back later."

"Sweetheart," I said, "do you see my friend back there?" I stepped aside so she could see Sam.

"Yes," she said. "Mr. Teriyaki?"

"Kuryakin," I said. "Mr. Kuryakin. Mr. Kuryakin is going to shoot you in the face if you don't let me in to see Father Eduardo. It's not personal. It's just what he's been told to do. You can understand that, right? Doing what you've been told to do? You do what you're told, don't you, sweetheart?"

She swallowed hard again. "You don't understand," she said, her voice a hoarse rasp. "People are coming who will kill you."

"I admire that you want to save my life," I said. "But don't you want to save yours?"

"No," she said. "I let you in, I'm good as dead, anyway."

"What about your son?"

"How do you know about my son?"

"How does anyone know anything these days? It was on *TMZ*."

Leticia slid her hands beneath her thighs. It was something a small child might do when nervous, and I realized Leticia wasn't that old, really. A sad remnant of a life lived too quickly. "I can't go," she said.

"Leticia," I said, "isn't there another building you could visit right now? You don't need to leave the state. You don't even need to leave campus. Just put up a note that says you'll be back in ten minutes and transfer your calls to voice mail. I'm here to help you. I really am. If I wanted you to be dead, you'd be dead. I don't want that. I just want you to let me in, and then I want you to disappear until you think you should come back. I think you'll know when that is. Won't you?"

Leticia nodded slowly, and then I saw something dawn on her. "That girl?" she said.

"That girl," I said.

"You really don't want to hurt me, do you?"

"I really don't," I said, "but my partner will unless you leave."

It was important that Leticia not know precisely what to believe, but also that she should believe me. She wanted out. We knew that. But I didn't want to give up too much. Not yet, at least.

Leticia grabbed her purse and started to get up. "Wait," I said. "Give me your cell phone."

She reached into her purse, fished her phone out and set it on the desk. She kept her eyes on me the entire time. Not scared. Interesting.

"You like what you see?" I asked.

"Why aren't you wearing a mask?"

"Because I don't care who sees me," I said.

"You're not a bad person, are you?"

"No time to find out," I said.

"That scar on your face," she said, "you get that shaving?"

Testing now. Even more interesting.

"You have five seconds," I said.

Leticia stepped around her desk and walked past me. Sam opened the door for her, and she never once looked at him.

"Tough girl," Sam said.

"Let's hope she's not stupid," I said.

We walked down the hall toward Father Eduardo's office. There was a conference room on the right, followed by three offices along the left-hand side of the corridor before you reached Father Eduardo's office at the end. I stuck my head in the first office and saw a young man of maybe twenty-five holding a Bible in his lap talking to a boy of no more than sixteen. The young man was dressed in a crisp white shirt with a tie. The name on the slider outside the office said CLIFFORD TURNER on it. Up the hall, I saw Sam enter another office and introduce himself as Chazz Finley, as we'd planned.

"Excuse me," I said, and Clifford looked up at me.

"Help you with something?" he said. He didn't seem annoyed, but clearly he was in the middle of a conversation and wanted to get back to it.

"Mike Michaels from the mayor's office," I said. I gave him the toothy smile every city employee with an ounce of desire to be a state employee can employ at a moment's notice.

"Okay," he said.

"I'm going to need you to clear out of your office for the next hour," I said. "The mayor is coming in for a meeting with Father Eduardo, and we're going to need your office to set up the media."

"What?" he said. "I'm in the middle of a counseling session here."

"I see that. I see that," I said, "but it's been a change of plans. Leticia just found out, the sweetheart, and so she's busy trying to find us some space elsewhere. But when the mayor says jump, you know how that is."

Clifford looked at his young charge. It would be imprudent to fly off the handle in front of the kid, particularly since the kid had a monitoring bracelet around his ankle.

"This is unusual," Clifford said. "But what are we as humans if we cannot adapt, right, Milo?"

The kid didn't say anything. He just stood up when Clifford did and made his way to the door with him.

"Real sorry about this," I said.

"I didn't vote for the mayor," Clifford said. "Don't expect my vote next year, either."

"Noted," I said.

Down the hall, another young man and kid with an ankle bracelet came shuffling out of the office Sam had entered. They didn't look happy, either, so when they passed me I said, "The mayor thanks you."

"The mayor will be hearing from me," the young man said.

"All letters are appreciated," I said.

Sam opened up the third office door and then stepped back abruptly.

"Problem?" I said.

"Mike, this isn't good," he said. I peered into the office. It was filled with bookshelves. On each of the shelves were approximately twenty Bibles. "That's a lot of judgment right there, Mikey."

"You're on the right side of the law," I said. "Generally."

"We'll keep this door closed," Sam said. "I don't want Fiona to walk by and burst into flames."

"Good call," I said.

When we reached Father Eduardo's office, I rapped lightly on the door and he opened it and, yet again, surprised me. Instead of the shirt and tie I'd grown accustomed to, Father Eduardo was dressed as the priest he was, collar and all.

"Jesus," Sam said.

"That's the idea," Father Eduardo said.

It was nice he still had a sense of humor. Even still, it was going to be hard to hit a man in a collar, which Father Eduardo had likely banked on. I'd done worse, and I had a feeling that Father Eduardo, at some point in his life, had done so, too.

Once we were in the office I said, "I emptied out the floor. What's above us?"

"Nothing until tonight," he said. "What did you do with Leticia?"

"Gave her a choice," I said. "We'll see how that works out."

Sam peered out the window. "Company's coming," he said. "Should we get out the nice china?"

I walked up behind him and looked out, too. Junior Gonzalez: his eyes were covered by black wraparound sunglasses, but his tattoos and scars and muscles, however, were on full display. He'd given up the pretense of pleasant businessman so well cultivated in his suburban home that I had to wonder how silly he felt changing into a wife beater, Dickies and white shoes. The lieutenant walking with him was a massive hulk of a man. Maybe six foot five. Close to three bills. He had on shorts and white socks pulled to his knees, and wore a button-down shirt opened up to reveal a plain white T-shirt. It always surprised me how these guys had such white shirts. Didn't they ever spill a Coke on themselves, like regular people?

"When was the last time you saw your brother?" I asked Father Eduardo.

"Nine months," he said. "Maybe a year. Maybe longer."

"You ready to see him again?"

"I am," he said.

Out on the street, a Miami police cruiser came to a stop at the corner. I called Fiona. "You see that cop?" I said.

"Hard not to," she said.

"Get his plates. He gets out of the car and starts heading toward the office before you make your move? Shoot him."

"Really?"

"Really," I said.

There was a pause. "You mean with the paintball gun?"

"Yes," I said. "How's Barry doing?"

"He's sweating through his pants," she said. "He's agreed to get my car cleaned so we won't have a problem."

"That's just great," I said. "Let me know if you hear anything important when Junior and Killa walk up."

"That's Killa?"

"Doesn't look the part?"

"I guess I imagined he'd be smaller," she said, and hung up.

Out the window, Junior and Killa were making slow progress across the grounds. Every person who walked by got stared at. "Not trying to be too inconspicuous," I said.

"Not Junior's way," Father Eduardo said.

"Open up your office door and stand there," I said. "Let your brother see you and let Junior see you."

"Should I look worried?"

"Are you?"

"No," he said. "I have faith."

"That's good," I said. I lifted up my shirt and showed him my paintball gun. "I have this."

"I told you," he said, but I put my hand up.

"It's a toy," I said, and handed it to him.

He hefted it a bit and then gripped it completely in his hand. "This feels comfortable," he said.

"It's perfectly legal," I said.

Father Eduardo looked down the barrel. "What is it loaded with?"

"That one is loaded with paintballs filled with a fun, flesh-eating acid. The one on my ankle has pepper spray. In case I'm mugged."

"Mikey," Sam said from the window, "they're getting close. Better have the padre move to the door."

Father Eduardo gave me back my paintball gun and then walked over to his double doors and opened both wide. His frame filled up the open space impressively. He might have been religious, but he was still hell to look at.

I sat down behind Father Eduardo's desk and placed my gun between my legs. Sam stretched out across the leather sofa to my right, leaving the conference table and the other sofa open for our guests. I closed my eyes, leaned back, relaxed and waited. In a few moments, I heard the slap of Junior and Killa's footfalls in the hallway.

Even if you can't see someone, you can tell a lot about them by listening to the way they walk. Put two people next to each other, and evolutionary science tells us that they will attempt to keep pace with each other. They will match speed. They will match stride. They will do all they can not to be left behind. From listening to the syncopated rhythms of the footfalls, I could tell that one of the two men was dragging a leg ever so slightly. Instead of making a definitive *clop-clop* sound, it made a *clop-clap-clop*, which meant he was dragging his foot instead of lifting it completely off the ground.

A weak knee.

Which probably meant a weak hip.

Since both men were rather physical specimens, my bet was on Killa, because his bulk looked more like something that came from a needle and not a dedication to working out. And that meant he probably had tendons and ligaments stretched beyond their normal limits. Which meant they could be snapped like a twig.

I opened my eyes in time to see the proof of my assumption. Killa was a half step behind Junior as they got to the door, all silent violence and dressed-down aggression and, it appeared, a bothersome medial collateral ligament.

Father Eduardo stepped forward and met both Junior and Killa before they could get inside. This wasn't part of the plan.

"Jaime," he said, using Junior's real name, and then he did the damnedest thing. He hugged him. The two men embraced for just a few seconds, and I thought, Oh, no, this is a setup. This is about El Salvador. Father Eduardo then turned to Killa and said, "Adrian, my brother," and hugged him, too.

Sam hadn't moved on the sofa. Or at least hadn't moved much. Just his hand, which held his cell phone. Neither of us had real guns on us, as per Father Eduardo's instruction, but I had a pretty good feeling that

Fiona had a MAC-10 in her trunk for a very special occasion.

The three men—all well over six feet, all well over 250 pounds—stood there in the hallway for a moment and stared at each other. They looked like triplets. "Come in," Father Eduardo said eventually, "meet my friends."

Father Eduardo stepped aside, and that's when Junior got his first look at me. He wasn't pleased.

"You," he said.

"Me," I said.

"You stole my BlackBerry," he said.

I reached into my jacket pocket and pulled it out. "You've got terrible coverage," I said, and tossed it back to him.

He saw Sam on the sofa. "Your girlfriend looks different," he said.

"Just a different outfit," I said. "You want your car keys?"

"I already got rid of that car," he said.

"You know these motherfuckers?" Killa said.

"Language," Junior said. "You're in a church."

"It's all right," I said. "This is my church now, and I allow for all kinds of language."

Junior looked mildly surprised. "Oh, really? Is that true, Eduardo?"

Father Eduardo began to speak, but before he could get a word out, Sam jumped up from the sofa, took two steps and slapped him. Hard. "You don't talk," Sam said. "Nobody talks but the big man. You hear? He wants you to talk, he'll tell you when."

Killa made a move toward Sam, which didn't surprise me in the least, but it was especially telling. Junior grabbed him by the shoulder and yanked him back. "Stop," he said. "You don't do anything unless I say so, remember? Same rules."

"Maybe you want to chain your puppy up?" Sam said. "I'd hate for him to get hurt."

"Do you know me?" Killa said to Sam.

"Yeah," Sam said, "I know all the pretty babies. Are you a pretty baby? I like all the pretty drawings you have on your arms. Did your mommy draw those?"

I didn't know where Sam was getting this stuff, but I liked it. Killa thought he was tough—and by the looks of him, he probably was, at least in the conventional street sense, which is a different scale—but Sam could put him down without breaking a sweat. That's the difference between striking fear in someone by looking tough and actually being tough. Killa was probably pretty good at shooting someone in the back of the head, but Sam didn't even need a gun.

"All right," I said calmly. "Why don't we all just sit down and then we can make threats to each other after everyone knows what the score is. Father, why don't you put your big ass down on a chair, and maybe your buddies will follow suit."

Father Eduardo, whose face was still bright red from where Sam slapped it, sat down at the table covered with blueprints. Junior and Killa didn't bother to move.

"Please," I said to Junior, "you're my guests here. Have a seat before my guy Finley puts you down."

Sam cracked his knuckles, but they didn't make any

noise, which sort of understated the effect he was aiming for, so he cracked his neck, too, and it sounded like someone dropped a piano down a flight of stairs. "Ah," he said, "now I'm loose."

Junior and Killa exchanged glances and then sat down in the two seats directly in front of the desk, not bothering with the empty sofa. At least they knew they wanted to be in front of me.

"Good," I said. "Now, I understand you have a proposal for me?"

"Who are you?" Junior said.

"I'm the person who didn't kill you in your own home," I said. "But you can call me Solo."

Junior laughed. "You have balls," he said. "In here, you have balls. There's two of you. And maybe you've got this snitching priest on your side. So you think, Okay, I got God working for me now, too, in addition to whatever you think you're going to tell me. But I've got an army. You heard? I make a phone call, and I can have two thousand people here. You step outside, you won't talk to me with such disrespect."

"I gave you back your phone," I said. "Why don't you go ahead and make that call? I'm happy to wait. And while you do that, I'll have my man Finley here make a call, too, and by the time you've hung up, Julia Pistell's throat will be slit. Nice girl, by the way. Ever met her? Sweet as can be. Yeah, we got her down at the Ace Hotel. She thinks she won a contest through her college. How long you think it will take the police—and not the ones on your measly payroll—to put her dead body and your house together?"

"Who?" Killa said. And when Junior didn't say anything, he said it again. "Who?"

"Nice you brought your owl with you," Sam said from the sofa.

"Shut up, Adrian," Junior said. "I'm trying to think."

I caught Father Eduardo's eye. He looked . . . impressed. But this wasn't anywhere near over yet.

"You said your name is Solo?" Junior said.

"That's what I said you could call me," I said.

"What's the nature of your business, Solo?"

"My business? You could say I take over distressed companies and then, when they're profitable, I sell them. Why, you looking for an investor?"

"I guess I'm trying to figure out why you'd align yourself with someone who has a history of selling his partners out."

"Align? You think this is an alignment? Father Eduardo works for me. You think you're the only person who ever tried to blackmail someone?" I said. "I understand you want to utilize Father Eduardo's existing infrastructure to run your business—would that be correct? I know you came in with this revenge-and-reward business, but the truth is that you see a good business model here. Right? Let's just be honest, businessman to businessman. I've done pretty well here, haven't I?"

"Eduardo is a Latin Emperor," Junior said. "He may think he serves someone else, but he serves us first. That's the oath. And he owes me much more."

"Yeah, yeah, I've seen the documentaries," I said.

"There was even one you were in. Did you see that one?"

"No," Junior said.

"Yeah, showed your picture, and then someone with a blurred-out face spent about twenty minutes talking about how you were the toughest SOB in the world and how you ran this and that and the other thing. But, shit, I just thought you looked like a guy who needed some nice Pottery Barn furniture and some chenille rugs."

I winked at Junior, because when you wink at people, it's a sign that either you're insane or you know they're insane and it's cool, really.

"Thing is," I said, "Eduardo has a new boss now. You have a problem with him, you take it up with me, and we'll see what can be worked out without you getting killed."

This made Killa laugh. He had an odd sense of humor. But Junior wasn't amused. "I. Am. Owed." Each word Junior said was its own sentence.

This day was not going as he had planned, I suspected, and I also suspected he wasn't used to being challenged. I also had a pretty good idea that if pushed hard enough, he'd try to do something stupid. We hadn't checked them for guns, but I was sure they were strapped. Or at least Killa was. In a moment, however, Fiona would be here to defuse that problem, if need be.

"You've got an outdated business model that needs some tweaking," I said. "That counterfeiting business you were trying to pull is example A, Your Honor. And this idea that Father Eduardo owes you something? You wipe that clean from your mind. You go to that happy place you live in, with those nice sofas and pieces of art and that gazebo. I really liked that gazebo, Junior. You ever seen his gazebo, Killa?"

"Who the fuck are you?" Killa said. "Who the fuck are these guys, Junior?"

"Shut up, Adrian," Junior said. Junior inhaled deeply and then tried to relax. "Eduardo belongs to me," he said to me. "You must understand that."

"Sure, sure," I said. "You think I haven't been in a prison or two? So he snitched you out. Big deal. He fell in love with the Lord—what did you expect? Let's just get beyond revenge and deal with the tangible, okay? Everything you see here? That's me. Father Eduardo and I made a deal. He had dreams, and I had means."

"You are not involved!" Junior said. It was as if I wasn't even speaking. Junior had his own script, and here I was interrupting it. He thought this was going to go down one way, and here it was, an all-new set of circumstances.

A rational man would change his tack.

A rational man might excuse himself and set up a new meeting at a later date.

A rational man might even just have his muscle pull out his gun and kill everyone. And Killa did have a gun. He walked like a guy with a bad knee and a gun shoved into his tailbone. Sam had noticed this, too, and was keeping a laser focus on Killa's every move.

I'd spoken rationally thus far to Junior, and it frankly

hadn't done much to defuse the situation. Junior was quick to boil. The problem with speaking rationally to criminally insane people is that at some point, no matter how much sense you've made, they just won't be able to process what you're saying.

We'd already reached that point and had been talking for only about three minutes. So, when that point of stasis arrives, you need to get down to the level of your opponent, ponder what his next move might be and then make it before he did . . . which is why, during the second or two it took Junior to process what I'd just told him, I decided to shoot Killa in the knee with my big shiny gun.

Except it wasn't a gun, of course. It was a paintball marker. But instead of paintballs, I'd filled this gun with rounds of a mixture containing primarily lortropic acid, which is a particularly voluble acid when it hits things containing water, since it actively repels the substance, which is why it works so well when you're refinishing your deck. There wasn't enough acid in the round to do much damage, apart from eat away a patch or two of skin, but when combined with the force of the shot, I knew in all likelihood the round would go right through Killa's pulled-up sock and into his skin, where it would burn and sizzle and be plenty dreadful to look at, which is part of why I decided to do it.

The advantage was that the acid would actually cauterize the wound so, on balance, I was really doing Killa a favor.

Plus, my real plan was to sever his medial collateral

ligament, or at least crack his patella. It would depend on how accurate the gun was. And that would help him in the long run, too. You can't be much of a gangster if you can't run after or away from people.

So, just as Junior was opening his mouth to respond, I slid my gun beneath the desk and with a single pop that didn't sound like a gunshot (which is good, because a gunshot is pretty distinctive and loud and tends to bring in uninvited guests) dropped Killa to the ground in a screaming mess.

"My knee!" he bellowed.

Sam walked over to where Killa was writhing, knelt down, put a hand on Killa's head to keep him still, and proceeded to pull a nice, little snub-nosed .357 from his belt, which he handed to me.

Junior didn't move. He just looked at Killa with something less than amusement. Killa's knee was cut open in a two-inch gash that was, as predicted, bubbling but not really bleeding. A clean shot. Mostly, Junior seemed confused.

"I'm sorry," I said to Junior, "but I don't allow guns in here. It's a church, you know? And I found his tone very disrespectful."

"You shot me!" Killa said.

"Shut up, Adrian," Junior said.

"Does that burn?" Sam asked.

"It's eating my skin!" he said.

Junior kept his eyes on Killa, but said to me, "It is eating his skin."

"Yes," I said. "He's got five minutes until it hits bone, so he should be fine provided we reach some kind of accord in, oh, four minutes and thirty seconds. He'll want some time for the antidote to work its way into his system."

"What did you shoot him with?"

"Trade secret," I said.

Junior finally pulled his eyes from Killa and looked over his shoulder at Father Eduardo, who, amazingly, seemed pretty content with everything. It was all working out perfectly, and perhaps he saw that.

The only problem thus far was that Killa's burning flesh smelled. The acid really wasn't going to eat away at him until it hit bone—it would only burn off a few layers of skin, and, mixing with blood and the oil in his skin, would cause a lot of visual fireworks, but no real permanent damage. His destroyed ligaments were more his own fault than mine. They would have popped at some point. I just brought the future forward for him.

"Here's what I want," Junior said. "I need the printing plant. I will pay no fee for it. It will be mine. Eduardo can still print his newspapers and his flyers and no-drug pamphlets and everything else he wants. But I need the operation from midnight to six daily. There is no negotiation."

"Really?" I said.

"Really," Junior said. "Or else I kill Father Eduardo's nephew."

14

The element of surprise is really an issue of controlling morale. Shock your enemy, and you can expect that a feeling of hopelessness will descend upon him. He will begin to feel vulnerable both mentally and physically. His training, both mental and physical, will come into question. He might even turn on his leaders, thinking they are incompetent for not knowing what to expect in the heat of battle.

Not killing all of your enemies is actually an advantage, since the myth of your power will ripple throughout the ranks of your enemy and then you have the mental advantage. A spy feeds off this advantage, because once you've defeated an enemy from the inside, it's much easier to defeat him from the outside.

The problem for Junior was that he probably wasn't aware of this maxim. Or maybe he thought he was surprising me.

He wasn't.

Maybe he'd surprised Father Eduardo, but since he was the one who used to control the Latin Emperors' message, maybe it was an old tactic brought back for a good cause.

The one person who was surprised was Killa, since Junior had just put a death sentence on his son with Leticia.

"What?" Killa said. He didn't quite have the language skills of his brother, but in this case there really wasn't much to say. His boss had just said he was going to kill his son. And then there was the issue that the skin on his knee was bubbling away.

"You heard me," Junior said to Killa. "Your son belongs to the Latin Emperors, and if I decide he dies, he dies. That's just how it is. You have a problem with that?"

Killa didn't know what to say. That was clear. He looked from Junior to Eduardo and even to me. He looked afraid, helpless—all the things you'd want your enemy to look like after launching a surprise attack. That Killa worked for Junior showed the level of depravity in the situation. Everyone was expendable. "He's just a kid, Junior," Killa said. "He's not part of this."

"Are you part of this?" Junior said.

"You know I am," Killa said.

"Then he's part of it," Junior said. "You ready to have him die for this? Aren't you ready to die? Because I know I spent a lifetime in prison willing to die for this, so you better be willing."

It was actually rather fascinating to watch the skewed reasoning of men, particularly powerful men, and here on display was the old school and the new doing battle over what was, in essence, the future of the gang. They needed this place for the long-term survival of their clan. But bringing in a kid was a level of devotion I wasn't familiar with and wasn't comfortable with. I knew we needed to protect Leticia, but hearing Junior threaten the kid's life in front of his father was a nihilism that told me all I needed to know about Junior: He knew this was his chance to make it. What "it" is to anyone is a good question, but for Junior, a man who'd spent thousands of days behind bars, clearly this was a chance at the life he felt he deserved.

"He's with it," Killa said, though he didn't sound all that affirmative. "He's with it. Just get me to the hospital, Junior, because I'm gonna lose my knee, man. I know it." He'd begun to bargain, which wasn't a good sign. He was actually going through all of the stages of mourning right in front of us.

"Adrian," Father Eduardo began to say, but then Sam started to get up, so he quieted down. He knew his role well. He also knew that his brother was suffering.

"Everyone settle down," I said. "Even if you kill the kid, what does that matter to me? What's the use? You hurt Father Eduardo? You think that matters to me?"

"Same use as all the dead bodies Eduardo put into the ground thirty years ago," he said. "It's good for *our* family. That's the only one that matters. I'm going to guess the good father doesn't want a dead kid on his hands, because I will make it look like his doing. And that you best believe. I lose; he loses. That's the new rule. I've got ways to make this happen. That you best believe, too."

"Right," I said, "you've got cops. I know. We all got cops. But, really, that doesn't matter to me. I'm happy to give you the plant from midnight to six. I get twenty-five percent of what you print."

Junior pondered for a moment. "Ten percent."

"This isn't a negotiation," I said. "I just gave you the terms. And you employ your own guys. I'm not compromising my operation here with your three-fingered technician."

I let that sink in, let him know I knew so much more than just the basics, that I was in on the minute details, too.

"He won't be working for me anymore," Junior said. "Or for anyone."

"That's good," I said. "I get final approval on your plates, too. You running the U.S. Mint through here, I don't want it to be a half-assed job. We all go back to prison if you're making that skunk money I saw at the hotel."

I let that sink in, too. I'd infiltrated all aspects of his life, and now he knew it. Maybe it was a surprise, maybe it wasn't, but it couldn't have been good news for him.

"Deal," Junior said.

"And from now on," I said, "I control your security operations. We got into and out of your life in two days. We know everything about you, and we're just businessmen. Right, Finley?"

"Business is our business, big man," Sam said.

"That's not happening," Junior said.

"You work with me," I said, "you work with me. Or you're going to be a liability, like Killa here."

A moan rose from the floor, where Killa was likely counting toward the five-minute mark, which was when he thought he'd see himself from the inside out. He was also likely considering the fate of his son, maybe himself.

"How much time has elapsed, Finley?"

Sam looked at his watch. He had no idea how much time had passed. Neither did I. "Four minutes and seventeen seconds. Eighteen. Nineteen."

Even though the acid that was currently biting into Killa's skin repelled water, the amount of acid was so insignificant inside the paintball that the best antidote *was* water, or a flush of water.

"Go ahead," I said to Sam. He got up, opened up the small fridge in the corner of Father Eduardo's office and came away with a bottle of Evian, which he dumped on Killa's wound.

"There," Sam said. "Unless you're the Wicked Witch of the West, you should be fine now."

"I'd go see a doctor, anyway," I said. "Since you don't have any ligaments in your knee anymore. And you'll probably get gangrene from the wound, too." Killa whimpered something that sounded like "Thank you," but I couldn't be absolutely sure.

The truth was that he probably wasn't in terrible pain from the shot or the acid. The torn ligaments would hurt and make it hard for him to walk, and he'd never play pro football again, but nothing that had happened to him was particularly torturous.

Killa was experiencing anticipatory pain. It normally happens to people in the middle of combat. A person gets nicked by a piece of shrapnel, sees that his flesh is torn and bleeding, and thinks he should probably be in terrible pain, even if he isn't. So he acts as if he is. The human brain doesn't realize that you look like the toughest man alive; it just realizes that you should be in pain by virtue of visual evidence, and the next thing you know, you're prostrate on the floor, clutching your knees to your chest and sucking your thumb.

I regarded Junior again. "Those are the terms."

"You protect me, then," he said, "but you leave the rest of the Emperors out. I'm not opening my books to you."

"Fine," I said, because it was precisely what I wanted. "What else?"

"I thought you made the terms?"

"I do, but you could do this without us," I said. "You're paying a twenty-five-percent tariff on your product just because it's easier for you. So you tell me what other low-down shit you want to do, and I'll tell you if it's possible."

"You're a smart man, Solo."

"No," I said. "I just got here first."

"I need an office," he said. "People see me working for Father Eduardo, they'll think he turned me. They'll think the LE are dead. I need that."

"What's in it for me?"

"I don't kill the boy," he said.

"Kill the boy," I said, "and I'll kill Julia Pistell, and then you'll have two murders on your plate. So I ask again, What's in it for me?"

The truth was that I needed to get Junior in the building. If this was all going to work, I'd need him to not just be counterfeiting money here in the middle of the night; I needed him to be in an office, doing the business of the Latin Emperors. It wasn't legal for the police to bug the church, but I'm not the police.

With twenty-five percent of the counterfeit money even for one day, I'd be able to put that bogus cash directly into the hands of someone who could make a difference, someone who would bypass the beat cops on Junior's payroll.

Someone like the mayor.

"What do you want?" he asked.

"I need some bodies," I said. "Some muscle to do a few jobs for me. I figure you got guys who could help me. Guys who know how to stay quiet if they get nicked. Guys who could do a year standing on their head if some shit went down wrong. I'm not anticipating that, of course, but that's the kind of soldier I need. Killa here wouldn't be a good choice, on account of his busted knee and his crying, but I think you get what I'm aiming for."

My plan was to not just get Junior in the building, but to get his men out on the streets in a situation I controlled that might just negatively affect the morale of the Latin Emperors. If you want to make a powerful leader vulnerable, make his troops think he's incompetent and leading them into slaughter. Natural selection tends to take care of the rest.

There was a sound out in the hall just as Junior was about to give me his answer. It was perfect timing: the sound was Fiona pulling Barry down the hall, the stockwhip wrapped around his neck. Barry's face was bright red, probably from lack of oxygen, and he had dried blood on his face, neck and white shirt, which I suspect Fiona had picked out this morning simply for the effect it provided.

"Hello, boys," Fiona said, and then flung Barry into the room by snapping the whip handle around in front of herself. Barry spun and then landed on the sofa with a thud. It was a neat trick. Sam tried his best not to show any concern for Barry, but, well, he's a chivalrous guy, so he gave Barry a shove in the chest for good measure.

Fiona stood in the doorway, admiring her work. She still had the whip in her hand. It made for a lovely image. "You left your trash out on the curb," she said to Junior, "so I picked it up for you."

Junior looked confused. Again. Which was what I was aiming for.

"Hope you don't mind," I said, "but I took the liberty of trimming a few of your loose ends before they ended up tying your hands."

Junior said nothing. He was too busy glaring at Barry.

"A guy like Barry? Really? This is who you go to? This is why I either control your program or you walk. So do we have an agreement?"

After a few seconds, when Junior still hadn't said a word, Fiona cracked her whip a few inches from his face, which caused him to actually cower. Most people, it turns out, don't know what to do with themselves when a person cracks a whip at their heads. The reason is that there's really no way to defend yourself. Put a hand up, and you could end up losing a finger. Put up your forearm in defense, and you run the risk of having your skin flayed open wide.

"Speak up," Fiona said, "or I'll come to your house and steal your throw pillows when you're not looking."

Junior shook his head; it was as if he couldn't figure all of the things he was being shown. "Who are you?" he said again.

"Not someone you want to be on the bad side of," I said.

He looked back over at Barry. "What are you going to do with him?" he said.

"I'm not sure yet," I said. "Killing him would probably make you happy, but the fact is, he's got some good qualities. We've done some business in the past, but not the kind you hired him for, that's for sure. But I feel like he might be able to provide us with some insight into a professional counterfeiting business. Would that be right, Barry?"

Barry nodded once. He knew his role, too, but in this case he was also scared. All that blood on him wasn't an actual indication of serious injury, though. It looked like Fiona had simply cut him on his scalp with a razor. It would hurt and it would bleed, but it would require only a Band-Aid. In fact, it had already stopped bleeding, so it was likely Barry wouldn't even have a scar.

"I want him dead," Junior said.

"I can understand that," I said. "But what you want and what happens now are irrelevant. He works for me until I say he doesn't work for me."

This was a lot for Junior to consider. Probably more than he'd managed to ponder outside of solitary confinement, at least. At his feet was his main muscle. Behind him was the man he thought he was going to juice. And surrounding him were people telling him how his life was going to be for the foreseeable future. If he was smart, he'd agree to all I'd offered him. He'd make his money. He'd take his revenge—albeit more passively than he might want—and he'd secure the future of his organization. If he was stupid, he'd agree, and then an hour later he'd come back with fifty guys holding automatic weapons and kill us all. There was no gain in that now, really, which meant if he was truly bright, he'd kill us a year from now. Maybe two. Long enough away that we wouldn't be expecting anything, as we'd all be happily in business together. Thirty years he'd waited. He could wait another one or two for the blood he wanted to spill.

"Fine." He reached across the desk with his hand extended. "Let's do this," he said.

I took his hand and said, "This is my bond here. I'm good to my word. You be good to yours, and no one gets hurt, except Killa here."

"He'll heal," Junior said.

We both laughed. Nothing like two homicidal maniacs agreeing that someone's suffering was damn funny.

"One other thing," I said, still holding on to him.

"Yeah?"

"You come within three feet of Father Eduardo," I said, and then I gave him a good squeeze, and then another to make him wince, which was surprising, since he wasn't a small man, "and I will kill you."

"And if you touch any of my men again," he said, and this time he returned the squeeze, "I will kill the girl."

That was the wrong thing to say.

Fiona cracked the whip around Junior's neck and yanked him toward her with a quick flourish of her wrist. He was at least a foot taller than she, but at that moment, it didn't really matter, since he couldn't breathe.

"I'm sorry," Fiona said, "I didn't hear you."

Junior let out a series of gurgles and gasps.

"Uh, honey," I said.

"Yes, darling," she said.

"If you're going to kill him," I said, "could you do it outside? It wouldn't be right to do it in the father's chambers."

Junior was scratching at the whip around his throat and gurgling even more. He had a good couple seconds of breath left before he passed out. Interestingly, Killa hadn't even bothered to move. Morale, it seemed, was low.

"I guess I won't, then," she said, "out of respect for Father Eduardo, and in light of our new business relationship."

She flicked her wrist again and, just like Barry, Junior spun out of the whip and then ended up on the floor beside Killa. I got up from the desk and walked around to where they both were and talked very calmly to Junior.

"I'm going to go out on a limb here and say that making threats to me isn't a good idea," I said. "I'll have an office ready for you tomorrow. Can we expect to see you here at nine A.M.?"

He didn't say anything. There was a chance Fiona might have done some damage to his windpipe.

"Noon would be fine, too," I said, "If maybe you need to see a physician between then and now."

Nothing.

"Make it two. But no later. I know how hard it is to get in to see a doctor on my HMO, so I understand where you're coming from. I'm going to go ahead with our mutual friend Barry here and see about getting you some decent plates to run from. Does that sound good?"

Again, nothing. Junior had tears in his eyes, which was nice to see. It's an involuntary thing when you're being choked, but it was still a pleasant reminder that he was human.

"And if you don't mind," I said, "it would be nice to get five guys tomorrow, too. I have a job I'd like to get started on."

Junior coughed, hacked out a clump of pink saliva and wiped his mouth with the back of his hand. The tears in his eyes were gone. All that was there was rage. This was not a man used to being beaten; certainly not a man used to being whipped, literally, by a woman. I think maybe his morale was low, too.

"Girl," he rasped, but then thought better of his choice to speak when he began coughing and gagging. Better all the way around, really.

"Well, you two have a nice day, now," I said. I gave Sam a look, and he got up and yanked both men up by their collars, which didn't seem to make either of them very happy, not since Killa couldn't really put any weight on his knee and Junior was having an issue with his throat, and pushed them toward the open door.

They both stumbled at first and then seemed to gain a bit of purchase after they bounced off each other and found their balance.

"You don't ever disrespect me like that," Junior said, though it was hard to hear him. It's hard to sound threatening when air keeps whistling out of your throat.

"I just did," I said.

"Never again," he said.

"Fine, fine," I said.

"And keep her away from me," he said.

"Can't promise that," I said.

The issue Junior Gonzalez was having, other than with breathing, was that no one ever talked back to him. He simply wasn't made to take orders.

"Tomorrow," he said.

"Tomorrow," I said.

All of us watched Junior and Killa drag themselves down the hallway. They looked like wild horses that had been broken. When they reached the front door, Killa looked back at us and held Father Eduardo's gaze for a few seconds before he shuffled back out into the daylight.

"That went well," Sam said.

"You think so?" Barry said. "Because I'm covered with blood over here. And, Michael, you didn't mention anything to me about Fiona wrapping a whip around my throat or cutting me. That was not part of any form of discussion you and I had, Michael, and I'd like you to know that I found both experiences . . . to put it mildly . . . upsetting."

"You loved it," Fiona said.

"A part of me enjoyed it," Barry said.

Father Eduardo took his rightful seat behind his desk and dropped his head into his hands.

"Guys," I said, "can you leave us alone for a minute?"

"Sure, Mikey," Sam said. "We'll get Barry cleaned up in the bathroom. And then maybe, Fi, you can show me that little trick with the whip?"

"Why don't you try something proactive," I said, "like bugging that empty office next door? Get it ready for Junior's occupancy."

When they were gone, I sat down across from Father Eduardo, in the same chair Killa was in prior to my destroying his knee. "I know what I'm doing, Father," I said.

"I know," he said. "I know. Ernie, he told me you might make it look like I'm in an impossible situation, but that you would be in control. I just . . . to see my brother that way. It was hard."

"I had to show them that I have no fear," I said.

"No, not that. That I understand. To see him sub-servient to Junior. To see him give up his own son to him. It made me sick. That's me there, Michael. That's what I used to do. I may not have killed directly, but I put that fear of suffering into other people. I have to make that right."

"You are. Right here."

"There's more. There has to be."

"We'll figure that out," I said. "In the meantime, it's business as usual here. We'll clear the storeroom next to your office and put Junior in there. We'll give him a computer and a phone and all of the bugging devices money can buy."

"How long will he be here?"

I had to think about that. "Two days, if everything goes according to my plan. If he's still here by the end of the week, that just means we've both been mur-dered."

Father Eduardo looked stricken.

"Kidding," I said.

"He'll come for you," Father Eduardo said. "That's his nature."

"I know," I said. "He won't get the chance."

"I hope you're right."

"I am," I said. "In the meantime, you need to be in a safe house."

"I am safe in the Lord's house," he said.

"I respect that," I said, "but I'm the only one who does. Sam will be your shadow for the next few days, but at night, you're sleeping elsewhere."

Father Eduardo nodded his assent. "Do you have a secure facility somewhere?"

"You could say that." I pulled out my cell phone and made a call. "Ma," I said, "you remember Little Eddie Santiago from the other day? Turns out he's getting his house fumigated and needs a place to stay for a few nights."

"Michael," she said, "is he in danger?"

"Of course, Ma," I said.

"I thought he was a priest."

"He is," I said. "But he's a priest who needs my help."

"You lead a very strange life, Michael."

"I know, Ma. I know," I said. I checked my watch. "Sam will drop him off in a few hours. That okay?"

"Do I have a choice?"

"No," I said. "You made me get the car washed, remember?"

"You just can't stop blaming me for one minute, can you?"

"Appears not," I said. "I appreciate this, Ma. And so does Father Eduardo."

"I'll put on some coffee," she said, and hung up.

"All taken care of," I told Father Eduardo.

"Fine, fine," he said. He reached into his desk and pulled out a Bible. "Would you mind leaving me alone for a few moments? I need to pray."

"Sure," I said. "Of course."

"You can let yourself out?"

I told him I could, and then got out of his office as

quickly as possible. It was hard to see him as the religious man he was when in my mind he was Eddie Santiago, not Father Eduardo. He was a man to be feared, and now he had the fear of God. It was a turnaround I wasn't practiced in, and not one I yearned to be overly familiar with.

I found Sam in the empty office, stacking extra Bibles. It was one of strangest things I'd ever seen.

"Take a picture," Sam said, "before I go up in flames."

"Where's Fi?" I said.

"She ran back out to get the bugs. Barry's in the bathroom, shaking and sobbing quietly."

"Really?"

"I dunno, Mikey, but he's not made for hostage situations. That's all I'm saying."

"I thought he did well."

"He's lucky Junior didn't plug him."

"We're lucky Junior didn't try to plug all of us."

"That won't be the case next time," Sam said. "How long we planning on pulling this off?"

"Couple of days is all we'll need. Get him on tape in here, get the counterfeiting operation up and running, which should take only a day if we get some decent plates, and then see about maybe pulling it all together with a police action that doesn't implicate anyone but Junior."

"How you planning on doing that?"

"I was thinking of starting out with a Chechnya-type situation in the printing press," I said, "but without killing anyone."

"Good luck with that," Sam said.

"You'll be helping," I said.

Fiona stepped back into the office then and set down a small container of bugs. One for the phone; a tracking device on the computer that would clone all of the work Junior did, as well as send cloned e-mails to a private server; and a small camera that would fit inside the spine of one of the Bibles.

"It's on you, Fi, to put the cameras inside the books," Sam said.

"Why, Sam, are you afraid?"

"You ever go to Sunday school, Fiona?"

"I grew up in Ireland," Fiona said. "Maybe you heard of the place? Years of armed religious conflict?"

"Well, wonderful. Then you shouldn't have a problem with doing things in the name of a greater good with religious icons. Me, it makes me a little nervous. My family came over on the *Mayflower*." Neither Fi nor I bothered to respond to Sam. He wanted us to, so we didn't. "So," he said, after it became clear to all involved that we weren't going to engage him on what had to be a lie, "I'm morally disallowed from bugging Bibles. Miles Standish runs through this blood, sister."

"But shooting people for the last thirty years has been fine?" Fiona said.

"Hey, sweetheart, those were all in the service of this great country," Sam said. "Or a lot of them, anyway."

"Michael, I expect that you'll speak for us at the pearly gates?" she said.

"I'll do my very best," I said.

"See, Sam? Nothing to be concerned about," Fi said. "Oh, and here." She handed me a sheet of paper with a bunch of numbers listed on it. "Your dirty work."

"What's this?"

"The license plate of the police cruiser, as well as the car number from the roof."

"Nice."

"I'm a professional, even when I'm saddled with a sweating Chatty Cathy," Fiona said. "You know, I actually think Barry really did enjoy me cutting him."

"Everyone is into something strange." I handed the numbers to Sam. "You got someone you can check these with?"

"I'll have to tread delicately here, Mikey. One wrong step, and these guys are on to our operation."

"I know you'll find just the right person," I said. "Maybe you can use your standing as a founding father of the country to sway the right people."

Fiona handed me a Bible. "Hold this open," she said, and I did. She took a bottle of nail polish remover from her purse and poured about a teaspoon of the fluid down the interior spine of the book. She then shoved two fingers into the spine and gently pulled the pages from the binding—the nail polish remover had made the fine gold threading far more elastic, which is what you want to do if you're going to hide something inside of a book instead of, say, cutting a hammer into the pages. Even people being spied on have seen movies, so they have a general idea what an amateur might do and may even look for a few telltale signs.

But what Fiona was doing was essentially the same process an antiquarian book restorer might do. Except that instead of restoring the Bible, she slid a small camera about four inches in length down the spine of the book.

Back in the Cold War—and in the 1990s, too—if you wanted to film someone, you needed to have a camera that was routed into a recorder somewhere, usually not too far from the camera itself. Any decent, paranoid person could discover these things in just a few minutes of frenzied searching. But the camera Fiona had just slipped into the book was no thicker than her thumb and was able to use motion-detection technology to record directly to a chip inside it. While we wouldn't have remote access, we would have a fine digital recording of all Junior was doing.

Or, since I saw that Fiona had ten of these cameras, several digital movies of the life and times of Junior Gonzalez.

Fiona sealed the book back up, poked several small holes into the spine so that the camera could view the activity and then placed the book back onto the shelf.

"Good work," I said.

"You should see what I put in your loft last week."

"You bugged my loft?"

"You'll never know without checking. Will you, Michael?"

I didn't know whether to believe her or not, and fortunately I was saved by Barry's appearance in the doorway. He'd washed his face some, but it was still a light pink color, and his clothes were covered in blood. He looked like a man who'd been strangled with a whip and beaten, essentially.

"Come on, Barry," I said, "you're going to help me with a secret mission."

"I'd like to go home," he said.

"You are home," I said, "for now."

"That wasn't fake blood, Michael," he said. "You let her cut me!"

"There is no letting," Fiona said.

"She's right," I said.

"Free country," Sam said. "It's what we came here for."

Barry looked like someone had just hit him in the back of the head, so I made it simple for him. "A little blood for a good cause, Barry. Namely, your life."

"That makes sense," Barry said. "And that it makes sense means that I have made some terrible mistakes in my life, doesn't it?"

"You can always change," I said. "Look at Father Eduardo."

Barry considered this. "Where are we going?"

"I need you to get me the best money plate your money can buy," I said.

"My money?"

"This is your problem we're solving," I said.

"I know a guy named Jacques," he said. "He's from the old school. He might not deal with you."

"I'm sure you can be persuasive," I said.

"I'm only saying I may need to take the lead here."

"Like you did with Junior?"

"Similar situation, possibly," he said, which meant to me that no matter what relationship Barry had with this Jacques, by the end of our time together, he'd understand who was really in charge, even if I didn't make a single move.

"All right," I said, "we'll do it your way."

"I'll need some new clothes," he said. "And is there any way we could get some lunch?"

When you're a spy, sometimes your toughest job is keeping your informants dressed and fed. It's not always about beautiful women, shiny cars and blowing things up.

Unfortunately.

15

Making money costs money. This is true as both a frothy maxim you might read on a poster and in reality. Each note the U.S. government prints costs four cents in simple materials, but the lead-up process is far more costly. The plates used in the production of money are hand engraved, a meticulous process that takes a substantial amount of time and dedication, but this is done for a very exacting purpose: You can re-create a computer's etchings very easily, but it's impossible to precisely emulate the hand of a human being. There will always be subtle differences.

So if you really want to counterfeit money, a printing system like the Latin Emperors had set up at the Ace Hotel would suffice only for the short term. You can print and press money using only computer software and a particularly detailed reproduction of an actual bill. But if you want to make money to make money, you'll need a hand-engraved plate.

And it would help if you had Barry, too.

While Sam and Fiona finished setting up Junior's

office with the appropriate listening and tracking devices (and to ensure that no one came in and made an
attempt on Father Eduardo's life), and to manage the
Leticia situation if she bothered to return to work, which
was not something I was sure would happen, I set off
to learn just how Barry handled his business.

Not that I didn't have a pretty good idea as it was,
but it was always interesting meeting new friends. Or
new friends of friends. And, really, Barry was eager to
help this project along. . . . Or, well, he was eager for
this project to be over so he could leave town for as
long as possible without worrying about his family
being killed.

I sat in my Charger and waited for Barry to come
out of the Dillard's department store he'd gone into to
purchase a new outfit, since the one he was wearing
just had too much blood on it. I opted not to join him,
figuring it would probably be better all around if security cameras picked up one shady, blood-covered indi-
vidual and not his friend, too. And since this Dillard's
was housed inside a nice suburban mall in Doral, I
really didn't want to have to fight off a SWAT team.

That, and I was afraid of watching Barry shop. There
are some things you simply do not want to do with
certain people, and I had a feeling shopping with Barry
would be a situation that might engender thoughts of
murder in me. But the real reason we were at this mall
and not some other clothing store was that Jacques, the
engraver Barry had contacted about our specific job,
told him he'd only speak to him from a certain pay

phone, and that certain pay phone was located just adjacent to the men's room on the second floor of Dillard's.

Finally, after at least thirty minutes, Barry came out of the store, wearing a cream-colored, short-sleeve button-down that was opened (none too discreetly) to the center of his rather clammy-looking chest, brown chinos and a pair of braided leather flip-flops. He looked like he was ready to play badminton in someone's backyard. He'd also purchased a new pair of sunglasses and, judging by the smell when he slid into the Charger, stopped by the cologne counter, too.

"That's a wonderful new fragrance," I said.

"You like it?"

"Not really."

"And I didn't like getting strangled by Fiona, so that makes us even."

"If that's what does it, fine."

Barry inhaled. "I think it smells fresh."

"Barry," I said, "did you talk to your guy?"

"It has a vanilla scent on the back end," Barry said. "You don't get that?"

The issue with Barry is that he's stubborn. He's used to doing things on his own timeline. Occasionally, you have to work within that knowledge if you wish to have a successful interaction with him.

"You look and smell just like a vanilla bean," I said.

"I appreciate that, Michael," Barry said. "I like to think that if you look good, you feel good, and I feel good now. Better than I have all week."

"That's wonderful," I said. I gave him a big, warm

smile. "Now tell me what your guy said before *I* strangle you, too."

Barry cleared his throat and then reached into his pocket and pulled out a torn out page from the phone book with scribbles on it. "You're gonna wanna get onto Sixteenth Avenue and turn left."

"Where are we going?" I said.

"I'm just following directions," Barry said. "My guy was very specific."

"Who is this guy?" I said.

"I've only ever known him as Jacques," Barry said. "Never seen him in person. But I told him I was in a bind and I really needed his help. He owes me a few favors."

If you're the kind of guy who knows how to move things on the black market—and Barry was pretty much the Walmart of the black market—you end up with plenty of acquaintances who owe you a favor or two. In that way, Barry wasn't so different than Sam. In all other ways, it was like apples and chainsaws.

"This is a guy who can keep a secret?" I said.

"He's a ghost," Barry said. "Really. The guy is Fort Knox. You think guys who can hand engrave plates for money just blab to everyone they meet about their special skill?"

I started the car and headed out of the mall and followed Barry's circuitous directions until we came to a stop on Aragon Avenue in Coral Gables, some ten miles from where we started, even though we'd traveled closer to twenty. I looked around for some obvious sign of the world's finest plate engraver, but all I saw was a taupe-colored strip mall that boasted a hair salon, a coffee place called Cliffhanger and . . .

"What did you say this guy's name was?" I said.

"Jacques," Barry said.

"Not Harvey?" I said.

"Why would it be Harvey?"

"I don't know, Barry. Maybe because we're currently parked in front of Harvey's Trophy World," I said. I pointed out the window to the storefront. A painted sign in the window announced that Harvey's was THE OFFICIAL HOME OF ALL YOUR LITTLE LEAGUE NEEDS!

"Everyone has a day job," Barry said.

"Yeah," I said, "what's yours?"

I got out of the car, and Barry trailed after me. "He said no guns," Barry said.

"I'm not coming to rob him," I said.

"He might pat you down," Barry said.

The door to Harvey's shop opened up and a young boy and his mother came out clutching an armful of awards. "Great," I said. I went back to my car and dumped my guns. I didn't even bother to pick up the paintball gun, for fear that I might shoot Barry with it. "You sure this guy is what you say he is? Because I don't want to walk into this place and find out we've wasted the afternoon."

"Mike, trust me," Barry said. "Have I ever steered you wrong where money was concerned?"

He had a point. Barry was especially good for his word with money, so I let him lead the way across the street and into the shop.

The interior of Harvey's was filled, wall to wall, with awards, trophies, pendants, charms, commemorative cups, water bottles, fake fish mounted above empty gold labels, tote bags that said YOUR LOGO HERE on them. There were also pennants, dish towels, sun visors and every other conceivable item that could possibly have a logo or saying or award declaration placed on it.

The store was a narrow funnel that led to a single counter in the back, where the cash register was located. Behind the counter was a double door that led into, presumably, Harvey's great factory of fame and recognition. All I knew for certain from where I stood soaking up the ambience of Harvey's was that he hadn't dusted in at least a decade, nor bothered to change any of his displays.

"Nice place," I said.

"Maybe he does a big mail-order business," Barry said. "Now, just follow my lead here. He was very specific in his directions."

"You're the boss," I said.

We walked to the back of the store and Barry rang the bell on the counter . . . the one that had a sign next to it that said PLEASE RING THE BELL. I MAY NOT HEAR YOU COME IN OTHERWISE, which to me sounded like an invitation to pull the cash register off the counter. Except, oddly, the register was bolted to the wall and down to the floor using thick titanium bars. Not exactly standard for a trophy shop.

And then I began to notice other details. The floor, while dusty, was lined with razor-thin metal piping that led directly into a series of small boxes built into

the floor at the front of the store. The only time I'd
seen that previously was in a vault inside a mansion in
Belarus, which is good, because once you see a floor
that's capable of electrocuting you with the flip of a
switch, you generally want to avoid a second occur-
rence.

The double doors swung open and out came a man
of about seventy. Maybe seventy-five. He did not look
like the kind of guy who would electrocute you without cause. Nor did he look like someone named Jacques.
Harvey? Certainly. He was bald except for a wisp of
gray hair in the center of his head, wore eyeglasses
with no frames and had on a dust-covered gray shirt
covered only nominally by a dust-covered gray apron.

"Are you here to pick up your trophy or to design a
plaque?" Harvey said.

Barry started to speak, stopped, started again, and
then reached into his pocket for the scrap of the yellow
pages he'd scribbled on, and attempted to read his
own handwriting. "Uh, we are here to pick up the trophy for, uh, the, uh, Desperados?"

Harvey didn't respond.

"The, uh, Diamondbacks?"

Still nothing.

Barry attempted again. "The, gosh, Destroyers?"

Harvey scratched at something on this nose.

"Mike, you wanna take a shot at this?" Barry said
and handed me the paper.

Anyone with this much patience and an electrified
floor probably didn't appreciate Barry's inability to

read his own words, so I decided to take a more direct approach. "Harvey," I said, "we're here because I need a plate to counterfeit money from. Is this the right place?"

Harvey pulled a cloth handkerchief from his pants pocket, took off his glasses and then spent a few moments cleaning the lenses, all the while breathing so heavily I thought he was having a stroke. When the glasses were finally clean enough, he put them back on and stared at me with something like recognition. It was a look I'd seen many times before, just in a different package, and usually not in a trophy store.

"Marines?" he said.

"Rangers," I said.

"CIA?"

"No," I said.

"No?"

"Not officially, no," I said.

"You lose your pension or something?"

"Something," I said.

"You going to pay someone to blow up a government building or fund a terrorist cell?"

"No," I said.

"You usually work for people like Barry?"

"*For?* No. Barry and I have some mutual interests. In this case, specifically, I'm trying to keep him alive."

"In the event it's possible, will you return the plate to me?"

"In the event it's possible, absolutely."

"Are you local?"

"Born and raised right here," I said.

"Back for a visit?"

"You could say I had a burning desire to come home."

Harvey cleared his throat and then spat on the floor. I had the sense maybe he'd found himself in a similar situation in the past.

"Yes," he said. "Well. I don't suppose you have a card or something?"

"My name is Michael Westen," I said.

"Oh. I see."

"Were you ever in Germany?" I said.

"East or West?"

"East."

"For a time," he said.

"There used to be a lovely pastry shop in the Ottersleben district of Magdeburg," I said. "Karl's, I believe it was called. You ever get there?"

"Delectable!" Harvey smacked his lips. Karl's was a drop spot for American and British spies for about fifteen years. If you did time in East Germany, you had yourself a few pastries at Karl's. "Wait here," Harvey said, and disappeared back through the doors.

Barry began to say something, but I put a hand up over his mouth. "Don't speak," I said.

A few moments later, Harvey appeared holding a chromium plate. It looked to weigh about fifty pounds, which meant either Harvey was in surprisingly good shape underneath the dust or he'd spent a lot of years lugging heavy plating. "Just the twenties?" he asked.

"The twenties will be fine," I said.

He pulled out his handkerchief again and wiped off his face and then he nodded at me. I nodded back.

And then I picked up the plate and made my way out of the store, with Barry trailing behind me.

"What just happened?" Barry asked once we were back in my car.

"I'm going to guess that old Harvey was a spook," I said. "Probably still is."

"You recognize him from the Masonic Temple or something?"

"His floor was electrified, Barry," I said. "You didn't notice that?"

"No," Barry said. "I don't even know what an electrified floor looks like."

"The only other time I've seen it in a domestic situation was in a house in Belarus owned by a former Soviet commissar. It's not a standard upgrade."

"And he just gave you the plate because you both know the secret handshake and had eaten at the same pastry shop?"

"Something like that."

"You gave him your name."

"It's all a man's worth these days," I said.

"Do you know what a plate like that is worth on the black market?"

"Barry," I said, "I told him I'd return it if I could, and I mean to do that."

"I'm just saying," Barry said, "that you and I could both be very wealthy men. I'd be willing to split any profit with you sixty-forty, and understand that extra ten percent on my end would be my standard finder's fee."

"Barry," I said.

"Just letting you know it's an option." We drove in silence for a few moments, until Barry said, "A guy like him, what's he doing running a trophy shop?"

"You said yourself that everyone needs a day job, Barry."

"An electrified floor?"

"Yes."

"So if he wanted to, he could flip a switch and sizzle everyone?"

"That's the idea."

"You have a weird life," Barry said. He was silent for a moment, and then said, as if it had just dawned on him, "Wait. Did you say East Germany?"

"Did I?"

"Didn't the wall come down in, what, 1990?"

"I don't recall."

"So you were there when you were in your teens? You left high school and ended up in East Germany?"

"Barry," I said, "if you ask me any more questions, I'm actually *required* to kill you."

That wasn't strictly true—at least not since I'd been burned—but it's nice to keep your associates guessing.

My cell phone rang. It was Fiona. "Sam is taking Father Eduardo to your mother's, and then he said he was going to check out the plates on the police cruiser," she said. "Am I free to spend the rest of my afternoon shopping, or would you like me to beat Barry some more?"

"Actually," I said, "I think it would be good if you joined Barry and me for a little recon mission."

"Really?"

"Yes," I said. I told Fiona about acquiring the printing plate, a fact she was as excited about as Barry was, which made me concerned that the two of them had more in common than I'm sure Fiona would be comfortable knowing. And then explained to her that I had another move planned. "When Junior's men take over the printing plant, we need to find a way to keep them there and keep them immobilized."

"You could have Sam tell them all about the pilgrims. People always love to hear about that."

"Funny," I said, "but no. I was thinking something along the lines of a chemical agent."

"Mustard gas?"

"Preferably something that won't kill everybody."

"You're never any fun," she said.

"Do you know where we might find ourselves a large quantity of fentanyl?"

"Do you need to stop smoking?"

Fentanyl is what comes on the backside of smoking-cessation patches, but when it's turned into a gas, it's also a very effective chemical for subduing a human being. Problems occur when people don't know just how much gas one might need to use to effectively render a human unconscious (or, in what is often a better outcome, exceptionally relaxed) versus the amount that will kill them, which is what happened in Chechnya, except that the Russians didn't just use fentanyl when they tried to smoke out the terrorists that had overtaken a school; they used a chemical derivative that renders the nervous system obsolete, particularly, as it happened, in the small children who'd been taken hostage.

But dissolve a small amount of fentanyl and the chemical portosyt together, which Lowe's and The Home Depot keep in the garden section in huge cakes to help with the growth of new strains of certain field grasses, and you end up creating a gas that will cause disorientation and drowsiness, followed, usually, by sleep, but that won't turn off your central nervous system. It's the perfect chemical agent to use when putting down a rebellion, provided the rebels don't have gas masks. It's also known to be a very popular party drug in parts of Belgium where, apparently, falling asleep is the height of fun.

"I need to stop the Latin Emperors," I said. "But what I'd really like to do is get them to steal the fentanyl for us."

"Oh, Michael," Fiona said, "I love it when you double-cross people."

"I'm looking for a warehouse," I said. "Something with cameras. Know of any?"

"I just sold some guns to some very nice Australian separatists who were planning several very interesting, nonlethal attacks on their government," she said. "Let me ask them if they have any leads and I'll call you right back."

"Australian separatists?"

"Everyone hates their government, Michael," she said, "not just burned spies."

Usually, planning a heist requires a certain amount of qualitative thinking mixed with just a hint of immorality and a dash of spite. If you're robbing something so large that you actually need to plan a heist versus just walking into a bank with an Uzi, the spite issue is paramount. Most criminals work quickly because they work from need. Out of drug money? Rob a liquor store. Or they work from specific, unreasonable obligations they've made for themselves. Like a billion-dollar pyramid scheme that needs constant attention. But in order to orchestrate a big score, to embark on the sheer amount of planning that goes into a high-level action, a driving personal desire helps keep you excited through the down times.

Sometimes, however, planning a heist comes down to a single word that has bedeviled bad guys since the beginning of time: opportunity. See a truck from Best Buy rolling through your neighborhood? Need a television? Need five televisions? Have a gun and some friends with dollies? You have an opportunity.

I couldn't help but think, as Fiona, Barry and I sat parked across the street from Harding Pharmaceutical Labs of America, that the opportunity to rob Harding glimmered like a diamond. The building was a one-story warehouse structure with a loading dock on the east end and was surrounded by a chain-link fence, atop which stood video cameras. A nice precaution.

There was also a sign that promised an armed response by a private security company, which was also a nice precaution.

When you're staking out a place to rob, it's important to know just what an armed-response sign means. And that means spending some time examining the cars in the parking lot of the place you're considering robbing. If you don't see any security-company cars in the lot, that usually means security isn't on-site, or if they are, they aren't armed. For insurance purposes, most security companies require their armed employees to check in at their offices first, receive their guns and then leave again in a company-owned fleet car.

If the parking lot has an empty space reserved for the security company, that means the security company tends to come by at prescribed intervals, or it means that there's a security guard on duty who also drives around the property, looking for criminals, when he's not sitting behind a desk, reading Harlequin romances. This person might be armed, but it's unlikely, and, nevertheless, if he's not there, it's irrelevant.

The mere sign itself indicates a response, not a presence. If you're savvy, this makes a difference. If you're a crackhead looking to steal a home theater system, it probably doesn't.

Harding had neither a space nor a car in the lot. Employees and visitors each drove into the facility through a big, open driveway that was on either side of the chain-link fence. They'd taken precautions here, but I had a pretty good feeling that's all it was. The building was certainly alarmed, but beyond that, an armed response was likely ten to fifteen minutes away, which was fine, as Harding Pharmaceutical wasn't exactly making nerve gas in their offices.

A simple look at their Web site told me that what the mythical guards were guarding was, in most hands, absolutely nothing of value. They warehoused various "stop smoking" products from a variety of corporate partners who used their fentanyl, but since the chemical wasn't being made in the building—they handled that in lovely Newark, New Jersey—it was merely a shipping port for a variety of Southern locations. The Web site also touted their frozen-storage facilities for products like chlorine dioxide hydrate, a product so volatile and toxic when defrosted that you'd need to be a chemical engineer to make it worthwhile to possess, unless, of course, you intended to bleach wood or process flour.

"How did your Australians find this?" I asked Fiona.

"They needed chlorine dioxide hydrate," she said.

"For what?"

"I don't ask questions," she said.

Sometimes, being a burned spy is actually a blessing.

"They break in?"

"No," she said, "they bought their supplies using a purchase order. They are very organized."

"Barry," I said, "what's the market value of fentanyl?"

"Pure? I could name my price. But if it's just on patches, it's worthless. I'd tell my clients just to go to Target and buy what they want."

"What about, say, half a truck full?" I said.

Barry thought about that for a moment. "Would the truck be included?"

"If need be," I said.

"There could be a profit," he said.

"What if we just needed the truck to be ditched somewhere after they took the product?"

"The truck could be stripped in this scenario?"

"Of course," I said.

"And who gets the money?"

"I thought maybe a donation could be made to Honrado," I said, "and then the rest could go to the charity of your choice."

"The International Barry Appreciation Society is holding a charity dance next month," he said.

"Make some calls," I said. "See if you can get someone ready on a moment's notice."

"I'll be in my office," he said, and then Fiona let him out of the backseat so he could walk down the street and conduct his business. Better I didn't hear him making his connections.

"How many guys you think we'd need to hit this place, get a truck and not get anyone killed?" I asked.

Fi pushed hair from her eyes and exhaled hard. "Michael," she said, "you bring the Latin Emperors here, and someone is going to get hurt. What time were you thinking of doing this?"

"Night," I said.

"So some custodian can get stomped to death?"

"Broad daylight would be a little brazen even for the Latin Emperors. They aren't exactly a tactical force. I need them to leave as much evidence as possible," I said, "but that doesn't include slugs in heads. You have a better idea?"

Fiona watched the delivery bay for a few moments before responding. "You might consider sending a pretty girl over with a problem. See if she can maybe lock someone in a closet."

"Too risky," I said. "We can't have you leaving prints all over the place or appearing on camera. But it's too risky having these knuckleheads out here when something might go wrong. We need a third force."

We spent another few minutes watching the building, until Barry walked back up and Fi let him back into the car. "I've got a guy who is happy to take on this complex project," Barry said.

"Good," I said. "This is a Barry project, right? I'll never see these guys?"

"They're New York Russians," Barry said. "They'll be selling smoking patches on Coney Island before the police have even begun investigating this."

The police.

Sometimes it's the obvious things that make the most sense. I pulled out my phone and called Sam. "Any luck tracking down that plate?" I asked.

"My special powers know no bounds," Sam said. "Or will have no bounds as soon as I meet a friend of mine in a bit."

"So you don't have it?"

"Not yet, no," Sam said. "But it's like all things, Mikey. In due time. Due time."

"It's due time," I said. "If we're going to make this all work out, I need to get that plate confirmed."

"No fear, Mikey. It's going to be like that time we took down that evil criminal mastermind."

"When was that?"

"You know, Mikey, any of the times. I'll call you when it's in hand."

I hung up with Sam and looked back out the window. "You see any police cars roll by since we parked?" I asked Fiona.

"No," she said. "Why would they?"

"Exactly. So it will be a good thing when one pulls up here and tells the night crew there's a problem."

Barry leaned into the front seat. "You got police on your payroll, too?"

"I do now," I said. I put my phone on speaker, dialed another number and waited for someone to pick up.

"Good afternoon, Harding Pharmaceutical. How may I direct your call?"

"Shipping, please," I said.

"One moment," the operator said. "I'll transfer you to Marty Delabate."

Fiona and Barry were quiet, but were clearly puzzled.

The call picked up. "This is Marty."

"Marty," I said, "this is Dan from Newark. How you doing?"

"Good, good," Marty said. If you're going to pretend to be someone else on the telephone, it's usually a good idea to assume an identity that is so common, it's likely the person you're trying to fool will think they're the one with a problem for not knowing precisely who you are.

"How's the season treating you?" I said.

"Fine, fine," Marty said.

"Looking forward to getting down there in the fall," I said. "You know how it is up here."

"Don't I ever," Marty said.

"Listen," I said. "I've got a note here on my desk

about a shipment of patches leaving there on Saturday. That still right?"

"Let me check the system," Marty said.

"Running slow today," I said, "or else I would have gotten on myself."

"It's crawling today," Marty said. "Okay. Let's see. Yeah, we've got a three P.M. headed up north, and then we've got a six P.M. going to shops between Naples and Tarpon Springs."

"That's the one I didn't have," I said. "Okay, great. Thanks a bunch, Marty."

"No problem, Dan," Marty said.

I turned off the phone. "Got any plans for Saturday night, Fi?"

16

Sam hated cop bars. It wasn't personal. He just preferred a bar where you could get something more than
a domestic beer and a shot of Jack Daniel's. And then
there was the issue of the kind of women who fre-
quented cop bars. Not that Sam kept up on all the latest hairstyles for the fairer sex, but he was pretty sure
that teased and crimped hair bleached to the point of
translucence was not being shown anywhere near the
runways these days. And yet sitting along the bar at
Cuffs were three women whose hair looked to be con-
ducting electricity. They weren't bad to look at otherwise, but Sam just didn't care for women who smelled
of Budweiser and Jack Daniel's and whose hair had a
separate area code.

Sam could have lived without hearing "Magic Carpet Ride" for the rest of his natural-born days, too, but
it seemed to be on heavy rotation on Cuffs' jukebox,
having already played three times in the past hour
while he waited for his friend Ross Angel to show up.
Ross wasn't exactly a cop; he was a meter maid. Or, as
his business card said, PARKING ENFORCEMENT OFFICER,

which meant he had a badge and access to the systems Sam periodically needed access for, as well. Sam didn't know Ross well—he'd been introduced to him by another friend, this one at the DMV, after Ross had a small problem with a loan shark over some gambling debts. It wasn't a huge debt—$500—but the shark was starting to make threats, and Ross couldn't very well call the cops. So Sam did what he could to help the poor bastard—which, in this case, just meant that Sam dug deep and paid off the shark. Now Ross owed him a periodic favor, one low enough on the totem pole that Ross could be of any use at all, which meant Sam mostly used him to help parking tickets disappear. Still, he felt pretty confident Ross could come through on something a bit larger, like the identity of the cop who drove the cruiser Fi spotted. But now Sam was worried, since Ross had chosen to meet at Cuffs, which meant his judgment had to be impaired.

The jukebox spit out the opening strains of "Back in Black"—easily the fifth AC/DC song played in the past hour, too—just as Ross finally entered the bar. Sam waved his bottle of Bud Light at him, and Ross sidled over the long way, making sure to pause by the bar for quick conversation with the ladies before sitting down.

"You a regular here?" Sam asked.

"No, no," Ross said. "They got trivia here every Tuesday, so I come in for that periodically. And on Wednesdays and Fridays they got half-priced wings, so I tend to drop by then, if I'm around. And Mondays they got a pretty chill DJ. Saturday and Sunday, if they got a game on, I might drop by. But that's it."

Meter maids, Sam thought, spent so much of their lives accounting for time that, apparently, they just didn't have a good sense of it in their personal lives. Either that or Ross was just a strange, strange man.

"Any luck with my errand?" Sam asked.

Ross put a finger over his lips and then looked over both of his shoulders. Because nothing conveys secrecy better than shushing someone and then looking over your shoulder. "You know where we are?" he asked.

"Yeah," Sam said, "you picked the place."

"I thought if we were here, no one would think it was suspicious that we were together."

Oddly, Ross' explanation actually made a bit of sense, but was also entirely senseless. "Listen," Sam said, "top secret mission here, Ross. Lives are at stake. Communists could be landing on our shores at any moment. So, do you have a name for that plate or not?"

Ross reached into his pocket and pulled out a slip of paper and handed it to Sam. "You didn't get this from me." It was as if everything Ross said was cribbed from a bad crime novel. It didn't surprise Sam. He suspected Ross had a lot of free time to read. "Unless there's a commendation coming. If there's some hero shit going down, it would be fine if you mentioned me. Just trying to get a leg up in the force, you know?"

"I know," Sam said. "If we get before the Hall of Justice with this, I'll recommend you immediately be made an honorary Superfriend."

Sam unfolded the paper and saw the cop's name: Pedro "Peter" Prieto. A pretty common Cuban name.

He had to hope that Ross' own latent desire to be a detective got the better of him and caused him to do some legwork.

"What do you know about this guy?"

"He writes off a lot of minor tickets," Ross said. "He's what we call a neighborhood guy. Everyone he grew up with comes to his house when they have a fix-it ticket or a parking ticket. Just one of those things."

Just one of those things. Of course, if you happened to be wanted for some larger crime and got a fix-it ticket, it would help to have someone there to write it off. "What's his beat?"

"Little Havana, mostly. I don't know much about him except for his daily logs I pulled. He does some traffic pickups over by the Orange Bowl, too. We don't exactly hang out. Cops and Parking Enforcement aren't on the same feed line, but I see him here and there and he's come to me with a couple favors over the years. You'd be surprised how much a ticket for an illegally lowered car can be, seeing as they mount up. That's one thing I've never understood. Lowering your car. Why do that?"

"To look cool," Sam said.

"Really?"

Sam wanted to say, "No, they do it to look like assholes," but decided against it. Let the poor man live in blissful ignorance. "This Prieto," he said, "how old is he?"

"Thirty? Thirty-five? Why?"

"Helping out neighborhood guys, that's something you do when you're not sure you want to be a cop long term. But get into your thirties? That's your career. Why jeopardize that for some kid on the streets?"

"Maybe he's cultivating confidential informants?"

Sam was going to guess that Ross watched a lot of *Law & Order*. Who ever called a snitch a confidential informant? "He's not working major crimes, is he?" Sam said.

"No," Ross said, "more like stolen bicycles and petty robbery. Pick up a hooker every now and then. That would be my guess. I see him on the street, he's just rollin' most of the time. You know, I'm trying to get into the police academy. Did I tell you that before?"

"No," Sam said.

"I just want to be a cop that no one has any issues with, right? Like, just a good person."

Interesting.

"Any rumors about him being gang affiliated?" Sam said.

"Everyone who grew up in Little Havana is gang affiliated in one way or another," he said. "But he's with the good guys now."

"If that's true," Sam said, "why didn't you have some moral objection giving me his information?" Sam hated to play hardball with Ross, but he felt like the meter maid wasn't giving the full story. That was the downside of dealing with sources: Sometimes they just don't want to give up what they know.

Ross drummed his fingers on the table. "Sweet Home Alabama" started on the jukebox and for a couple minutes Ross seemed to get lost in the music, but Sam was pretty sure he was trying to figure out how to say something he didn't want to say. "You know what's crazy?" Ross said. "Neil Young and the guys in Skynyrd? They were actually good friends. So everyone hears this song and thinks the guys in Skynyrd hate him for all that 'Southern Man, don't need him 'round' shit, but it's not true."

"Really?" Sam said, thinking, Okay, now what?

"Yeah," Ross said. "It was just hype. Something to sell records."

"I guess sometimes that's the case," Sam said. "Things aren't what they appear."

Ross drummed his fingers again and then stopped and looked around the bar one more time. "The thing is," Ross said, "people in Miami, you know, everyone has a past. So I had a friend of mine in the juvenile division just run a search on Pedro Prieto, you know, see if anything popped, because I'm thinking if you wanted his information for something, it must be some bad news. And, you know, you helped with that problem and I can't repay you enough. You know, that was some Donnie Brasco stuff you did."

Every meter maid wanted to be a cop, Sam knew, and every cop kind of wanted to be either a hitman or a mafia don, so when Sam paid off the shark, he went back and told Ross he went all the way to the top of Miami's biggest crime family and informed him that Ross was a protected guy and to lay off. It was the kind of stupid story someone would believe only when they didn't want to possibly imagine the path of least resistance—in this case, paying off the debt—but it also served their relationship well. Big Bad Sam knew mob bosses! In this case, though, that reputation meant Ross ended up sticking his own neck out. It was more admirable than Sam could have imagined.

"He's been involved in some shady things," Sam said. "Let's just say he's part of the problem in the United States today." Ross' eyes got wide for a moment, and Sam could almost hear Ross screaming Conspiracy! in his mind. "Let's just say, he's no friend to the hardworking, lunch-pail Americans I think we both look up to."

Ross nodded in agreement, though Sam suspected Ross ate most of his lunches at Chick-fil-A.

"Well," Ross said, "listen to this. When he was thirteen, he got picked up for running drugs for the Latin Emperors. Just minor stuff. A little weed. Misdemeanor stuff. He went to college, passed all his exams, and Miami PD, you know, they want guys who know the law of the land. But knowing how serious this might be, in light of your involvement, I poked back on some fix-it tickets and a few parking jobs in the last couple months and found a lot of crooked guys there, Sam."

That was a good piece of information . . . but also so juicy Sam had to make sure Ross understood it wasn't something he could pass onto anyone else, no matter how many times they made him listen to "Magic Carpet Ride" as torture.

"I'm sure it's nothing," Sam said. "Most of these guys, Ross, they just want to feel respected and tough.

It's not enough that they are the law of the land, my friend, they want people to *need* them, too. It's a sign of narcissism. But you know what? It's human. I'm sure it's all a big misunderstanding." He paused and let that sink into Ross' mind. He pondered, adding, "These are not the droids you're looking for" into the conversation, just to give it a little context, but felt like Ross might not grasp the allusion. "Anyway," Sam continued, "this helps with what I'm looking into. Just a hit-and-run case. One of those things that sticks in my craw, you understand, makes me distrust my fellow man."

Ross looked relieved. "That's good," he said. "Because, you know, we have a code of silence and, well, I feel weird breaking it. But a hit-and-run, that's low down."

"Meter maids have a code of silence?" Sam said.

"Law enforcement in general," he said. "You got a badge. You keep your mouth closed."

"That's good to know," Sam said, but didn't bother to inform him that not only had he talked, but so had his guy in juvie, too. Maybe it was a code of occasional silence. He pocketed the piece of paper and stood up to leave. It was getting late in the afternoon, and that meant more cops, more women with teased hair and more Steppenwolf on the hi-fi, as it were.

"You don't wanna stick around? See if maybe we can get a few of these ladies to dance?"

"Next time," Sam said.

"And, Sam, just hypothetically," Ross said. "If I happened to run into trouble with someone in the gambling trade again, would you be amenable to my calling you for some advice?"

"Here's my advice," Sam said. "Stop betting on sports."

"It was strictly hypothetical," Ross said.

"Good luck on the academy," Sam said, and then walked outside, certain he'd be hearing from him as soon as football season started again. He made a mental note to put aside a few hundred dollars just in case, of course, he needed to help his friend.

Though, the more Sam thought about it, the more he thought that maybe the best way to help Ross would be to give him an in on some actual police work. If things worked out, maybe he'd be able to do just that.

Normally, Sam preferred to do his own legwork so that he could get a definitive answer to his questions. Depending on people like Ross always ended with more ancillary work than he really wanted to handle because of the nature of the source. He trusted Ross. Was sure Ross had given him nothing but the straight dope, but even still, old Sam liked to depend on his eyes for things.

So after he left the bar, Sam drove down to one of his favorite spots in Little Havana—a restaurant called Ozzie's that sold the absolute best plantains north of Cuba—and enjoyed a leisurely meal outside, to see what the police presence was like. There were a few squad cars that came through periodically, which wasn't unusual for the area, but none of them were Prieto's.

Ozzie's was considered a neutral spot, on account of the food and the fact that Ozzie himself was still behind the counter, eighty years old and known to be one of the sweetest men alive. Well, sweet provided you didn't make him pull his sawed-off shotgun from beneath the counter. His restaurant was given the ultimate respect: There wasn't a single tag on the outside walls, nothing even on the sidewalk.

If something jumped off at Ozzie's, it was usually some tourist making a complaint about his pork chop or some such thing. Ozzie didn't care much for people complaining about his food, and that included the grave offense of asking for salt. But gangs? No. They liked his food, too, and Sam could even remember an occasion when he'd dined at the counter between a Crip and a Blood who had both decided to make the drive in for some lunch, and found themselves separated only by an ex-Navy SEAL. Sweet, really.

If Peter Prieto was what he appeared to be, he'd be the first responder to any Latin Emperor situation here on hallowed ground. So, after his meal, Sam walked back to his car and made a call to 911. "There's about fifteen Latin Emperors getting ready to storm Ozzie's in Little Havana. Yeah. I'm sure. I just saw them out front with guns and everything. Heard one of them say it was time Ozzie got his for giving his mama congestive heart failure. My name? Aldrich Rosenberg."

Sam closed his phone, pulled out the SIM card and replaced it with another, and then sat back, swallowed a Tums—thanks to Ozzie's spice predilection—and waited for the sirens to begin wailing.

Four minutes later, a cruiser came screeching down the block but with no siren. Sam sat up and took notice. The car came to a halt in front of Ozzie's, and Sam made note of the car number and plate, and then when Peter Prieto hopped out, he wasn't all that surprised. Tall and lean, Prieto moved like a cat when he stepped from the car, all coiled energy and spring—he was looking for something, anything, but also seemed nervous. He didn't pull out his gun and he didn't even bother to go inside Ozzie's. He just swept the area quickly, checked the ground a couple of times and, presumably, upon seeing nothing amiss, immediately got back into his car and pulled away from the curb.

Sam followed him around the block and watched as the cop parked his car beside a FedEx truck idling beside a CVS pharmacy, but with an easy view of Ozzie's. Sam parked in the same lot and pretended to be very busy with the machinations of his phone, but really was just watching to see what Prieto was seeing.

It wasn't until three more cop cars pulled up, sirens blaring, that Prieto finally backed up his cruiser and drove away. Sam had a pretty good idea what was going to happen next, so he kept his vigil in the parking lot. Sure enough, a few seconds later, Prieto's cruiser came screeching around the corner, siren blaring.

You sneaky bastard, Sam thought. He opened his phone and called Michael. "Mikey," he said, "we have ourselves a company cop."

17

When you're a spy, it's bad business to put your faith in anything you can't control. Everyone and everything becomes suspect.

Whom do you trust?

Yourself and maybe your gun, but even your gun can run out of bullets or jam.

When you're a spy, a day might come when your government disowns you, your partners turn out to be your enemies and the world you once knew to be true ends up being a terrible, terrible lie.

Your only opportunity for survival then is what exists between your ears. That means tamping down impulsive behavior in favor of well-planned counteraction. Can't shoot your gun? Then use it as a blunt-force weapon. Or trade it for money or shelter or food, because if there is one thing that is true, it's that there's always a market for a gun. And there's no more lethal weapon than a man who is willing to wait for someone else to make a mistake.

This was wisdom I was well acquainted with and, as I explained to Father Eduardo Santiago, a strategy that would work well for us. All he had to do was wait, and Junior would trip up and we'd be ready to pounce. In the meantime, we'd put into place all of the nets that would ensnare his fall.

It took three days of waiting. Three days of watching Junior's every movement in his office. Three days of listening to his every phone call. Three days of reading his e-mails.

And three days of me actually going into an office every day, which was far more taxing than I could have ever imagined. Each morning, I picked up Eduardo from my mother's and drove him to his office, where he conducted his business as usual. This meant keeping all of his appointments, which typically started at eight A.M. (which automatically excluded Sam from duty).

Father Eduardo taped his part for the community news program on Thursday morning, spent Thursday afternoon having lunch with two city councilmen who wanted his opinion on a new land deal that would give jobs to inner-city kids and on Thursday night, it was a charity dinner where he served as the MC. And then there was the actual managing of the day-to-day business of Honrado and the business of being a priest: the café, the auto shop, the job placement services, the people who need not just a word with you, but a lifetime with you.

And then it was Friday.

For three days, Father Eduardo conducted this business with me standing very near to him.

"He is writing a story on me for a magazine in Nevada," he told the news program people and the charity organizers who noticed my presence.

"He is here to oversee the architectural development of our new buildings," he told the Honrado employees who noticed me in his office day and night.

"He is here to protect me," he told himself and, when Leticia called Fiona, it's what I told her to repeat. It was Saturday morning and Father Eduardo was at my loft, along with Sam and Fiona, while we piled through all our surveillance of Junior. Barry was busy upstairs snoring through the important discovery process, which was fine. There was plenty of incriminating evidence, none of which Barry needed to see or hear, since a lot of it mentioned how they were going to kill him as soon as they had the opportunity. My mother had been kind enough to offer him a few of her horse tranquilizers to help him calm his jitters, and now he was on hour number eleven of sleep. We'd wake him when we needed him, which would be soon, as we had to make our moves today.

Saturday was to be a big day: Barry and Sam would train Junior's men on how to operate the printing press and utilize the money plate. Sam had no actual facility with this skill set, but sort of wanted to learn, and also happened to be pretty good about shooting people who needed to be shot . . . even if he'd sworn to Father Eduardo that he'd only shoot them with a paintball gun. And that meant today would also be the day I had Junior's men pull the job I wanted done at Harding Pharmaceutical, so that by Sunday, if everything worked according to plan, Father Eduardo might just have his day of worship.

But then Leticia called.

She'd been missing since Sam and I showed up to Honrado three days earlier, which meant she likely saw her boyfriend Killa and Junior arriving in one condition and leaving in a slightly different version, and knew that this might be her only opportunity to steal away with her son. But she could only go so far—a fact Fiona had predicted too well, so that when Leticia phoned her, she wasn't all that surprised.

After she answered the call, Fi put her hand over the phone and whispered, "It's Leticia."

"She'll want to talk to you," I said to Father Eduardo. "You ready for that?"

"Yes," he said.

"Let her know Father Eduardo wants to speak to her," I said to Fiona. "And make sure she knows he's not angry with her."

Fi spoke with Leticia for just a few moments and explained to her what had probably grown to be obvious: it wasn't an accident that they'd met up that afternoon earlier in the week, and that it was all part of a larger plan to disrupt a conspiracy she'd been unwittingly pressed into, one best explained by Father Eduardo. Fiona handed him the phone and he spoke with the girl as calmly as possible.

"They are here to protect me," he said to Leticia. "They are here to protect you and your son. Whatever you might have heard that is the contrary is rumor and innuendo. They will protect my brother, too, if it comes to it."

Father Eduardo looked at me when he said that. It wasn't something I was entirely certain was possible, not because it was physically impossible, but because it might be morally and ethically impossible. I'd already hobbled him, which would likely preclude him from taking part in anything involving standing for a few weeks, effectively keeping off the production line for the money and out of the heist, too. The rest? That would have to be up to him.

But, in that particular moment, there wasn't a lot of space for nuanced thought. I just nodded my assent.

"Pardon me," Father Eduardo said to us, "but I need some privacy to continue this conversation. I'm going to continue this call outside."

We waited for Father Eduardo to step outside before we continued our previous conversation—which was just how we were going to position Junior to fail.

"You think he'll be able to keep it together?" Sam asked.

"Right now? Yes," I said. "If we keep him out of the lines of fire, he'll be fine. But when we turn this information over to the authorities, and they call Father Eduardo as a witness? Well, that will be up to him. But my feeling is that he's led a dual life before. A little white lie here and there to the police will be fine."

The bugging of Junior's office, just over the course of three days, had provided all the information needed to get Junior put back in prison and people like Peter Prieto into prison for the first time. There were phone calls, all recorded, between Junior and Peter. There were e-mails between Junior and "clients" in other countries ensuring delivery of product as soon as production was resecured. There was video of all of this, too.

And Sam had gone back to the Ace after our first meeting with Junior and managed to pick up the two missing fingers, too. Physical evidence is always a bonus.

"What's our move?" Fiona asked.

"Our first one is to get Junior's people positioned," I said. I put my cell phone on speaker and called Junior at his office. Just like every other office drone, he answered on the third ring.

"What do you want?" he said.

"Is that how you greet a business partner?"

"We are not partners," he said. "You wouldn't happen to know where Killa's son is, would you?"

"Why would you ask me that?"

"Because he and his mother disappeared on the same day you showed up," he said.

"Let's just say," I said, "that maybe I'm more careful than you are."

There was silence on the other end of the line, but I could tell that Junior was trying to contain his anger. He wasn't the kind of guy prone to long, contemplative silences.

"What do you want?" he said again.

"I need your guys," I said. "And your cop."

"When?"

"Tonight," I said. "There's a shipment leaving Harding Pharmaceutical at six P.M. that I'd like to own."

This got Junior's attention. "What is it?"

I decided being honest was the best policy. "About a thousand stop-smoking patches."

"There a market for that?"

"There is in Bolivia," I said, thinking that a quarter century in prison might have made Junior a little dim on the black markets and geography. Or where people still smoked.

"What's my cut?"

"You don't get a cut," I said. "It's the price of doing business at Honrado. We discussed this right before my friend choked you out with her whip."

"Change of rules," Junior said.

"You don't make the rules," I said.

"You think I'm stupid? I spent some time looking into you, Mr. Solo," he said. "You don't exist."

"And yet here I am, talking to you on the phone."

"You think you're the only person who can run a license plate?"

I looked at Sam. He was the man in charge of making sure I had plates on the Charger that couldn't be traced back to anything prudent. It had been so long since we'd changed them that I had no idea whom or what they belonged to. I gave Sam a look that I hope conveyed this. He just shrugged.

"I trust that Officer Prieto can do all sorts of services for you," I said. "But do you think I'm the type of person who just rolls up into the DMV and registers my ride? You better have your man dig deeper."

Junior sighed. It was an odd sound. You never want to think of terribly menacing people feeling resigned. It ruins your idea of ultimate evil on all levels.

"We either start understanding each other on a better business level or one of us is going to die," Junior said.

"Are you speaking euphemistically?"

"I'm speaking bullets to heads," he said.

I laughed. It wasn't a funny thing to be hearing, but it's always nice to give psychopaths reason to believe you're just as crazy as they are. "I like how you think, Junior," I said. "Look, we can only both bleed this whale for so long and then we'll have to fight for his oil and blubber once he's dead; that's what I'm hearing. So why don't we do this. You send your guys and your cop over to Harding Pharmaceutical this evening, grab the truck, don't kill anyone in the process, and in good faith, I'll give you forty percent of my take."

"Fifty percent."

"What are you willing to give me to get fifty percent of a score you wouldn't even know about without me?"

"You can keep the girl. What's her name? Leticia. She's yours. But my man wants his kid. That's Latin Emperor property."

Fiona was already angry, but this last demand got her ready to blow. So I did the only thing I could do. "Deal," I said. "Why don't you and me go to the job tonight, too. Make it a real gentlemen's agreement, and that way I can make sure none of your boys goes crazy and caps someone and then we both lose."

"When do we get the kid?"

"Sunday morning," I said. "I've got buyers ready tonight. They'll inspect the truck, see if it's all kosher, we'll get paid and we'll make the trade in the morning at Honrado—that way no one goes gun crazy. No one gets cut. Father and son are together. We all go get some Jesus together, maybe. Make it real easy. And I've got one less crying kid to worry about. You ever listen to a kid cry for an entire night? And then there was the food he ate. You can have him, Junior. You can have him."

Junior considered all of this. "Where do we meet tonight?"

I told him to meet me a few blocks from Harding at four forty-five. "The truck is scheduled to leave at six," I said. "I want you to send Officer Prieto there to clear out the building well before then. Tell them there's a bomb threat."

"I don't tell him what to do," Junior said.

"You won't. I will. He can tell them whatever he wants. Just get the people out. I don't trust that your boys won't stomp the shit out of someone just for kicks."

"Then what?"

"You just make sure everyone's out of the facility, and then have your boys take the truck from the loading dock. Your boys know how to steal cars, right?"

"I'll find someone," he said.

"Be good if they knew how to drive a truck," I said. "You got any kind of program in the Latin Emperors that teaches manual-transmission driving?"

"Why don't you just do this yourself?"

"Because I don't trust that you wouldn't have your officer Prieto arrest me. Or shoot me. And we're a team, Junior. Remember?"

"Where do I tell them to take the truck?"

"Bring it to the back of Honrado," I said. "Park it

next to loading bay by the press. One of my people will be waiting. The truck doesn't show up, you don't get your money plate."

"How much is this job worth to you?"

This I had no idea about, so I came up with a number that would make Junior interested. "Fifty g's, easy. Maybe more. And this is real money. Not your photocopies."

"Four forty-five," he said and hung up.

Leaving the planning and execution of the job to Junior meant that I could keep my hands clean. But it also meant that there was a better chance Officer Prieto wouldn't let anything go wrong.

Dealing with Fiona would be enough for me to handle.

"Michael," Fiona said, "what are you thinking? You can't give them Leticia's son!"

"I'm not going to," I said. "But we just got him on tape agreeing to buy a child. Well, actually, he's trading a child. Either way, it's a crime."

"Oh," Sam said, "you're a fast one, Mr. Westen."

"I'm trying my best," I said. "You want to tell me where they traced my license plate to?"

"Well, if my memory serves me correctly here, he just traced your existence back to a wrecked Dodge Charger I saw out at the dump a few months back."

"No idea who owned the car?"

"I ran the plates, and they came back as being owned by a gentleman named Cy Rosencrantz, who currently resides in the Shayna Grove Assisted Living Facility in Ventura, California. I think you're safe."

"That's fine work there, Sam."

"There's only one of me," he said.

Father Eduardo came back inside the loft then and handed Fiona back her phone.

"Where is she?" I asked.

"She's got a homegirl lives near Coral Springs. So she's there for right now."

"She going to stay there?"

"You can't tell with these girls," he said. "All she knows is the streets. I've tried to help get them a new life, but when things get tough, they slip back into what they know. She's scared, but she understands the situation now. And she's been forgiven for what she's done. That helps."

"Look," I said, "tonight it's going to happen. Either we'll have the Latin Emperors where we need them— and that means Junior, too—or people are going to start dying. Junior's about three steps behind right now, but he's gaining speed."

I didn't bother to tell him about his demands, which showed he was emboldened now, and which also showed he was beginning to get close to the truth of who we were and what our intentions were. It helped to have a cop on the payroll for these purposes.

"What do I do?"

"Today," I said, "you go into your church and you do your job. We'll tell you if and when you need to move."

"What are you going to do?" he said.

"All due respect, Father, if I told you, it would put you into a bad position," I said.

"With the law?"

"With the law, with God, probably with yourself. Just know no one's getting killed on my watch, and all crimes committed are for a greater good."

Father Eduardo seemed dubious about my claims, but wasn't in much of a position to argue. "What about my brother?"

"That will be up to him," I said. "If I can keep him out of the endgame, I will. But no promises. If he's at the plant tonight when Sam and Barry start running the money with Junior's men, we can see if we can pull him out. That's the best I can offer, because I'm not going to look for him."

"Fine," Father Eduardo said. "It will have to be." He looked at his watch. "I need to get to the church. We're having a bake sale today."

"Sam's going to go with you to work today while I do all that greater-good stuff."

"I'm handy at a bake sale," Sam said. "And if you have any overflow of people needing holy advice, I'm happy to help in that capacity, too."

Father Eduardo still looked distressed, but agreed because he had to. He and Sam started to make their way for the door. "Wait," I said. "Sam, are you armed?"

"No, Mikey. I know the rules."

"Sam," I said, "are you armed?"

"I have a .22 on me. It would hardly do any damage," he said. He turned to Father Eduardo. "Little more than a pellet gun, really."

"No guns," Father Eduardo said.

I walked upstairs and came back down with two

paintball markers and handed them both to Sam. "Both are filled with pepper spray," I said. "Try not to shoot anyone at the bake sale."

Through the window, I watched Sam and Father Eduardo drive away. In any other circumstance, they'd make for enemies, but here they were, in the same car, going to church. You never know when the occupied will rise up and become the enemy, and when the enemy will become the ally.

"Fi," I said, "why don't you make Barry's life complete and wake him up from his golden slumber?"

"Does this involve me kicking him?"

"He's got work to do today. Let's try to keep his internal injuries to a minimum," I said.

So Fiona tramped up the stairs to the top of the loft, where Barry was still snoring away, and shouted "Alarm!"

One thing about Fiona: She can be subtle when she wants to be. It's just an issue of how often she wants to be anything but what she is.

While Fiona made Barry alert, I went about assembling what we'd need to either convict, imprison or kill Junior Gonzalez. There's no joy in this sort of work, the gathering of evidence to ruin a person, but if you're willing to do the crime, as the adage should say, you have to be willing to be outsmarted by a spy.

When working with someone for the first time, it's wise to let them feel like they have the freedom to express themselves without fear of rebuke. So when Fiona and I arrived at the meet-up spot with Junior that evening—the parking lot of a Steak-N-Shake a few blocks from the industrial park that housed Harding Pharmaceutical—I decided not to get angry with the man if he reacted poorly to anything.

Like, say, the presence of Fiona.

"You didn't tell me you were bringing your poodle with you," Junior said. He sat at one of the outdoor tables with a half-eaten burger and a pile of fries in front of him. He took a sip from his milkshake and then set it down beside his plate of food. The shake probably made his throat feel better.

"I thought it would be good for you two to settle your differences. In the spirit of teamwork, of course." I motioned to the other seats around his table. "Mind if we join you?"

"Yes," he said. "I chose to sit outside to avoid the noise inside."

We sat down, anyway.

Inside the restaurant, a little girl's birthday was in full swing. There must have been twenty kids running rampant. Even outside, the high-pitched squeals were enough to make me want to swear off sex permanently.

"My friend has something to say to you," I said.

"I am truly sorry for choking you with my whip," Fiona said. "Though there are places in this world where the service you received would be the culmination of a lovely night out. It's all about how you appreciate the finer things."

Junior grunted. "Save it," he said.

"So, we can't be friends?" Fiona said.

"I don't deal with you," he said. "Just Mr. Rosencrantz."

"I told you," I said. "You have to dig if you want the truth, Junior. I didn't buy my security at Staples, like you did. And maybe, if we become good friends after tonight, I'll just show you my passport. And next thing you know, we'll be having Thanksgiving dinner together. Your family of gangsters. My family at the Shayna Grove Assisted Living Facility. It will be lovely."

Junior made that grunting noise again. "Why'd you pick this place to meet?" he asked.

"I like the fries," I said.

"When I was in the joint," he said, "I used to have dreams about this place."

"Then you should be happy," I said.

"Funny thing is," he said, "all those years, and when I got out, I forgot to come to this place."

"Too wrapped up in your little plans for revenge?" Fiona said.

Junior actually smiled. I think we might have been having a moment of some kind. "Just happy to cook for myself again. You get a little tired of burgers and fries in prison."

"You do have a lovely kitchen in your house," Fiona said.

Junior checked his watch, but didn't say anything.

"You late for something?" I asked.

"I asked a friend of mine to stop by, too," he said. "You have a problem with that?"

"No," I said. "Any friend of yours is a friend of mine."

"We'll see," he said, and just then a police cruiser, followed by a tow truck, pulled into the lot beside my Charger. "You may not want to tell me who you are, but I'm going to bet that you have fingerprints on file somewhere. I got to watch a lot of *CSI* in prison, so I asked *my friend* Officer Prieto to get a few . . . what do they call them? Latents?"

I had to hold myself back from clapping. It was a great move by Junior. Instead, I said, "Junior, if you attempt to move my car without using the key? It will blow up."

"You bluff."

"One way of finding out," I said. "But from this distance? We'll all be dead, too. So if you don't mind, I'm going to go behind the building. I'll pop inside and see if I can get the birthday party to cower beneath the tables."

Officer Prieto and the tow-truck driver stood behind my car, presumably waiting for some sign from Junior. He didn't make any, so I went ahead and decided to rectify the situation on my own. "Just tell *our friend* that I'm happy to give him my prints."

The advantage of being a covert operative, and one that has had certain nebulous organizations proctoring his work recently, is that I happen to know my prints aren't in the system. Or if my prints are in the system, they don't come up as belonging to Michael Westen.

But Fiona's just might be. Not that she couldn't handle herself, but it probably wouldn't do anyone any good to have certain government agencies aware that she was in town.

Junior stood up and whistled. Officer Prieto and the tow-truck driver exchanged a few words, and then the truck drove off. "Give me a minute," Junior said, and started off toward the policeman.

I got up from the table when Junior was far enough away that he couldn't hear me. "Here," I said. I handed her my phone. "Take some candid photos for our memory book, won't you?"

"Love to," she said.

"Keep my face out."

"That officer is very handsome," she said. "I'll focus on him."

"Good," I said. "When I go over, you wait here. But keep snapping photos. You never know when we'll want to relive this experience."

"That was a smarter move than I would have anticipated," Fiona said. "The fingerprints? The car? Very savvy."

"He's had a lot of time to think of great ideas."

"Are you sure you'll be fine?"

"What's the worst that can happen—he finds out I'm a spy? Spy trumps local cop every day."

"I hazard to remind you that you're not a spy anymore," she said.

"You know what I mean."

Officer Prieto dipped into his car and came back out with something small and square. Probably an ink pad. Junior waved me over.

"I'm allowed to use a real gun here, right?"

"Try not to shoot the kids," I said.

By the time I reached the Charger, Junior and the

cop were already back in conversation. "You must be the crooked cop," I said. I extended my hand to shake, but instead, Officer Prieto pressed my fingers into the ink pad and then onto a piece of paper. He did it in under ten seconds. It was fairly impressive. Since I knew it was coming, and since I thought maiming a cop would be more trouble than I needed that afternoon, I opted not to stop the process by breaking his arm in two. All that, and I don't even think Prieto made eye contact with me, though it was hard to tell, since he wore mirrored aviator glasses.

"You got anything to hide?" Officer Prieto said.

"I'm a criminal mastermind," I said, "but that's probably pretty apparent. Other than that, you now have all the clues you need to my existence."

"I find out you're not who you say you are, I'll bring your whole world down," he said.

"Yeah," I said. "Good luck with that. I can tell you right now, I'm not really Cy Rosencrantz."

The three of us stood there for a moment without saying anything. It was a nice form of posturing, one usually only seen in the wild. I decided to wait it out a few moments longer and then said, "You done?"

"A real joker here," Prieto said.

"I'm just concerned that we have a job about to jump off, and you're trying to stare me down. Either you're a crooked cop or you're not. If you're not, just go on and run my prints. If you are, you need to decide how you're going to get everyone out of that warehouse in the next twenty minutes or so."

Prieto reached into his pocket and pulled out a cell

phone and a phone number. "You want some diversion? You make the call," he said, and gave me the cell. "My voice isn't appearing on anything. I'll do my job, but you do yours."

I examined the phone. It looked like a burner, but I wasn't taking any chances. I went into the Charger and took out one of my own disposables from the glove box. "I come prepared," I said, and then dialed the number.

"Harding Pharma, this is Dan."

Huh. Dan was a good choice.

"Dan," I said, "this is Kirk Peterson from Diagnostic Partners. You in the warehouse?"

"Yes, sir."

"We've got a report here that the cooling systems are going nuts there. What do you have?"

"Uh, well, I'm just on duty for the loading dock, sir. You got the loading dock on the line."

"Then I need someone in the lab," I said.

"No one like that here. It's a Saturday."

"Son," I said, "I'm going to make your life real simple for you. You're about fifteen minutes from a stage-three collapse in the CDH units. Who's on call?"

"Uh, uh," he said. Panic. It makes you sputter.

"Settle down, son," I said. "Just calmly get everyone out of the dock. I got a call in to the police. They're on their way."

"We've got a truck leaving in the hour," he said.

"Leave it," I said. "And get your ass out of there, son. Police will be on-site in a few minutes. God help you all if this gets into the water."

I clicked the phone off, took out the SIM card, and then crushed it on the pavement.

Junior and Prieto just stared at me.

"I told you," I said, "you're dealing with a criminal mastermind. So, why don't you get moving there, Officer Friendly, before someone gets smart and starts actually thinking over there at the warehouse?"

Officer Prieto got into his car without saying a word and drove off. Within a few seconds, we could hear his siren.

"Nice work," Junior said. He extended his hand.

Old friends. That's what we were. I took his hand and said, "You ever try to corner me like that again, and I'll torture you to death in a way that will make your ancestors hurt. We got a deal, hoss?" Junior said nothing. "Great." I patted his hand lightly. "Good talk."

I waved Fiona over. She sashayed across the parking lot, and when she got close to Junior, she gave him one of those smiles she normally reserves for men she's about to hurt. "Always a pleasure," she said, and then she got into the car.

I looked at my watch. "If that truck isn't at Honrado within the hour, I'll assume you want that ancestor thing early."

When we drove off, Junior was still standing in the middle of the parking lot, looking for all the world like a man without a country.

18

The final execution of a counterinsurgency plan is to not just defeat the insurgency, but cripple the will of anyone who might want to follow in the insurgents' footsteps.

For a man like Eduardo Santiago, there would always be people gunning to bring him down. *He was too powerful now. He'd forgotten where he came from. He was no more than a crook with a collar.* And then people really gunning for him: The Latin Emperors were not going to disappear. As long as there were prisons, as long as there was poverty and drugs and violence, there would be the Latin Emperors. And as long as Father Eduardo was alive, there would be a Latin Emperor who would think that the way to earn his stripes would be to get the man who snitched out Junior Gonzalez.

Unless they were too damn scared of the power Father Eduardo still had from his perch in the church. That meant creating a mystique of fear. And the only way you scared hard knocks like the Latin Emperors was to attack them in a way they could not quantify.

Like through the air.

Fiona and I sat idling in the Charger across the street from Honrado when we saw an eighteen-wheeler roll tentatively down the street. I couldn't make out the face of the driver in the cab, but thought that the tattooed arm draped out the window was a pretty good sign that the driver wasn't under the employ of Harding. It was seven P.M. and the Honrado campus was clear of people . . . except for the ones Barry and Sam were training in the art of counterfeiting this fine evening.

I called Sam. "Delivery is here," I said.

"That's great," Sam said.

"You sound a little distracted," I said.

"Mikey, we're printing money in here."

"I'd like to remind you that you're a federal employee," I said.

"You know that pension I was worried about?"

"Sam."

"I just saw it roll off a press and get cut into exact replicas of twenty-dollar bills. And that was just on a practice run."

"Where's Barry?"

"He's holding forth with the gangsters," Sam said. "You know, in another life, he might have made a pretty good professor. The kids really respond to him."

"Don't let him leave with anything in his pockets tonight," I said.

"Mikey, I'm not going to frisk him."

"Sam, I will have Fiona frisk both of you," I said.

"Fine, Mikey, fine. Just know that I have seen temptation and I have walked away from it a better man. Or I will. I will. Yes, I will."

"Where's Father Eduardo?"

"He finished up the bake sale at three, and I brought him back to your mother's. He's far away from here."

"No one followed you?"

"There was a car that picked us up leaving here," Sam said. "And then another that picked us up at the corner. So I had Father Eduardo call the mayor and see if he could pop into the mayor's quarters for a quick talk about something pressing. But the mayor wasn't in."

"So what did you do?"

"Drove over there, anyway, and sat around for twenty minutes while Father Eduardo chatted up the security detail and mentioned that it looked like some gangsters were loitering around out front. So the security detail went out and arrested them. Turns out they were bad guys. I gotta tell you, Mikey, it's hard to be a covert operative and a hard-core gangster at the same time. Tough to be inconspicuous while you're thumping your bass."

"Occupational hazard," I said.

"I got the truck in my sights here," Sam said.

"Let it back into the loading dock and then get rid of the driver. Don't open the container until the driver is gone. Got it?"

"On it," Sam said, and hung up.

Outside, a young woman pushed a baby in a stroller. A man sat on the porch of his apartment and read the newspaper. Two boys rode by on matching low-rider bicycles.

"What's the point of that?" Fiona said.

"The bikes?"

"Yes, the bikes."

"Look cool, I guess," I said.

"Father Eduardo needs to start talking to these kids from the moment of conception."

In the backseat of the Charger was the residue from fifty cakes of portosyt. We'd stopped off at Lowe's on the way over and purchased enough of the chemical to either stave off an entire football field of wild grass or render unconscious, with the help of fentanyl, an entire generation of gangsters. It was now stacked innocuously inside a garbage can just beside the loading dock where Sam was.

"You sure we have the right combination of chemicals?" I asked.

"If not," Fiona said, "what's the worst that could happen?"

"Fiona, I'd prefer not to deal with those kinds of scenarios. It's the grounds of a church."

"Oh, Michael, always so pious," she said. "We'll need at least five hundred fentanyl patches' worth of gel to dissolve with the portosyt."

"We should be fine," I said.

In an optimum situation, we'd pump the gas into the ventilation system of the printing-press room, but the entire facility was enjoined by the same system, which meant that we'd need to dissolve the chemicals in the same space as the gangsters in order to control it.

Our plan was extraordinarily high-tech: We'd combine the two chemicals, along with the appropriate amount of distilled water, in this case two jugs, which we'd already poured inside the garbage can, and place it in the facility while they worked. It would take about five minutes for the chemicals to become a strong enough gas to knock them out. The sustained propagation of the gas, combined with the oxygen in the room, would keep them under like an anesthetic for the duration of the dissolve time. Which in this case would be about three hours.

Or enough time to alert the proper authorities to a bunch of gangsters who'd broken into the plant and started making counterfeit money.

Provided nothing went wrong, which seemed to be the case until Junior Gonzalez and Killa pulled up in front of us in the parking lot, hood to hood. Except that Junior and Killa were in a lowered Honda Accord and we were in the Charger.

"Act natural," I said through my smile to Fiona. "And by that I mean don't shoot them until it seems like the last resort."

"Always with the rules," she said.

I got out of the car and walked to the driver's-side window and peered in. "Something I can do for you, Junior?"

"Just wondering what you were doing sitting here on point," Junior said.

"Wanted to make sure the truck arrived," I said. "How's your knee, Killa?" Killa kept staring forward. His eyes were hidden behind a pair of black wrap-around sunglasses.

"Where's the boy?" Junior asked.

"Safe," I said. "You'll get him tomorrow. As we previously determined."

"You see, that's funny," Junior said, "because Leticia doesn't know anything about that."

Shit.

"Why would she?" I said.

"You separate a mother from her child, maybe you think you'd let her know," Junior said. "You think I'm stupid? You think I can't get to her? You think her home-girls will keep her secrets? You've never had her or him, have you?"

"Junior," I said, "you really want to play this game? You're an old man working in a young man's game now." I looked over my shoulder at Fiona. Her focus was unwavering. I didn't know how to tell her with simple body language that she needed to let Sam know that he needed to rush the chemicals *right this very instant*.

"And something else," Junior said. "Julia Pistell? She's on a cruise right now. Yeah. Summer at Sea, her mother called it. You wanna know how I found out? I picked up the phone and called her. Four-one-one. Still works."

Shit again. I looked back at Fiona, and this time she had her head down for just a brief second. When I looked back into Junior's car, Killa had a nine pointed at my chest.

"Why don't you get in the backseat," Junior said. "And you and I can have the conversation we should have had a week ago."

"And if I say no?"

"I got five guys in the printing press with your two friends," he said. "They don't hear from me, your friends are going headfirst into the pulper."

I looked back at Fiona again, but this time more deliberately.

"Don't worry," Killa said, speaking for the first time, "we'll come back for her later."

I had a couple choices. I could run and get shot in the back. I could reach into the car, attempt to break Junior's neck and disarm Killa, but there was a high likelihood that Killa would get off a shot in the process, since the angles of attack were difficult because the Honda was at about hip level for me.

Or I could trust that Fiona would do the right thing.

"Fine," I said, "let's have that talk."

I reached for the door handle at the same moment the Charger slammed headfirst into the Honda Accord, the airbags exploding immediately into Junior and Killa's faces. Fiona, from the passenger's seat, floored the Charger into the Accord, shoving it across the street like a toy, spinning it around back to front as it careened toward the grassy area in front of Honrado. Fiona kept ramming the Accord, finally spinning it into a tree, where she then pinned it with the front of the Charger.

If you're going to be a menace to society, it's wise to think of the car you drive. A lowered Honda Accord, stripped for racing speed, as it appeared this one was, weighs about 2,600 pounds. A 1974 Dodge Charger weighs about 3,800 pounds. It's a significant difference if you happen to be sitting in a Honda Accord when it's hit by a Dodge Charger.

I ran up to the Charger.

"You okay?" I said to Fiona.

"Of course," she said. "I buckled up first. You might have a small transmission problem, since I just threw it into park while it was running. My legs weren't long enough to reach the brake. And I think I heard one of the lights break."

"It's all right," I said. I reached into the glove box and took out one of the paintball guns, shoved it into my belt, and then walked toward the Honda. Inside, I could see that both Junior and Killa were a bloody mess. Junior was knocked out. Killa was blinking and gasping for air. I walked around to the passenger's side and pulled him out and put him on the pavement. His nose was broken for sure—it was turned at a terrible angle on his face—and his right arm, which had held the gun, was broken in at least two places, and was roughly the shape of the letter S. I went back to the Honda and found the gun in the backseat. I picked it up and walked back over to Fi and gave it to her.

"Put this somewhere safe," I said. "And call Sam. Tell him to set off the . . ."

Before I could finish my sentence, a fireball erupted from behind Honrado. It billowed up a good fifty feet into the air and set off every car alarm in the neighborhood.

"What the hell was that?" I said.

"I'm going to guess Sam didn't quite know the right

prescription for setting off the chemicals," Fiona said. "Like maybe he didn't bother to use the fentanyl at all and just set fire to the portosyt."

"Why would he think to do that?" I said.

"I have no idea," she said.

"Fiona," I said, but I couldn't be too angry. She had just saved my life, after all. Whatever had just happened had likely saved Sam and Barry's lives. "Get behind the wheel."

I ran back over to Killa and grabbed him by the face. "Can you talk?" I said.

He nodded weakly. "What happened?"

"You got played," I said. "Your brother is a nicer man than me, and he has an offer for you. You want to be reformed?"

Killa's eyes darted back and forth. "Am I dead?"

"Not yet," I said. "You have to listen to me. Do you want to be reformed?"

"I just want to be with my kid," he said.

"Good enough," I said. I hefted Killa up and dragged him to the Charger and shoved him into the backseat.

"What are you doing?" Fiona said.

"I promised Father Eduardo that we'd give his brother a chance," I said. I walked around the trunk of the Charger and dragged out a small box of items that would be of interest to any law enforcement officer who might come across Junior. Any box that contains a severed finger wrapped in counterfeit bills tends to draw attention. I'd FedEx another box of items the next day, just to be sure.

I reached inside the driver's-side window of the

Accord and placed the box on Junior's lap. I reached down and grasped his left wrist, which caused Junior to moan. A good sign. He was alive enough to be in pain. I checked his pulse—it was strong and steady, but judging by the amount of broken teeth in his mouth, the cuts on his face and the way his left leg was crumpled over his right leg, I was going to guess he had a broken pelvis, which is no fun. I had a good sense that he wasn't going to be waking up anytime soon, with any intention of going through any boxes on his lap. The one thing I needed to make sure of, however, was that Officer Prieto wasn't the first on the scene.

I was about to hop into the passenger's seat of the Charger when the eighteen-wheeler, this time not being driven very tentatively at all, and now down to just ten wheels, since the payload had been left behind, therefore allowing it to barrel down the street with far more ease, did just that.

"That would be Sam," Fiona said.

"I would have never guessed," I said. "Call Father Eduardo and tell him we have his brother, and then take him wherever Father Eduardo says, okay?"

"If he tries anything, I will shoot him," she said.

"I don't think he'll try anything," I said. I looked over at him in the backseat. "Especially since he's passed out from the pain again."

"Where are you going to be?"

"Finishing this," I said. I pounded on the roof. "Now go. And thank you."

"You're welcome," she said, and then she backed

the Charger away from the wreckage of the Honda and drove off. It was nice to see that there wasn't too much damage to the front end of the car. The benefits of solid, American craftsmanship.

The truck screeched to a stop, and Barry opened up the passenger's door and let me in. We eased down the street as if there wasn't a smoldering fire somewhere behind us. "What the hell just happened back there?" I said once we were safely away.

"Fi texted and said you were in trouble and that I should set fire to those chemicals," Sam said. "I was just following orders."

"Where are Junior's guys?"

Sam looked at Barry. Barry looked at Sam. "They might be locked in the payload trailer."

"Might?"

"They came at us. One thing led to another, there was a big explosion, they ran into the trailer and, well, that's where they sit," Sam said.

"Barry?" I said.

"Whatever Sam says," Barry said. "The man is a ninja."

"All right," I said, "Barry, I'm afraid your friends are only going to get a truck, not a payload."

"They're flexible," Barry said. "And I'll pay them. Whatever, okay?"

Sometimes, Barry makes more sense than I give him credit. "We need to take care of Prieto," I said. "I've got photos on my phone. We can't have him messing this up."

"Aye, aye," Sam said, and he took out his phone

and made a call. "Ross? Ross, it's Sam Axe. Listen. I just saw someone illegally parked inside a tree in front of Honrado's headquarters, over by the Orange Bowl. Yeah, looked serious. Can I e-mail you some photos that might be of interest to you? Great, great. I'll send them right over. And Ross? Get there quick. I think your friend Officer Prieto might be the person involved here. Maybe another hit-and-run."

When he hung up, Sam had an odd smile on his face.

"What is it?" I asked.

"You ever do something for someone and you know it's the right thing even before you do it?"

I thought about pulling Killa out of the car and offering him his brother's salvation, even when I knew I didn't have to, and probably shouldn't. "I guess I do," I said.

Barry sighed.

"What?" I said.

"I guess I do, too," he said. He pointed his thumb over his shoulder. Sitting in the sleeping compartment of the truck was the money plate.

Epilogue

Nothing inspires the great wealth of giving more than turmoil. So after spending a month on the front page of the *Miami Herald*, detailing how he'd been duped by his old friend Junior Gonzalez, a man who came to him seeking reformation but who really had hatched an insidious plan to counterfeit money just under his nose, Father Eduardo Santiago was flush with donations for all of his pet projects. And why not? The story that was unfolding was as bizarre as anything on the television that week. There was even a police officer who'd been found on the payroll of the Latin Emperors, discovered by the dogged research of a meter maid, of all things. It even looked like the cop and the gangster were party to the theft of high-grade chemicals. Could they have been domestic terrorists?

It was a Sunday, and I was reading all about the news while I ate lunch in my mother's kitchen. I was working on the Charger in her garage, pounding out a few dents, replacing a broken light, and bleaching blood from the backseat (again), and had come in to eat a cup of yogurt and a piece of toast. Twenty minutes later, I was still there, reading all about the exploits of the good, the bad and the meter maid.

"Compelling little tale," my mother said.

"It's a good one," I said.

"Can I ask you a question, Michael?"

"Probably not, Ma," I said.

"Don't you ever get tired of all of this?"

I set the newspaper down. "No," I said. The fact was, I had one more job to do with Father Eduardo planned for that evening. "This is what I do. This is what I was put here to do. Either I'm a spy or I'm not a spy. But I'm not sitting around waiting for bad things to happen, not if I can stop something from occurring."

My mother came over and put a hand on my face. "Please, Michael," she said, "be more careful. These people? They sound crazy."

Aren't they all?

That night, I went to Father Eduardo's house to pick him up. It was close to midnight, and Father Eduardo was dressed in a sweat suit when I met him at his door. I hadn't seen him since the day everything had gone down, though we'd spoken several times.

"You ready?" I said.

"I am," he said.

We drove for a long while in silence, headed out past Homestead and toward the Everglades. I finally asked, "How is your brother?"

"Healing," he said. "I sent him to Nevada. I have a

friend in a church there who is understanding of these things."

"You're not worried he'll go back to the life?"

"I'm worried I'll go back," he said. He laughed, but I think he meant it. "I can't control him. I can only give him a choice. He loves his son. That is worth something."

"Where is Leticia?"

"Somewhere safe," he said.

"You're not going to tell me?"

"The more people know, the more people know," he said. "I trust you, Michael, but she wants no one to know her anymore. A fresh start."

"Does she need money?"

"Your friend Fiona has been very generous," he said. "So, no. She's fine." Every day, a new surprise. "Turn left here," he said, and pointed at an unpaved road that led off toward farmland. We drove for another few minutes, until he motioned for me to stop.

"Here?" I said.

"I think so," he said.

We got out of the car, and Father Eduardo looked up into the sky, took a deep breath and then walked farther on, toward an old barn in the distance. I followed behind him at a distance.

Father Eduardo began to speak, his voice barely audible at first, and then slowly it rose in tenor as he delivered the last rites to a field of dead men, long ago buried by Junior Gonzalez and the Latin Emperors— a final act of contrition. I couldn't help but wonder who'd delivered the last rites to all the men I'd left behind over the years.

I walked back to the Charger and waited for Father Eduardo to return, so I could drive him back to Miami, so I could return to my loft and wait for my next assignment, be it from the people who'd burned me or someone who only needed my help.